The Porcupine Boy

& Other

Anthological Oddities

Edited by Christopher M. Jones

Struggling to rise, Ben's legs failed him and he fell forward. On his knees, he crawled between the rows of seats. His mouth felt full, his teeth bit down on something chewy that reeked of blood. The faint chatter of the projector had disappeared. In its place were the sounds of heavy grinding and the plop of blood and gristle as it flowed copiously into a shallow trough. As for the creature alongside it, Ben had managed one glimpse before his eyes had skittered away in terror. However, it continued to evolve in his mind's eye, regardless—hunger, anticipation, and desire—hair, horns, teeth, and tongue. It coalesced with a disturbing familiarity.

Dedication

This book is dedicated to Jack Ketchum and Charlee Jacob.

Table of Contents

Introduction

This past February for Women in Horror Month, my mother came to the Lovecraft Arts & Sciences bookstore in Providence to hear me read. It was the first time she ate the fruit of her daughter's dark imagination. I was anxious about what she'd think, and how she would perceive my writing and storytelling.

"That wasn't really horror," she said later in the car. "It was just good writing."

She was wrong about it not being horror, but my heart nearly burst with joy that she liked it. It dug at me a bit that in order to appreciate it, she had to separate it from something "scary," from what she'd been exposed to as mainstream horror just because it invoked a strong emotional response from her that wasn't fear. Not exactly.

It was a story about witches who hex their common ex-lover, a tale born not only from my love of horror, but also the pain of a recent breakup. Falling in love with someone who hurts you is scary. Leaving someone who has abused you and your child is darkness. Joining a coven of witches to take revenge is horror. Good writing invokes both emotions *and* can throw in a well-done trope or create a new vision that compliments the pain and fear.

To the general public, horror has a narrow definition, but to those who love the genre, it is a vast, rich, dark soil for word-smithing, sewn with the strongest emotions, because horror is a carnival of extremes: fear, love, hate, joy. All these emotions give stories their power. The creatures and villains are no more than cardboard cutouts or jump scares without the deep well of the human experience to draw from and create empathy in the heart of the reader.

The stories in THE PORCUPINE BOY AND OTHER ANTHOLOGICAL ODDITIES are a kaleidoscope of what the horror genre can be and how far into the imagination it can stretch while remaining true to its roots. FERAL by Priya Sharma personally touched me as a woman and someone who has struggled with infertility. Perhaps she meant to invoke these themes, or perhaps my experience read into them. Either way, it's a beautiful tale of relationships and femininity, but with Sharma's subtle vision of werewolves, unique and powerful in their metaphor of the strength of women to endure.

ADRENALINE JUNKIES by Ray Cluley is a tale of heartache and loss, but also of monsters that claw and rip and devour. The relationship between the protagonist and her girlfriend is sweet and tender, and serves to raise the tension and anxiety to an almost unbearable level, a mood that is appropriate for a tale about skydiving.

ROADKILL by Meryl Stenhouse is a story of friendships, guilt, betrayal, and invokes the horror trope of the "hungry house," or in this case, a "hungry motel." When a group of friends with secrets end up in a motel where dead things come looking for them the experience will change them in ways they never could have imagined.

Author Janet Joyce Holden has invoked Clive Barker and Ramsey Campbell with the story THE DARK WINDMILL. Ben follows his interest in a silent filmmaker to the man's family home, where the director's daughter and granddaughter are hiding a horrifying family secret. The quiet dread that slowly escalates to deep anxiety and fear is perfectly timed in this tale. Through description and character development, Holden is able to build a distrust that amplifies the narration exquisitely.

And finally, the title piece, THE PORCUPINE BOY is another example of storytelling where relationships are forefront, namely the one between a patient care advocate with some skeletons in his closet, and his client with secrets of her own. It is a terrifying tale of monsters, but also a sweet and endearing tale of belonging and acceptance. The juxtaposition is a perfect example of how horror isn't always "scary." It's not always about fear, but sometimes about the lengths people will go to for the deepest desires of their heart, even if that desire requires something monstrous.

Come to this anthology looking to be moved by the tales I mentioned above, and many more. The emotions invoked are powerful, as are the terror of the monsters, both supernatural and human. Maybe pass this anthology on to someone who doesn't read horror and tell them it is a book of scary tales. Tell them the stories in this anthology are also examples of good writing. They can, in a world where all things are possible, be both.

Warmest Regards,
Catherine Grant
Writer, Editor, Assistant Director of Core Programming
NecronomiCon Providence

Outside

By Gary McMahon

Now…

Terry sits quietly at the window and stares out at the street. Dusk is falling like a dirty curtain across the rooftops and the swan-necked streetlights are coming on one by one, spraying a muted yellow wash along the desolate stretch of pavement.

Seerdale Crescent is a quiet pocket of normality located three miles outside the city, a neat little suburban enclave whose semi-detached tranquillity belies the frenetic bustle of the nearby city. The houses and gardens are all neat and well maintained, each car parked either at the kerb or on one of the tasteful gravel drives less than three years old, and most of the residents have full-time jobs. A lot of his neighbours are white-collar workers in high-rise offices inside the rigidly defined city limits, or they work from home, huddled over flickering computer screens in cramped spare-room offices.

It is a nice place, a safe place, somewhere to raise a family.

Terry often sits in the bulging bay window of Number 20 and watches the daily dance of commuters, school runs and childcare drops. It is hypnotic, in its own small way; and it helps him to keep his mind off his own worries.

For example, right now, as he sips his coffee, he watches the attractive young mother of two from across the street as she pulls up at the kerb in her sturdy four-wheel-drive vehicle. The woman fusses like an anxious hen as her offspring spill off the back seat; then she corrals her chicks indoors, looking slightly stressed and loosening the collar of her suit jacket so that she can breathe. All the ground-floor lights go on in unison, as if it is a previously co-ordinated act meant specifically to announce their arrival.

Terry smiles sadly; family life is something that has so far eluded him. Depending on his mood, he can never quite decide if this is a good or bad thing. Perhaps he'll never know.

The TV murmurs behind him, a newsreader chanting a litany of discontent: more terrorist-attacks in Central London, the body of a middle-aged woman found strangled in a south Leeds council house, two twelve-year-old kids caught in the act of trying to hang a third child by his neck from a tree in a park near Halifax.

Is it any wonder that he stays indoors all the time? His refusal to go *out there* is, in his eyes, completely justified.

His cup is empty, so he takes it into the kitchen and places it in the sink, alongside a small plate and a butter-smeared knife— the tuna fish sandwich he enjoyed earlier is still sitting heavily in his stomach, and the coffee has left a bitter aftertaste on his tongue.

He fills a glass with cold water directly from the tap and drinks it slowly, savouring the chill as it slices a route down his throat. The kitchen window is located above the sink, and as he drinks he watches a thin grey cat slink across the lawn. The cat is stalking a small brown bird, which sits on a paving slab near the pole that supports one end of Terry's unused washing line, and he begins to feel tense as the cat readies itself to pounce.

Without thinking, he raps on the glass with the knuckles of his free hand. The bird takes flight; the cat chooses that exact moment to leap, and lands in the spot the bird has just vacated.

The cat glances towards Terry, its narrow eyes blazing with casual feline hatred. Then it drops its shoulders and slouches away.

The party invitation is still on the dining table, propped up against the empty fruit bowl with Terry's address facing out-ward. The handwriting on the front of the envelope is rather fancy, almost like calligraphy, and slopes dramatically to the left. He barely knows Cousin Winston and the invite to the man's fortieth birthday party came as a surprise. Terry often thinks that the remaining strands of his geographically scattered family probably consider him long dead and buried, but this development seems to disprove his theory. They know he is alive; they just don't care.

He wrote off the idea of travelling to Liverpool for the family party as soon as he opened the envelope, but for some reason at that time he felt unable, or unwilling, to throw the letter in the bin.

Despite not having left the house for eleven months, Terry still clings to the idea that one day he might venture outside. In his clearer moments, he admits the folly of such a thought, but the idea of it still carries an almost erotic charge.

In dreams, he walks confidently out of his front door and says hello to that pretty working mother or conducts a brief conversation with the middle-aged housewife who lives next door—the one who always does her gardening in a pair of cut-off denims and a halter neck top, whatever the weather.

The attack, along with Stephanie's subsequent departure, has left more than physical marks.

He closes the blinds at the kitchen window and walks back into the living room, where he sits down in his armchair and fumbles for the remote control. He turns up the volume on the TV and flicks the channel to something safer than the news—a bland mystery set in a fictional country village that soon proves to be tainted by the same casual threat as every other show he attempts to watch these days. It is everywhere: danger, violence, the promise of pain.

He turns off the TV and decides to put on some music, crossing the room to push a CD of Beethoven's Symphonies into the stereo. At least Stephanie left him with an appreciation of classical music. Before he met her, his listening pleasure consisted mainly of 1960s pop, with a smattering of blue-eyed soul.

He sits down and closes his eyes, wary of the images that never fail to assault him whenever he is least ready for them. Whenever he is least protected.

They hover now at the edges of his vision: a vast mélange of flying feet and fists illuminated by the sudden flash of a listless blade. The leering, featureless faces of beer-swilling wife-beaters, tyre-slashers, housebreakers and carjackers, all leaning forward to stain his perception with the muck of their regard. All the ignorant products of a culture obsessed with the cult of the individual and lost in a landscape shaped by insane, unchecked greed; all the ugly monsters who lack basic empathy and compassion.

The scum of the earth: the dregs of society.

Terry rubs at his ribs and remembers the pain. It has gone now, merely an echo of violence, but his body still hears its dour music.

Then…

He was completely blameless in the incident. The bus was late that evening, so he decided to walk to the supermarket. He only wanted a frozen meal and a four-pack of beer for his dinner (Stephanie was away on a business trip; she was often called down to London on training courses sometimes three or four times a month), so he felt quite capable of carrying his meagre purchases home.

He cut across the patch of waste land behind the garages at the end of the street, hopping over the shin-high tubular metal fence that prevented vehicular access, and was only mildly disconcerted to find that the streetlights were out. Probably defective bulbs or a problem with the power supply; the local council was notoriously lax in their attention to such matters.

Terry passed the brick backs of the garages, trying to ignore the vulgar graffiti daubed there by local hoodlums. There was an infamous housing estate nearby—one of those places known in the local newspaper as a hotbed of petty crime and teenage gang culture—and the grim reality of problem families living on a combination of benefits and bitterness sometimes leaked across the uneasy borders between the two worlds.

When the lone figure stepped out of the shadows, Terry considered turning around and heading back, perhaps waiting for the next bus after all. But no, why should he? It was only one person, not a loitering group, and these were his streets as much as anyone else's. There was no reason that he should be forced off them by fear and intimidation.

(Now, looking back, he smiles at his own naivety. Those streets out there are not his; they belong to the brutish and the feckless, those who seek only to destroy the fragile peace and order of his existence.)

"Give me your fucking money." It was a blunt request; there could be no confusion regarding the meaning of the man's words.

"I...I'm sorry?" Terry felt tiny, like a gnat just before a palm fell and smeared it across glass.

"You fuckin' will be, mate. Give me your wallet. *Now*." This last word was punctuated with the snickering sound of steel as a blade emerged from a stubby switchblade handle that protruded from an unseen hand. The youth swung the knife in a lazy arc, his teeth gleaming almost as bright as the burnished steel.

"Here...take it. Take *everything*." Terry took his wallet out of his pocket and offered it to the advancing figure, which was rendered anonymous by way of the uniform of the streets—a loose-fitting tracksuit and a baseball cap.

In Terry's haste, some of the contents of the battered leather wallet (a birthday gift from Stephanie) spilled out and fell onto the ground. He bent over to pick up the store cards and credit cards and folded photographs, one arm held aloft in an attitude of both protection and supplication (and exactly how much does it still pain him to admit to the latter?). The boot impacted with such force that he was knocked sideways, gasping for air. The second blow caught him on the side of the head, the third and fourth he could not say where. Then he was consumed by blackness...

Now...

Terry crosses again to the large bay window; by now it is almost fully dark outside. He clutches the party invitation in his hand despite possessing no recollection of having returned to the kitchen to fetch it. He has taken the slip of paper from the envelope and is rubbing it between forefinger and thumb like a lapsed Catholic with a string of rosary beads.

"Why?" he asks, already knowing the answer: that there *is* no answer. He has been chosen; his time has come. The grinning gods of random violence have sent a messenger to take what they believe is owed to them. It is the price of living in today's society, where even the word is a mockery of its original meaning. Culture is now so debased, so knocked out of whack, that this kind of thing is considered just another aspect of modern life.

People read the newspapers or watch the news reports, shrug their shoulders, and get on with their lives. These days they do not even pray that they will not be next; it is assumed that eventually it will be their turn to suffer, and they prepare themselves for this inevitable moment of truth.

Is this what we have become—just cattle awaiting the slaughter?

Once again, he already knows the answer to his question.

Shadows scrawl chaotic messages across the window glass, but Terry is too uneducated to understand their meaning. Perhaps names are being written in the air or etched into the pane: the identities of fellow victims, or of those who might be next.

He turns away and is puzzled to find tears in his eyes.

Stephanie left him when it became apparent that he was not going to leave the house again. She begged. She pleaded. She bargained. But in the end, even she was forced to admit defeat.

Terry refuses to speak to anyone about what happened; the blade scraped away something that once lived deep beneath flesh and bone, and it left a deep mark on his psyche.

A man out walking his dog found Terry that night, bleeding and unconscious; an ambulance was summoned, and it took almost an hour to arrive. He lost a lot of blood, but luckily his injuries were not serious. Cuts and bruises. A knife wound where the thin blade had slipped between two ribs, scraping the bone.

Again, no one was surprised or outraged or even particularly bothered by what happened. His is another name on the list written in the ink of night, just the latest victim to be treated and sent packing to pick up the threads of his life.

But some threads, once severed, cannot be repaired. So the only sane response to an insane situation is to lock the door and remain indoors, never setting foot outside again.

It is simple to achieve, really, in the modern age: Internet shopping, email communication, television piped into people's homes twenty-four hours a day. It is more difficult, he thinks, to actually engage with the world outside world. Cutting it off is so easy.

Just then, the telephone rings, interrupting his thoughts. For a moment he considers ignoring the tone, but then picks it up because only one person ever calls him these days and he wants desperately to hear her voice.

"Hello, Terry." The sound of his name is a little like that knife, dragging quickly and sharply through flesh.

"I was just thinking about you."

"I think about you all the time, Terry. This is hard for us both. I just wanted to hear your voice; to check that you're okay."

There is a pause that stretches into a silence. Terry knows that it is his turn to speak, and exactly what she wants him to say, but he can't quite find the words.

"Have you been… you know… *Have you?*"

"Have I been *outside*? No. No, I haven't. Not yet."

Stephanie's sigh is audible down the line. "I know this isn't what you want to hear, and it isn't what you believe, but you're showing all the signs of agoraphobia. The doctor said this might happen, remember? I wish you'd call that number they gave you at the hospital and speak to someone."

"I don't need counselling, Steph."

"Then what *do* you need?"

"I need you." He fears that he has said too much, that she will simply hang up the phone and he will be left here listening to the empty crackle of static on the line.

"Come and see me any time, Terry. You know where I live, and I'll be here waiting for you. All you have to do is—"

"Go outside," he finishes the sentence, sensing her sad smile.

"Bye, Terry. See you soon?"

"Perhaps you will."

The line goes dead.

"I love you, Stephanie..."

Terry gently replaces the receiver in its cradle and stares at the mute plastic device, still hearing Stephanie's voice in his mind, holding it inside his skull for as long as he can manage, hanging on to the echo until he can no longer hear it.

She is clever, trying to lure him out like that. But he isn't sure if he has it in him to even try. It has been a long time since he flexed those muscles. And if any muscle is left unexercised, it can slide easily into atrophy.

But what if he tries to change all that?

After all these months—and specifically after he and Stephanie's difficult parting—perhaps there is still enough of him left to fight back. The knife did not flay him completely; tatters of his former self still cling to the resilient bone. If he has enough strength to simply put a foot outside the front door, then maybe he can convince Stephanie to come back.

She'd certainly hinted as much on the phone.

The music dies but he does not replace the CD. Silence is better for what he is planning: it clears the mind and focuses the will.

Terry gets up and strides out into the hallway, trailing his fingers along the wall, as if hoping that something will snag them and prevent him from moving any farther towards the front door, holding him there until the moment passes.

The door looms like an ancient edifice; it is a symbol whose significance he can no longer quite grasp, a lonely artefact belonging to a forgotten religion. The door seems to buckle as he stares at it; the square glass panels bevel inward and threaten to shatter. The white door handle squirms like a snake, and as he reaches out towards it he expects it to rear up and strike out at his dithering hand, drawing blood with tough white fangs.

He still clings to the creased party invitation, and the paper writhes like a trapped bird caught in his hand, wings flapping, savage beak pecking at his fingers.

Terry takes a step forward and lunges at the door. Its unnatural movement ceases and the door seems to stiffen and then open at the mere suggestion of his touch. A rectangular slab of night stands on the doorstep, a solid obstacle through which he must somehow pass. Beyond this are the streetlights, the other houses on his street, his neighbours, waiting behind their own closed doors and locked windows. With this single heroic act, he might set them all an example and show everyone what is possible: that a victim *can* fight back and rebuild his life, then reclaim the streets and disown the cruelty that dwells there.

His foot hovers over the step, and then falls, the sole of his shoe striking the lower part of the door frame and sounding like a memory of some other time and place that threatens to impinge on this one.

"Out there," he breathes, his voice taking flight.

Then he stumbles across the threshold, punching through that twitching wall of blackness and falling out the other side, aching and breathless, blood pumping like superheated fuel through a well-tuned engine.

Terry looks around, seeing lights go on up and down the street. It is almost as if his re-emergence has triggered some kind of response: he half expects to hear distant applause.

Then, flushed with his own sense of victory, he pushes on and walks down the cement path to his garden gate. He leans on the concrete gatepost and glances along the street, breathing in the outside air that has been denied him since the day of the attack. It smells wonderful, that air; it is the scent of everything that he's been missing. The fear is still there, discolouring the world, but he feels that if he really tries, he might be able to at least tame his terror, if not defeat it entirely.

He glances again up and down the street, inspecting his new environment, savouring its sights and its smells. The road is empty of traffic, and no one walks the narrow footpaths. If he senses danger, it is entirely of his own creation.

Then the streetlights flicker off. Not one by one, but in a single dousing of brightness. Darkness descends like a blanket thrown over a corpse in an empty room, and Terry suddenly realises the error of his ways, the huge mistake that he has made.

He turns to run, to flee back inside, but it is too late.

It is far, far too late.

Before he can even cry out in alarm, before he can emit the

dry sound that is lodged like gristle in his throat, they are upon him.

Instead of Terry going to the party, the party has come to Terry.

And the guests are terrible.

Stepping forward, appearing out of the air, they descend upon him. Too many to count; too many to fight off. A crowd of tall, thin, dark figures with wide hands and blunt fists, mocking mouths and sunken onyx eyes set into flat sneering faces. Base, artless things forged from a nameless fiery hunger that is never truly satisfied. Their flat brutish faces suggest nothing but a hideous banality; their bodies are formed from twists of shadow born in the corners of derelict buildings and empty midnight car parks.

Terry opens his mouth to scream, but something grabs his tongue; it is a hand, a slim dark hand with shadow-fingers that crawl down his throat and into his chest.

Something chuckles; the figures close in.

This, he realises, is a surly, idiotic species that will never, ever go away, no matter how far you run or how long you hide from them, hoping and praying that they will forget your name and where you live.

They squat in the bins outside fast food restaurants and stalk the aisles of Pound Shops and cheap European supermarket franchises, destroying the very things that they covet. They were human once or something like it, but now they have become like beasts.

He backs away, spitting out that insubstantial groping hand, and tries to shuffle back towards the door, but finds that once he's crossed the threshold there is no way back inside. No return. So instead, he crouches down and waits for them to pounce.

The vandals. The muggers. The burglars. The rapists. All the casual assailants who have waited so patiently for him to join their own private celebration of terror, in the dark, in the shadows, in the streets...

Tomorrow…

He sleeps all through the next day and into the night, and when he wakes in the dark he is one of them: an Outsider.

He climbs out of bed and walks through the rooms of his house—a place he no longer recognises, where he no longer feels at home. He feels too enclosed; claustrophobia soon sets in and he is overtaken by a sudden and all-consuming urge to leave, to be far beyond these confining walls. He has changed, altered. He is no longer afraid.

In a final symbolic act, he defecates in the corners, pisses on the kitchen workbenches, and trashes the TV and stereo. These acts of vandalism make him smile; the wanton destruction feeds him, just as blood might sustain a vampire.

After a short time, he steps out into the night, stalking like a hunter, keeping out of sight and listening to all the new sounds of freedom. He sniffs the darkness and it smells good, like something he might come to enjoy.

Soon he finds a place among the others and squats down in the shadows, wanting to see what the night would have him do.

And he waits for you to come outside.

Feral

By Priya Sharma

Kush led me into the bathroom on our wedding night. The white tiles and mirrors made me nervous.

Then I saw he'd already laid out a steel tray on the marble counter containing syringes, needles, ampoules and packs of dressings. The scalpel looked small and innocuous. My lip curled, revealing my teeth.

After Kush's funeral, we go back to the house that he and I shared. This self-designed exemplar of modernity was his dream, built it at the edge of the forest against all advice, because I'd been pining for the trees.

Lisa and I lay out the food in the kitchen, ready to carry through to the mourners. The kitchen was Kush's domain. He loved to cook.

"What do you think?" Kush asked when the first worktop was fixed in place.

The worktops were made of highly polished concrete. I laid my cheek on the silky, cold surface. Kush copied me, looking into my face, his dark eyes full of thoughts.

"Which platter for the prawns?" Lisa speaks to me like I'm an injured animal.

"The blue one." I resent her interrupting my train of thought.

An hour before the funeral Lisa brushed my hair and tied it up. I wanted my grief to trump hers, to rub her face in it. When she reminded me to put on shoes, as I tried to walk out to the car in stockinged feet, I realised what I was feeling was real, not just a righteous affectation.

"Where are the breadsticks?" Lisa asks.

"The pantry."

Kush had been insistent on a pantry. I like it. A store for lean seasons.

"I can't see them."

I join her. We rifle through the boxes and packets without looking at one another. What's between us feels leaden. I freeze when I hear voices from the kitchen. Maria and Naomi.

"Poor Ava." That's Naomi. "She's devastated."

"I'm not sure I'd have as much self-control as she's shown today." Maria is one of the few women I've met who is truly in love with her husband.

"She's in shock." Naomi pauses. "Do you remember the netball?"

She sounds fond, not mocking. I've learnt to laugh about that, too. Lisa had taken me to the club. They were trying to teach me how to play. Few women work, so they must fill their time. I was so excited by the chase that I leapt on the ball, trying to bite it.

"Kush was such a good man." Maria sighs. "What's she going to do now?"

Dr Garston told me about periods but I wasn't prepared, not really. He didn't mention the pain for one thing.

I woke with cramp low down in my stomach, as if I'd eaten something rotten. I waited for diarrhoea but nothing came. I felt uncomfortable. Wet between my legs. I smelt iron, not good and fresh, but old and decayed. The amount of blood surprised me. I stuffed toilet paper in my knickers and went to the supermarket. I took all my allowance, unsure what having a period cost.

I stood in front of a wall of sanitary products. Tampons. Towels. Liners. Winged, unwinged. Light, medium and heavy flow. I picked up a packet bearing a photo of a girl on a bicycle. I wanted to tear it to pieces so I wouldn't have to see her idiotic smile.

In fact, the whole supermarket put me in a rage. Soap. Bread.

Water in bottles, of all things. A dozen choices of each and yet no choice of how to live.

Women are sacrosanct. Dr Garston said. *Scarce. You're protected at all costs. You must perform your duty in return.*

I wanted to run but my newly remodelled body wasn't fast as it once was.

A pair of women carrying shopping baskets walked up the aisle, slowing as they approached me. They stank of fake flowers. One of them stifled a giggle. I whipped around, my back to the shelves, quick enough to see one of them wrinkling her nose in disgust.

I flushed with shame. They wore uniforms; tight jeans and long jumpers, belted at their waists. I was short and stocky by comparison. I didn't have their sleek hair or a painted face.

Out in the woods, my sisters and I would've run them to ground. I would've have put my teeth to their necks, not to break their skins, just to bring them into line.

"Do you need any help?"

A third woman approached. She smelt of sugar and was styled like the others, but she sent them on their way with a look filled with nip and growl.

"You're Ava, aren't you?"

I was notorious. Ava-the-dog-girl. Raised by wolves escaped from zoos, or feral mongrels. I was unmistakable. Large eyes beneath a marked widow's peak. Big hands and feet.

She tried again, gesturing to the pack of towels in my hand. "It can be daunting."

She pulled a scarf from her bag. "Here, wrap this around your waist. You've got blood on your skirt."

I flinched, but she spoke gently as she reached around me and secured the scarf with an artful knot at my hip. "This is your first period, isn't it?"

I nodded.

"Let's get you some things." She threw boxes into her basket with the assurance of a women well versed in menstruation.

That was how I met Lisa.

"I'm staying here tonight."

All the mourners have left, even Lisa's husband, Paul. I can't imagine him touching her. He'd keep her on a shelf like a trophy if he could. He doesn't like me.

"No. Thanks for the offer though."

My formality confuses her. It's enough to hurt her but not enough for her to take offence. Widowhood is a sword and shield.

"I'll help clean up." Lisa starts scraping a plate as if to demonstrate. I've always refused to have any staff. I don't want strangers on my territory.

"Leave it." I take the plate and fork from her and put them down. "I need to keep busy. Here, take these. I've run out of vases."

I hand Lisa the fat pink blooms. Peonies from one of the bachelors, presented to me as if he were already a suitor. I hate cultivated flowers. Give me snowdrops or wood anemones. Give me clumps of primroses. Better still, a soft rash of bluebells. My sisters and I rolled in them and the fragrance clung to us for days.

Lisa takes the bouquet but they slide from her hand and land on the floor. It's the first time I've looked her in the face today. Her shoulders hitch up and down with her gasping sobs. I don't know who she's crying for.

I know I should reach out for her. It's what people do in these circumstances.

"I'm sorry." She searches her pockets and pulls out a crumpled tissue to dab her eyes with.

"It's been a hard day for both of us. Go home. Get some rest. Your husband's waiting for you."

The barb finds its place. I can tell from how she tries to compose herself. She's about to say something but I don't want to do this with her. Not now. Not yet. I hurry her along with, "I'll phone you tomorrow."

"Okay, Ava. If that's what you want."

"It is."

The house falls into a lull when I close the front door after her. I listen to its quiet murmurs. They used to make me look over my shoulders to see who was there.

Kush is in every detail. People always comment on his eye for things. Each room is a careful curation of beauty. Lines of porcelain on recessed, underlit shelves. Antique dip pens on a malachite tray. Books arranged with care rather than piled on shelves.

I load the dishwasher and wipe down the surfaces. I push the vacuum around the lounge. Something too large for the Hoover's appetite gets sucked up inside it. The machine makes a whining noise that rises to a high pitch. I fall to my knees and howl back at it.

Since Kush's death I find it easier to fall asleep with the blinds open so that I can see the outline of the trees. The forest is my friend. I imagine that their dark depths hide rabbits, foxes and owls. The natural world replenishing itself without the blight of man, now that the reduced population clusters in cities.

Not that I sleep well. I lay awake, marking time, then doze fitfully only to wake again an hour later.

It takes a few heartbeats to realise that Kush isn't beside me and will never be again. Now that he's gone, and I have what I came here for, I should leave.

The security lights snap on. Sometimes a foraging animal does this. I wait for the lights to turn off but they don't. I go to the window.

The world is bright white under the floodlights. From my vantage point I see a flash of movement on the footpath beneath me. Whatever it is, it's fast. The lights snap off and the ones on the other side of the house go on, their brightness shedding in a diagonal across the grass.

I'm alone out here in my glass box at the edge of the trees.

I run downstairs, my feet thudding on the steps. The lights follow whoever it is as they circle the house. A fox wouldn't do that.

I reach the dining room just before the lights go out completely and I get a flash of something disappearing between the trees.

I pull the bifold doors open and run out. The flood lights come on again, this time because of me. Bare legged, the wind tugging at the hem of the old shirt I'm wearing, I'm exposed. They're out there, watching me.

"Come on!" I scream. "Come and get me!"

But there's nothing, except darkness and threat of rain.

Habit carries us when the heart's given up.

I get up and shower. Kush and I had separate bathrooms. He said he didn't mind sharing but I did.

I spend ages in there. I tried to make a joke of it.

That's because you're a woman.

I open the cabinet that contains my daily rituals. The things I didn't want Kush to see. Despite the vials of hormones, the syringes and the packs of pills in there, I still need the depilatory creams, razors and shaving oil. Slant and pointed tweezers for the most stubborn hair.

There aren't mirrors in the wilderness. Self-consciousness is a human trait. My reflection's that of a woman just shy of middle age, her waist starting to thicken and with a bit more heft to her buttocks. Her breasts, though slight, sag.

My body is fighting back since Kush's death, my nature trying to reassert itself. An alarming amount of new hair covers my chest and stomach despite the cocktail of chemicals I take to keep it in check.

I collect everything from the shelves and dump it all into the bin.

The phone has been ringing all morning, but I can choose who I speak to. All hail caller-recognition.

It's Jamie.

"Is this a professional call?" The brushed aluminium receiver is cold against my ear.

"Of course not. I stopped being your therapist a long time ago. I hardly got a chance to speak to you yesterday. I wanted to see how you're doing."

"I'm as okay as I can be."

"I think of you. A lot. I want you to know how much I admired Kush. What happened to him was terrible. You shouldn't have had to see it."

Memory is cruel. Of all our years together, the first memory of Kush that jumps into my mind is of the fresh blood coming from his mouth in waves every time he was sick. The paramedics put up a drip, pouring in fluid to replace the blood lost from his stomach ulcer, but eventually he started to vomit that up too as he had no blood of his own left.

I screamed for my sisters, somewhere deep inside my mind.

"Ava, are you still there?"

Jamie taught me to speak. I can imagine his expression now, the same as then, when he was trying to get my attention.

"Yes."

He's reluctant to hang up.

"Can you believe the cheek of some of those men?" He means the ones at the funeral, with their flowers and overtures.

"One of Kush's colleague has already left me a message about going to dinner."

"They don't know you, or anything about you. How dare they?" Jamie sounds angry.

These single men are desperate enough to cruise funerals for a potential mate. A widow's grace period is short. *You have to choose or they'll choose for you.*

"Is there anything I can do to help you?"

"Not right now."

"Okay. Keep in touch." The hurt in his voice surprises me. "But call me if you need anything."

The beginning of a headache covers my right eye. I go back upstairs and curl up. I realise that my head isn't the only thing that aches. It's funny how you don't realise how much you need someone until they're gone.

Dr Garston always frowned at me. I don't think he realised he was doing it.

"I'm a specialist in women's health. Do you remember me? I came to see you with Dr Phipps when you first arrived."

"You were wearing the same red bow tie then, too."

That startled him. When he first saw me I was pissing on straw because the porcelain toilet frightened me.

"You're a fast learner."

"That doesn't sound like a compliment."

Jamie Phipps chuckled. Dr Garston wasn't as amused.

"Her capacity for language is supernatural."

I smiled at Jamie, even though I didn't know what supernatural meant.

Dr Garston's mouth twitched. "Then she was with people for longer than she remembers."

"Maybe. Maybe not."

They both looked at me as if to settle the argument.

"I've told you, I don't remember."

"No matter." Dr Garston got up from behind his desk. "Would you step outside, Dr Phipps?"

The word *doctor* was infused with contempt. Jamie was only a doctor of words. He squeezed my shoulder on his way out.

"Get undressed. The nurse will help you."

"I don't need help."

"I'm Carol. Come through here." The nurse, white haired and thin, took my elbow.

I undressed in the cubicle. She didn't react to my abnormalities. My breasts were flat and clitoris engorged to manly proportions. Dark hair covering me in varying degrees. As she fastened the ties of the thin blue gown, she leant in close to my ear. "Don't let him see that you're scared of him."

"He looks at me like I'm an animal."

"He looks at all women that way."

The general barrenness of women. We were all a problem to him.

After Dr Garston inspected me, he kept me standing while he told me about the regime he'd planned to make me *more normal*.

"You will bleed from your vagina every month. That's called a period. That's good."

My forest-sisters and I knew about that already, although it wasn't a monthly event. Spots of blood that dripped on our thighs as we walked. The afflicted retreated until the others found her and licked the imaginary wound clean.

"I might as well chip you now."

"Chip?"

"A tracking device. It's so we'll always know where you are. All women have them." He relished my discomfort at that. "It's for your own good."

"Why?"

"Men here are civilised. They treat women like jewels. A man who attacks a woman risks execution." He didn't say *women are only for the wealthy*. "There are places where men live without women. If they abduct you, they'll keep you on a chain like a dog and regularly rape you."

The only time I ever saw Dr Garston smile at me was when he said the words *like a dog*.

The trill of the phone wakes me.

"You said you'd call." It's Lisa.

"What time is it?" I wipe the crusts of sleep from my eyes.

"Five o'clock."

"I fell asleep."

"You promised you'd ring me."

"You sound angry."

"Worried. Not angry."

"You worrying won't help me, so don't."

"Don't be ridiculous. You're my friend."

There's a fraction of a beat before she says the word *friend*. I don't reply.

"We are friends, aren't we?"

"Yes." I use my most ambiguous tone.

"It doesn't sound like it, not anymore. This is more than shock over Kush. Why are you—"

"I'm not up to this now."

That stops her dead. Her breathing's ragged.

"Okay."

I want to cry after talking to Lisa but I can't, so I rip the phone from the socket and smash it against the wall. It doesn't break, just makes a mess of the wallpaper, which frustrates me even more.

I wish Kush were here. I'd do the same to him. Instead, he's left Lisa to bear the brunt of it all.

I sit, nursing my numbness until it's dark.

I'm not startled when the security light goes on this time. What makes me jump is the wet *thump* as something hits the window pane. It comes again, then again. *Splat. Splat. Splat.*

All the ground-floor windows and doors are secure. The security lights make it worse. It creates halos around the dark patches on the glass. I wrap the quilt around me so I'm rolled in it, as if this can block everything out.

Go away, go away, go away.

My bravado of the previous night has gone. If I looked out I'd be able to see who it is in bright glory, which makes me more afraid than of the shadows. I'm not ready for that. Not yet.

The problem is that I can tell from the volleys that there's more of them down there flinging balled-up mud. There's a whole pack of them.

They stop as the morning light comes in, and I fall asleep for an hour or so. The bedroom windows are completely muddied, drying in patches to pale brown.

They've been busy out there. Every ground-floor window has been pelted, too. They've made a mess of the wooden cladding that Kush had chosen because it weathered silvery grey with age. It's a façade to make the house more at home in its surrounding.

The pond that runs beneath the decked walkway has been polluted with faeces. Most of the fish have been flicked onto the path, their bright colours dulling.

I grit my teeth and pull out the power hose and spray off as much muck as I can, leaving the glass streaky but cleaner.

A distant engine gets closer. It roars as it approaches. It's Jamie, on his motorbike.

"What the hell happened here?"

He follows me in, carrying his helmet.

"I don't know." I'm about to ask him why he's come but he interrupts me.

"You shouldn't be alone. Not out here. It's dangerous." He takes off his jacket and lays it on the arm of a sofa.

"Not to me. And I'm getting used to being alone."

"Yes, you're a fast learner. Words fell from your mouth like flowers."

"You've got a selective memory. For the first few weeks, I pissed in corners, and ate food from a bowl on the floor."

I bit anybody who came too close and they finally tranquilised me with a dart. I awoke to find they'd shaved my fur, clipped my nails and bound me in clothes. How I howled.

"Don't cry."

"Am I?" My own tears confound me. I'm more tired than I realise.

"Shh, I'm here, it's okay."

Jamie puts his arms around me. He presses his forehead to mine and his voice is soothing. He smells of sandalwood and leather. The softness of his nose pushes against mine, the pressure helping to close the distance between our mouths.

I scuttle backwards. He follows.

"Let yourself feel this. Go with it." He pushes against me.

Perhaps he thinks he's generating sexual tension. I strike his chest with the heel of my hand as a warning. It's an impotent gesture.

"I'd never hurt you, Ava."

His mouth searches for mine again. I jerk my head out of reach.

"It doesn't matter how much money Kush left you. If you don't take a husband, they'll choose for you. It's the law. You're rich enough to choose for yourself. Why not me?"

Jamie's hand is on the back of my neck. He's determined.

"You can't say no. Not forever."

"I'm saying no *now*."

"Who knows you better than I do? I can't afford you but now you can afford me."

Arousal comes off him in waves.

"I love you, Ava."

He puts a hand in my hair and clutches at the roots. He pushes his face into my neck, his other hand pulling at my shirt buttons. He's risking a lot, considering the punishment for rape outside marriage. Maybe he thinks that nobody will believe Ava-the-dog-woman, or this is a forceful seduction rather than an assault. Jamie isn't going to stop.

To think when I was first found that I was prepared to submit to such violent invasions for the sake of my sisters.

Not now.

Disbelief is a paralytic, preventing fight-or-flight. You have a series of moments in which to act, after which you're lost.

"Wait."

He pauses and I reach up and take his head in my hands, tilting it. His lips part in anticipation. Then I twist, a powerful jerk to the right and he falls like all the bones have gone out of him.

It's been years since I killed anything.

I put down my cutlery. I wanted to lick my plate to get at the last of the steak juices and the salt crystals, so I distracted myself by looking out of the window at the trees. Salt. What a marvel.

"Do you miss it?" Kush asked.

The pain in that question made me turn to him. He'd never asked me that before, not even in our most unguarded, intimate moments.

"You built a house in this beautiful place for us. I can go outside whenever I want to."

"It's not like living out there though, is it? Tell me what it was like."

There was no way to tell him what was out there. Escaped pigs grown to boar-like proportions, armed with tusks. Horses that thunder along the dried-up river beds, too wild to ever be ridden. It's not just mammals. There are elm saplings deep in the forest. There are abandoned towns in the great forest. The foundations have been torn up by roots. Broken roads lead nowhere.

So the real world regrows.

"Let me show you."

I slid open the doors. The fresh air energised me after the air-conditioning within. I ran. Kush was behind me.

"Come on!"

I ran between the oaks and the beech trunks, along an irregular line of young silver birches. I threw off my shoes. Paused to undo my skirt and let it drop. I peeled off my t-shirt and flung it down. The cool air chilled my skin. I laughed.

"Be careful!" Kush called after me.

I laughed with joy as I ran headlong, like I'd die if I stopped. I felt damp moss and bracken beneath my feet, punctuated by the crack of dead twigs. I could smell leaf mould. I scrambled over fallen logs and felt the mud between my toes. The fecund smell of home.

I still run but not as fast as I once could. My heart pounded. The light through the leaves found my flesh as dappled patterns.

"Ava, stop!"

I looked back to see Kush trying to keep up. He held a stitch in his side, wincing with pain.

"Don't move."

I was so exhilarated that I didn't see the danger ahead. I'd been running blind. The trees stopped at a precipice. The forest was no more. The drop was unforgiving.

Once I would've known it was there half a mile away from the thinning trunks, the roll of the land, the change in natural light and the resulting lichen growth on the bark. I would feel it in the breeze on my face. How I'd forgotten myself.

Kush closed the distance between us at a walk, panting and sweaty.

"I thought you were going to fall."

"I knew it was there."

Kush always knew when I was lying.

"You've hurt yourself."

Both my feet were bleeding. He made me sit down and he pulled out the thorns. I'd forgotten my soles weren't thick and calloused anymore. My arms and legs were scratched.

Kush glanced up at me like he was seeing something in me for the first time, something he took to be a sort of madness. It made me sad, because men had once been wild and free, too.

Taking Jamie up to the cliff-edge is heavy work. I can't bear to look at him. He falls like a broken doll.

His motorbike is heavy and cumbersome and I wonder if

it's worth the effort. In the end I dump it in the undergrowth and cover it as best as I can.

There's a van outside the house when I get back. The delivery man gets out when he sees me and thrusts a clipboard at me to sign. He's unhappy at being kept waiting. I don't apologize.

"I didn't want to leave this on the step."

It sounds like reproach. I hand back his pen without a word.

The package is from the crematorium. Kush is returned to me in a plastic urn. He would've hated that. He was a big man but I wasn't expecting his ashes to be so heavy.

I put most of Kush's remains into his beloved ginger jar. He brought it home one day, his eyes round with fascination.

"This is hundreds of years old. It was made on the other side of the world. This colour is called celadon."

"Celadon." I rolled the word mouth around with my tongue. It was a beautiful pale green that contained grey and blue. I traced the vein of gold that ran through the porcelain like jagged lightning. "It's been broken."

"In Japan, damaged things are sometimes repaired with gold. It's called Kintsugi. The flaw makes it more precious."

"Are you a collector of flawed things?"

The jar is the most fitting resting place for Kush, but I want part of him to be outside too, to be free. To nourish the ground and the trees so that I can taste him in the rain dripping from the branches and smell him in the sweet chestnuts.

I put some of his ashes in an old jam jar and go out.

Our weekend guests would admire the forest from the panoramic windows, as if trees were dangerous animals. The human race is gradually dying in concrete enclaves, only they don't know it.

For me the trees are company. Each type has their own discourse. Their leaves speak differently. When Kush was working I'd come out here and lie between the roots of the giant oaks. I imagined the pack surrounding me, our chests rising and falling in unison. We'd all dream the same dreams of rabbit flesh and the dark haunch of deer. Of rootlets pushing their way through the soil and the uncurling of ferns. Love knots of diamond-backed adders and the clinging, climbing ivy. Fat blackberries. Burnished, brown conkers.

I sit on a fallen log when I reach my favourite clearing. It's been colonised with wood beetles and bracket fungi. A centipede crawls out from between the rotting bark and then over my hand. How life survives.

It's time. Kush's ashes are soft in my fist. I let the wind take him.

I walk back slowly and stand at the forest's edge looking at the house. A chill sets in.

The huge windows reflect the moving clouds. The house is a piece of art in itself. As much an art gallery within as a house. I can't imagine a future there without Kush.

Then I realize that the front door's wide open.

I stand at the threshold, listening. Silence.

They've been busy. The canvases in the hall have been slashed in parallel lines. Strips hang off them. Clothes are strewn down the stairs, reduced to rags.

The smell coming from the lounge is so pungent that my eyes smart. The sofa seats have been torn open and the stuffing scattered. The sofa carcasses reek of urine and other musky signatures. Magazines and coffee table books are confetti. There's snot smeared on the mirrors and the windows, as if someone's pressed their faces against them.

Kush's collection of porcelain has been pulled from their shelves and smashed with utter disrespect for their provenance.

Except Kush's urn. It sits in the centre of the low table, placed carefully amid the debris. I wrap my arms around him.

I'm sorry, I'm sorry, I'm sorry. I'm sorry I was angry at you. It doesn't matter if you loved Lisa. It was my fault. I resented loving you. Every morning I thought, today is the day that I'll leave. I'll go home. But when I saw your face all I could do was stay one more day.

When Kush proposed marriage, I explained to him what Dr Garston had told me about my *abnormalities*. My eggs were few and my uterus misshapen. It contained a pouch that he couldn't remove, and it would interfere with artificial insemination.

Kush kept his head down as I spoke, only looking up at me

when I finished.

"That doesn't matter to me."

I thought I'd got the measure of Kush then. Even wombless women were wanted for pleasure.

"But are you sure it doesn't matter to *you*?" He gestured to my bookshelf, piled with books on reproductive anatomy, physiology, and theories on our lamentable infertility.

I waited naked on the edge of our marriage bed. My clothes were laid out on the back of a chair. Kush stood in the doorway, frozen. We stared at each other. His gaze stayed on my face. It took all my strength not to drop into a crouch and bare my teeth, even though I'd agreed to this arrangement.

A few times sister, that's all we need. Lie still and submit. Then you can come home.

I was aware of everything about Kush as he crossed the room. The movement of his Adam's apple. The eyelashes framing those dark eyes. The confusing smells of arousal and restraint on him. I'd never been so aware of the clothes that covered him. The security of those second skins didn't seem so false anymore.

He reached over to the chair and picked up my knickers. He knelt before me and put them over one of my feet and then the other.

"Stand."

He pulled them up like I was a child in need of help. He slid the straps of my bra up my arms and reached around to do up the clasp at my back.

The dress came next. I held up my arms and the supple fabric slipped over me like a caress. I shivered.

"I'm yours, to have whenever you want."

"I want you," I'd never seen him so fierce, "but I want you to want *me*, too."

I couldn't move. I couldn't speak.

"Ava, there's something I need to do."

Kush led me into the bathroom. The white tiles and mirrors made me nervous.

Then I saw that he'd already laid out a steel tray on the marble counter containing syringes, needles, ampoules and packs of dressings. The scalpel looked small and innocuous. My lip curled, revealing my teeth.

"Please, Ava. It's important to me."

I didn't understand what it was he wanted. He put a hand on my shoulder, the new wedding band glinting under the bright, clinical lights. He placed his other hand on the back of my neck and pushed my head down. "I'll try not to hurt you, I promise."

There's the crunch of someone stepping on eggshell porcelain behind me. I should be on my feet, ready to fight, but all I can do is clutch the ginger jar tighter.

"What happened here? Are you hurt?"

"No. I came back to find it like this."

"Pack a bag. You're coming to stay with me."

This is the Lisa I know. Maternal, calm, taking charge. It would be easy to let her sweep me up and carry me out of here.

"No. Forget this. It's not important. There's something we need to talk about." I have to say it now, while I still have a chance. "I know about you and Kush. I forgive you both."

Her mouth forms a surprised circle.

"There's always been a part of me that I held back from Kush. I don't blame him for turning to you. And I know how things are with you and Paul."

"Kush loved you absolutely. There was only ever you."

"I *know*, Lisa. You'd become so awkward together, like you didn't know how act around each other."

Lisa's low throaty laugh is clogged with tears. "It wasn't because we were having an affair. It was because he realised that I was in love with you."

Love. How much love have I had in this lifetime? Love that I wanted. Something that I thought was love but wasn't. And this, love unrecognised.

"Say something. Please."

Lisa. Friend. Sister. I lean in, ignoring her sharp intake of breath as I put my lips to hers. An undefined kiss. She tastes of heartbreak.

"I can't stay here anymore."

Colours rises in her cheeks.

"I can come with you."

"You won't survive out there."

"They'll find you."

I take off the long necklace that I always wear. The vial that hangs from it contains the chip that Dr Garston put under my skin.

"Kush?" Lisa asks.

"Yes." What better wedding gift could he give me than freedom?

I lift the ginger jar lid and drop the necklace in. Let it rest there, at least for a while.

"You'll be alone out there."

"I won't be alone." I'm not a foundling. I'm forest born.

"*What* are you?"

Lisa's hesitant. She wants to know but is afraid of the answer. It's a question that nobody ever thought to ask.

"I'm a woman."

"Not like me. Not like anyone else I know."

"No, you're right, I'm different."

"How?"

"I'll show you. Come outside."

She follows me. The earth is not the only thing to thrive in being left fallow. Out in the woodland, women have flourished, too. We've found another answer to our failing fertility.

I shed my clothes and stand as when my mother spilt me, screaming and thrashing on the dark earth. I stand as tall as I can and wait.

My sisters heard me crying when Kush died. They came from far away. Our strange gift allows us to hunt as one and subdue our enemies. Words are superfluous. I don't know if it's something primaeval in our genes or not.

They come out of the trees, some on hind legs, some on all fours. They're all short and stocky, just like me. They grin and grimace by way of greeting. Our thoughts buzz. Oh, you men and women, with your limited language that's so clumsy and veiled.

Our communication is instant. It's full of vision and nuances. I pull at the threads of their thoughts.

You've grown fat and old, sister.

We've missed you.

You're so bare.

Indeed I am, for all my regrowth. They have no shame in nakedness and I must learn that skill again. I lift my head, despite my deficit of fur.

We've been waiting for you. For years. Why have you taken so long?

We need to go north before the winter.

Their pelts are thickening in readiness for the snow. Before the freeze sets in, we'll find the breaches in the ground and explore the crevasses and cracks. We'll crawl on our bellies through the narrow passages into larger caverns where clean water pours through. We'll sleep in the safe arms of the dark.

What's that? They're all looking at Lisa, who's behind me.

Lisa is watching us all, unable to hear the silent dialogue.

Sister, I say.

Can we trust her?

Yes. One sniff of doubt from me and they'll tear out her throat.

Hmm. They're bemused by her pallor, her height, her smell. *Can she run?*

Not like us.

Can YOU still run?

One of them lowers her head as she approaches, sniffing me. Her face mirrors mine in her widow's peak, her pointed chin and her heavy brows.

I pissed all over your den.

I cuff her for that and we both grin.

Are you full of seed for us?

Yes.

If you have a limited supply of eggs, it's wasteful to squander one each month in hope of it being fertilised. It's more efficient to save them for optimal conditions.

That's the reason that I came here. We'd occasionally found a man living in a house as derelict as his mind, somewhere deep in the woods. We were kind to him, even if he couldn't father children. When we ran out of those we had to take men from the margins which was dangerous. None of us wanted to be caught and forced to live in cities, even if it meant there'd be plenty of mates.

We all want to be free to run.

I was chosen for my strength, speed and ability to endure. My vestigial pouch, bemoaned by Dr Garston, everts into a spout.

Captivity has made a reproductive theorist of me. Although hot inside my womb, tiny swimmers can survive for several months, by what I can only imagine must be chemical means.

I will share Kush's hoard with my sisters. I'd expected to be a vessel for sperm, not to find love. I hadn't expected a man, who was man enough to let me be free, to choose for myself.

Lisa wants to know what we are. Uncanny evolution. We're the future, not the past. The world will be ours when you're all gone.

I'll miss Kush. I'll miss Lisa. I'll miss your beautiful, arcane words. But when I run, I don't look back.

The Coldness of His Eye

By Brian Evenson

1.

There they were, Jens and his father, again together, after so many years. The same as it had always been, only so much had changed. Jens was much older, as old as his father had been when they had last been together, hair white and wispy and fugitive, complexion sallow, hands thin enough to display the articulation of his bones.

And yet his father looked like he always had—face hale and hearty, figure large and looming, unbent by age. It was as if his father had not aged at all. Which, in a manner of speaking, he hadn't, since he'd been dead now for thirty years.

Hello, Jens, his dead father said.

"Hello," said Jens, because he did not know what else to say. He was not, he was surprised to find, frightened. More than anything he was curious: *Why now?* And also curious to see if his father turned around, would the back of his bald skull would be solid and smooth or, as he had last seen it, broken and soft.

"What do you want?" Jens asked.

His father did not answer. He just smiled in a way that didn't move the muscles of his face. It was as if a smile had suddenly been painted on.

"It's been a long time since I've seen you," said Jens.

The painted smile flicked to a painted frown. *Not that long,* said his father. *Only yesterday.*

It had not been just yesterday. It had been three decades before. Should he correct his father? He wasn't sure. What was the etiquette in such a situation, when you were made to interact with the dead?

"Why are you here?" asked Jens.

Don't I have a right to be here? his father asked, indignantly. *Isn't it my house?* His lips when he spoke, Jens realized, didn't seem to move.

No, it wasn't his house. It wasn't a house the man had ever been in, but a place Jens had purchased shortly after his father's death, with the money the insurance paid out.

"How exactly can I help you?"

Help me? said his father. He gave that same painted-on smile. *Isn't it clear that I'm beyond help?*

And then he held out his hand, beckoned.

2.

He came to himself downstairs, beside the front door, his hand attempting to turn the knob as his wife shook him. When she realized he was awake, she stopped.

"What was it?" she asked. "Some sort of dream? Why were you going outside?"

"Did I want to go out?" he asked. "I was having a nightmare," he said, though he wasn't sure that was exactly what it had been. "How did I get down here?"

"You were sleepwalking," she said. "Muttering, too. Saying something."

"What was I saying?"

She shook her head. "I don't know. I couldn't understand."

"Good," he said. Inside, he winced. It did not seem the right thing to say.

"Come back to bed," she said, and he let himself be led. On the stairs, she asked, "What was your nightmare about?"

He waved his hands in dismissal. "Hard to remember," he said.

He lay there in the bed, beside her. In no time at all, her breathing deepened and her body relaxed, and he was sure she was asleep.

Did *he* want to go to sleep? Not really. It didn't seem like a particularly good idea. It was not that he was afraid of his father, of his father's ghost, but he did not particularly want to spend more time with it either. He had not missed his father since he had killed him thirty years ago, had hardly even thought about him. Which made him wonder again, *Why now?*

He slid out of the bed, careful not to wake her. He felt his way to the door in the dark and out onto the landing.

A shaft of moonlight shone down through the skylight. He couldn't see well but he could see enough to know where he was going. He made his way down the stairs and to the entryway below.

There was the door, the handle he had been touching when his wife stopped him. Where had he been going, and why?

Hello, Jens, he heard his father say behind him.

He flinched, then froze. Gathering himself, he turned around. There the man was, just visible, half in and half out of the dark, his lit eye glittering coldly. He wasn't asleep now, Jens was almost sure. Hallucinating, maybe? Or was he really here? Had he been asleep before?

Hello, he managed.

You don't look good, son, said his father. *You haven't been taking care of yourself.*

But he *had* been taking care of himself. It was just that he was three decades older.

"What do you want?" Jens asked.

Do you remember where you killed me? asked his father.

"I didn't..." Jens started, by reflex, and then fell silent.

So his father knew he was dead. And that Jens had killed him. Did that change anything?

"I was... cleared of any involvement in your murder," Jens offered.

Of course you were, said his father. *You're clever. You have good genes. I would expect no less of you.*

"I…" Jens trailed off. "Yes," he finally said. "Of course I remember."

Will you do something for me?

"I don't know."

His father ignored him as if he hadn't spoken. He stared at Jens. He had been staring the whole time, never blinking, his one lit eye never moving from Jens' face.

Go back there.

"Why?"

It is important, said his father. *Go back there.*

"But your body isn't even there. You're buried in the grave-yard off Twenty-sixth. I can show you your headstone."

I'm not talking about my body. I'm talking about the place where you killed me. Go there. Now.

3.

It was crazy, he told himself, even as he pulled on his boots. There was no point going, no point taking instruction from his father's ghost. That was one of the reasons he had killed his father; he was tired of taking instruction from him. Well, that and the insurance money.

What does my wife know? he wondered. She knew he had been interviewed by the police—she had been there when they arrived. She knew he had been cleared, partly due to her testi-mony. She had been asleep when he had killed his father—he had made sure of that, a pill crushed and mixed into her wine. His wife knew he had gone to bed with her and that he had been there, when, in the morning, she woke up. Why would she not think he was there beside her the whole night?

No, it was foolish. He had lived nearly thirty years believ-ing his wife had no idea he had killed his father. There was no reason to reconsider that now.

Besides, his father was waiting, in the dark near the door, watching him. No matter where Jens moved his father was always looking at him.

"Shall we go?" asked Jens.

After you, said his father.

"No, after you," Jens answered.

They had had the same exchange the night his father died, Jens realized once the door was locked and he was cutting through the grassy field and moving toward the forested mountain beyond. *After you. No, after you.* His father had shrugged and gone first and Jens had followed close behind him. He had watched the back of his father's bald head as the man climbed the switchbacked path up the mountainside and to the cave.

"A man?" his father had said.

"Yes," Jens had said. "A man. I think he's dead."

"Did you check his breathing? His pulse?"

"I couldn't find anything."

His father grunted, kept walking.

"The thing I don't understand," his father said a moment later, "is what you were doing up there yourself."

Yes, he had had to admit to himself, there was a flaw to his plan and his father had found it. There was no sane reason he would be up in the cave in the middle of the night. "I go there sometimes," he had claimed. "To think."

"To think," his father said flatly, not even bothering to turn around. "This is a strange place," he said. "I'd reconsider before coming up here to think."

True, his father had often told stories of the cave and the woods around it, as a way of making it difficult for Jens, when he was young, to sleep. Which was one reason it had given Jens a certain amount of satisfaction to kill him there. His father had been a good storyteller, he had to give him that, even if he was a sadist. Though now he wondered if killing him here was what had allowed his father to eventually come back as a ghost. If so, he had taken his time about it.

Back then, he had seen nothing but the back of his father's head, bald and featureless. Now, however, the dead father in front of him showed only his face. He wasn't walking backward exactly—it was more as if, motionless, he was always exactly the same distance ahead and looking back, always keeping an eye on Jens.

"Aren't you interested in knowing why I did it?" asked Jens.
Did what?

"Killed you."

The face flicked into a frown. *No,* his father said. *At this point knowing would make no difference.*

"Sometimes you think you know the world," one of those stories had begun, "and that's your first mistake." Now, hiking up to the cave, it was hard not to think of these stories of his father's:

A man goes into the woods and lies down. When he wakes up again, years have passed for him, but only minutes for the rest of the world.

Or, another: a man enters a cave. He twists and turns through its passages and comes out again. For him, no time has passed, but in the world at large, thirty years have gone by. And when he hikes back down the mountain and back to the town he has always lived in, he discovers that another man who looks just like him is living with his wife, that someone else has been imitating him.

Perhaps that was why his father had come back. Because it had been thirty years.

How had that last story continued? He had not thought about it all this time. All he remembered was the original man trying to convince his wife that she had lived with an imposter for the last three decades, and failing. Obviously, if there was an imposter, she reasoned, it would be the much younger man. It would be him.

"But he would not listen," his father had said—he remembered now. "He kept insisting until the townsfolk had little choice but to slaughter him."

Thirty years earlier, they had reached the cave at last, Jens breathing heavily from the climb and perhaps from anxiety as well.

His father was barely winded. He played his flashlight over the walls. "Where is he?" he had asked. "This man you claimed you saw?"

"He was right there," said Jens. "In that."

On the floor, a line of pale sand traced a circle, with a slightly smaller circle made of dirt just within it.

"What the hell is that?" his father asked.

"I don't know," Jens claimed. He moved forward and reached out to touch the twinned circles with his toe, but his father stopped him.

"Don't," said his father. "You don't know what's inside it."

But Jens did know. He knew nothing was inside it since he had drawn the circle himself. Unlike his father, he was not superstitious.

His father crouched down to get a closer look, still careful not to touch or cross the circle. And that was the moment Jens chose to strike the back of his head with the rock he had pre-pared just for that purpose. His father groaned. He fell into the circles, breaking the lines. A few more blows to the back of his skull and he was dead.

Here we are, said his father. *Again.*

"Yes," said Jens. "Here we are." He played the flashlight around the cave. It was empty, nothing there at all. If he looked carefully, he thought he could see the traces of the circle he had made, but little beyond that.

But of course there couldn't be traces of the circles: it had been thirty years. And yet, it seemed to him that that was what he was seeing.

His father's body had been found quickly, almost impossi-bly so. He'd expected a month or two of his father being missing and him having to pretend that, like everyone else, he didn't know where he had gone. But shortly after his wife awoke, the police had arrived at his door looking for him.

"What is it?" he had said.

"We have a few questions we'd like to ask," said one. "Can we come in?"

"Is anything wrong?" he replied.

"When was the last time you saw your father?"

For a moment he thought his father must have survived, that he wasn't dead after all, that he had stumbled his way down the mountain, bloody and broken, and called the police.

"Two days ago," he managed. "Maybe three?"

"Three days," his wife said from beside him. "He came over here yelling like a lunatic."

Their attention sharpened. "What was he upset about?" they asked her.

"Is anything wrong?" he asked again before his wife could answer. His panic from worrying that his father was still alive was exactly right for allowing him to convey anxiety and shock when they finally told him his father's body had been found. He tried to hold on to that panic, to not let relief wash over him until they were finally done with him.

He walked around the remnants of the twinned circles without crossing into them.

Remember how quickly I was found? his father asked, as if he knew what Jens was thinking. Perhaps he did.

"Yes," said Jens.

Who drew the circles? he asked. *Was it you?*

Jens hesitated, then nodded.

Why? Did you know what they would do?

He had suspected the circles would interest his father and cause him to let down his guard. He had, too, thought it might set the police off on the wrong track, thinking it an occult murder, a ceremony gone wrong, rather than bringing them after him. But neither, he felt, were what his father had in mind.

"What do you mean?" he asked slowly.

His father didn't answer, just stayed watching him as, restless, he kept circling, with that same unblinking expression.

You're afraid of it, his father taunted. *You made it and yet you're afraid of it.*

"Don't be stupid," Jens said.

All right then, said his father. *Prove it.*

He could see the circle clearly now, shimmering in the dim light, the lighter line and then, within it, the darker line. Perhaps it was not a circle but only the ghost of a circle. In either case, it could not hurt him. He was not superstitious. He had made it: something he had made could not hurt him.

He stepped across the lines and into the center.

And then, abruptly, his father was very close indeed.

The first mistake you made, his father's voice said softly, *was assuming I was your father, rather than just someone or something resembling him.* And when Jens turned to flee there was his father, or the thing that resembled his father, both in front of him and behind.

4.

When she woke up, she saw that her husband was still asleep. He lay on his left side, crumpled up, which seemed strange to her. He never slept on that side because, when he was younger, his father had broken that arm in one of his rages. His father had been a real bastard, a brutal man. Her husband never spoke of him. Just as well he was gone.

She shook her husband a little and he groaned. He rolled to his back, winced, then opened his eyes. They wandered a little then came to focus on her.

"Good morning," she said.

"Yes."

"Feeling all right?" she asked. "Over the nightmare?"

"Nightmare?" he asked, and seemed to search his memory without finding anything. "What did I say it was about?"

"You didn't say," she said.

"I'm just fine now," he claimed. "Better than I've been in a long time."

There was something about him, something different, something she couldn't quite put her finger on. Or maybe it was just that she also was sleepy from being awakened in the middle of the night.

She sighed. "What shall we do today?" she asked.

"You don't have to go to work?"

She furrowed her brow. "Silly you," she said. "I haven't worked for years."

"I'm off today?"

"It's Saturday. What's wrong with you?"

There was an expression on his face she couldn't read. "I

don't know what I'm thinking," he said.

She didn't say anything in reply, just lay on her side with her hand propping up her head, watching him. There was something, she felt, that she was trying to see, but she couldn't see it.

After a while he looked away, stared up at the ceiling.

"What to do…" he mused. "A walk," he said.

A walk? she thought. *That's a first.*

"Or a hike. Up to the mountains," he said. "To a little place I used to go. A special place. You'll love it." He turned to face her. "You'll love it so much," he promised. "Once I take you there, you have a hard time dragging yourself away."

The Porcupine Boy

By Lucy A. Snyder

Eddie Bellweather got out of his Honda Odyssey with his satchel, locked the door and grinned at the glossy new graphics he'd gotten his buddy Rafael to paint on the van's side. The logo bore the words "PORCUPINE BOY PATIENT SERVICES" in a blue circle around a cute cartoon porcupine in a Superman-style caped crusader costume with a fists-on-hips pose and a red PB on his chest shield in place of Supe's stylized "S". Rafael had promised him that DC couldn't sue him over his new mascot, and it was exactly what Eddie had envisioned. It was bold and friendly, and Eddie figured it perfectly conveyed the little-guy heroism he strove for when he started his business. People were counting on him. He was *needed*. And that was something he'd grown up thinking could never happen.

"It is a *great* day to be alive." He booped his mascot's flat black nose with his index finger and then headed up the tree-shaded walkway to Dr. Shanahan's office.

He hadn't set foot in this particular office in at least three years, and remembered it as having a cozy, unassuming waiting room with office furniture from the '80s. Only one of his clients was a patient here—old Miss Dorotka—and Dr. Shanahan was fine with renewing her prescriptions without making her take the stressful trek to his exam table. Until now, for whatever reason. Eddie was confident he could get it sorted out.

But when he pushed through the glass doors, instead of the outdated chairs and plastic-framed public health posters he saw fancy new seating, potted plants and expensive-looking oil paintings. And, on one wall, an ostentatiously large crucifix of a sheet-pale Christ nailed to a mahogany cross. It certainly wasn't there before. The sight of it made Eddie's stomach tighten. He didn't have anything against Christianity, not exactly. Not *officially*. But the cross was the kind of thing his mother would have put up in the living room, not as a reminder of any of the things that Jesus lived and died for, but as a stern reminder to all visitors (and particularly Eddie's few friends) that This Is a Christian House And We Don't Tolerate That Kind of Thing Here. Her version of Christianity had little to do with goodwill towards humankind or turning the other cheek, and everything to do with shame and fronting piety.

Eddie had plenty of Christian clients who weren't bent the way his mother was; they were good folks of faith. He had no reason to think that the owner of this cross should be less like them and more like his mother. But he *also* had clients who were Jewish, Muslim, Buddhist, or atheist, and a huge, hard-to-miss cross like this was likely to make them feel a bit unwelcome. So many Christians had done so many terrible things in the name of that crucifix: The Inquisition, the Crusades, the Magdalene Laundries. Dr. Shanahan seemed like the kind of man who'd cracked enough history books to realize that, and who just on basic principle would want to avoid alienating patients for no reason. So what was going on here?

If Eddie was being honest with himself, the cross gave him a twinge of envy. What must it be like to so firmly believe in a higher power, to have faith in the existence of a grand supernatural order that transcended the mundane bullshit that made up so much of everyday human existence? Eddie wanted to believe; he *craved* belief, at times. But he was fundamentally a man who could only believe in what he could see, taste, or touch. Even the powerful hallucinogens that his friends swore would open his inner eye to the wonders hidden beyond the limitations of fleshly senses left him queasy and agnostic. Eddie figured that the right thing to do was the right thing to do, regardless of whether God existed to give you wings for it or not. But some days, he'd have nearly been willing to give his right nut for proof that there was more to the world than met his eye.

                              Lucy A. Snyder

Eddie turned away from the cross and focused on the check-in counter. The receptionist during his previous visits had been a plump older lady who reminded him of his great aunt Judy, the one person in his family who never treated him like a loser. But now, the receptionist was an extremely pretty woman in her mid-twenties who looked like she should be in a toothpaste commercial.

She gave him a frosty-white smile. "May I help you?"

"Hi, I'm Eddie with Porcupine Boy Patient Services," he replied. "I'm helping one of Dr. Shanahan's long-term patients, Dorotka Nowak. I tried to get her maintenance meds refilled at the pharmacy, but they said they couldn't get this office to fax in a new script. So I'm here to check on that."

Her eyes narrowed suspiciously. "What's your relation to Mrs. Nowak?"

"As I said, I'm with Porcupine Boy. I'm here in my capacity as her patient advocate." He opened his satchel, pulled out the medical power of attorney form Miss Dorotka signed and showed it to the receptionist.

"Let me bring up her file." She turned to the computer and started keying in a query. "Porcupine Boy is kind of a weird name for a company, don't you think?"

Eddie's smile didn't waver. "My great-grandfather was Zuni. In his religion, porcupines symbolize the power of faith and trust, both of which are critical for patient advocacy."

He tapped the logo on his polo shirt. "And the 'Boy' part represents the idea that I'm getting out there and fighting for my clients like Beast Boy, or Astro Boy."

Eddie hadn't told her any lies, but none of those were the reason he got the nickname Porcupine Boy back in the day. When he was sixteen, his parents kicked him out of their trailer for going to the movies with a black girl and he ended up living in a downtown Granite City flop with a bunch of crust punks. One night, he watched a torrent of *Hellraiser* on a stolen laptop while he got blitzed on meth and cheap gin. He ended up shoving a hundred sewing needles into his forehead, cheeks, and arms before he passed out. His flopmates found him a couple of hours later, and one of the older guys in the house—who'd never seen the movie and didn't know what a cenobite was—started calling him "Porcupine Boy".

The nickname stuck harder than the needles. Even though it was a misunderstanding, Eddie felt like getting a real nickname was a sign he'd been accepted into the local punk community and wasn't just another gangly white-trash throwaway nobody gave a shit about. So he just rolled with it, and when he scraped together a few hundred dollars, he got a huge tattoo of a porcupine on his chest along with his nickname in black gothic lettering.

It didn't matter to Eddie that not everybody understood or cared about his personal brand. What mattered was that *he* knew what it meant, and he'd been able to change the meaning of his nickname to adapt to whom he had become as a person in the decade since.

"Huh," said the receptionist. "Looks like she's never actually seen Dr. Shanahan. She'll need to come in for an exam before he can write her a prescription."

"What do you mean she's never seen Dr. Shanahan?" Eddie blinked at her. "I brought her in myself right after she became my client."

"Oh, well, she probably saw Dr. Shanahan's uncle. He owned the practice before, but Dr. Shanahan bought it from him last year when the old guy got pancreatic cancer."

Shit. Eddie's stomach dropped. Not that any cancer was a day at the beach, but pancreatic cancer was particularly brutal. Dr. Shanahan seemed like a thoroughly decent guy and didn't deserve a terrible disease like that. "I sure am sorry to hear that … how's he doing?"

"I think he died." The receptionist shrugged indifferently, and Eddie decided he didn't like her very much, regardless of how pretty she was. "I never met him, so I don't know. Anyway, your client's going to need to make an appointment."

"Are you sure that's really necessary? She's very elderly, and her immune system is compromised. Getting out to appointments is hazardous for her. She's been doing telemedicine for urgent care, and she's got a USB blood pressure monitor and such. I'm a registered nurse, so I can do a blood draw if the doctor wants labs done. Can we arrange for a remote exam instead?" He hadn't drawn Miss Dorotka's blood before, but he'd done that for other clients and there hadn't ever been a problem with the doctors or the labs.

The receptionist looked bored and a little irritated. "She'll have to see the doctor in person if she wants to be a patient here."

Eddie tried to swallow his growing frustration. There was no point to making the old lady come in. She was frail but stable and in pretty good health considering her advanced age ... but that depended on her getting her medications. Particularly the ferropentin, which she had to take for recurring fevers she'd suffered ever since she'd gone on an archaeological dig in Egypt when she was a young woman. It was some kind of parasitic infection in her blood that couldn't be cured; she'd described it as being like malaria. Eddie hadn't gotten a lot of information about whatever the pathogen was, but the important details as far as he was concerned were that she wasn't contagious, and the ferropentin was critical for her well-being. Without it, she got moody and started suffering memory problems. Her mobility took a serious hit, and her immune problems worsened. One of the worst symptoms was a terrible, ulcerated rash on her skin; out of self-consciousness she'd started wearing long sleeves, gloves, and a veil. She denied feeling pain, but Eddie didn't believe that for one second; she walked like every step was on broken glass.

He was sorely tempted to tell the receptionist that they'd just find another doctor ... but he also knew there was no way he could find one before Miss Dorotka's medication situation became dire. "Could I speak to Dr. Shanahan about that?"

"He's with a patient. You can leave a message for him and he'll get back to you later, but I promise it's standard office policy and he'll tell you exactly what I did."

Eddie took a deep breath and forced his smile, reminding himself that if interactions with medical offices were easy and logical, nobody would need to hire him for anything. "Ok, well, she's almost out of her medication. She'll be in a bad way in a day or two. How soon can I bring her in?"

Miss Dorotka lived in a late-1800s Victorian up in Polish Hills. The neighborhood had begun as a blue-collar immigrant enclave—her place originally housed several families—but gentrified in the 1960s and became a favorite of Ford and Buick executives before their auto plants moved to Mexico. Now, many of the once-grand houses on her street were boarded up. Both her neighbors had abandoned their homes and mortgages years before. The old lady's physical isolation worried her great-niece Krystyna, who'd found Eddie in the Yellow Pages and contracted with him to check on her every few days.

Krystyna was an enigma, through and through, and during his occasional bouts of insomnia he found himself thinking about her. Wondering. They'd met just once at a coffee shop to discuss Miss Dorotka's situation. She was ash-blonde, athletically slim, looked to be in her late twenties but carried herself like she was the forty-something CEO of a megacorporation. Not arrogant, but someone who was in control, wise to everything happening around her. But despite her expensive clothes, she wore an old-fashioned wristwatch and carried an older flip phone instead of a smartphone. She had the faintest Polish accent, and wore all black in a way that probably just came across as very put-together and professional to most people, but he could smell the clove cigarettes on her clothes. Djarum Blacks.

And *that* familiar smell always made him nostalgic for the times he'd ended up at the local goth club. He'd liked the music okay, but there was something mystical about the scene that attracted him, even though he knew that his sunny punk self could never fit into it. There, in the dark under the blacklights surrounded by strangers in black lace and shiny black vinyl, the air filled with clove smoke, it felt like more was possible than met his eye. Something strange, something supernatural.

There was far more to Krystyna than met his eye, he was certain. If America had a throne, she'd belong upon it. On those late nights when his imagination got the better of him, he wondered if she was a hotshot business woman by day and a gothic domme by night. Breaking ordinary men with ropes and violet wands to turn them into something extraordinary. Not that he could ever find out. She'd never be into a guy like him, but knowing he was doing something to help her made him feel that he was in service to something greater than himself.

Eddie parked at the foot of Miss Dorotka's steep driveway, and walked up the blacktop to her house, stooping every few feet to collect bundled newspapers. He hadn't been able to get her on the phone when he was at the doctor's office, but that wasn't so unusual. The neglected papers worried him, though. One of her favorite activities was doing the daily crossword while she drank her morning coffee, so he suspected that either walking down the concrete steps hurt too much, or she was too mentally foggy to work the puzzles now.

The front door wasn't locked. He opened it a crack and called inside, "Miss Dorotka? It's Eddie. Are you okay in there?"

He heard a muffled "Yes" followed by something in Polish. Something wasn't right, and his stomach churned at all the dire imaginations crowding into his brain. Perhaps she'd fallen and shattered her leg and was struggling to shove the broken bone back into place in the living room. Or maybe she'd spilled boiling water on herself in the kitchen trying to make her tea. But he pushed all those grim thoughts away: it was a great day to be alive, and she was alive, and that was most important.

"I'm coming inside, okay?" He stepped through the door and pulled it shut behind him. The foyer looked as it had four days ago: mail piled on the dark wood console table, boots and shoes rowed neatly in plastic trays on the scarred hardwood floor. The house was eerily quiet compared to his other clients' homes, where infomercials and FOX News blasted so loudly day and night he could barely think. Miss Dorotka didn't own a television or a computer or even a radio, preferring to listen to old LPs and read even older books. Her rotary phone was an ancient, solid hunk of Bakelite built to survive a nuclear war.

Though everything looked to be in order, the air carried a sour, spoiled odor—probably the garbage needed to go out. But there was something else, a carnal rot like long-spoiled meat, and another stink that reminded him of when the old flop got a nightmarish roach problem. The memory of wandering blearily into the bathroom, flipping on the light and seeing the walls blackened by the skittering little monsters made his skin goosepimple unpleasantly. He hoped the old lady didn't have some kind of infestation, because then whoever did pest control would have to spread poison everywhere and it wouldn't be any good for her health. One of his patients got Parkinson's after exterminators fumigated her place for fleas. Not that cockroaches were any better for Miss Dorotka's health, either; salmonella would kill her a lot faster than low-grade nerve poisoning. A gross situation either way. He hoped his nose was mistaken.

He found Miss Dorotka standing in the middle of her living room with her back to the doorway. She wore a long-sleeved black dress and a heavy funeral veil, remaining so still that he wasn't sure she hadn't just dressed a mannequin and set it to stand watch in the room.

"Miss Dorotka?" he asked.

The figure stirred and turned her head toward him. "Oh, Eddie, so nice to see you."

Her voice was strangely distorted, hoarse and dry. She didn't sound like herself at all. How could she have gotten so bad in just a few days?

"I went to the doctor's office to see about your prescription," he said. "Bad news is, they won't renew your script without an appointment. Good news is, I got you one for this afternoon. But we need to leave soon."

"I don't want to go outside." She swayed back and forth as if she were suspended from invisible wires. "I don't want to be seen like this."

"I know you don't." Eddie felt a fresh pang of frustration. "I tried, I really did, but Doctor Shanahan's nephew is running the office now, and apparently he's kind of a hard-ass about things."

"Do we really need a doctor? My medication doesn't hurt anyone. All they need is a slip of paper with a signature on it, yes?"

Eddie felt a guilty heat rise in his face. He could forge a script; that was one of the many illicit skills he'd honed back in the old days. He knew all the local pharmacies that didn't bother checking too closely. Hell, he still had an old prescription pad from a defunct office hidden in a pocket of his satchel.

"I'm not allowed to write prescriptions," he said. "I know some nurses can, but I can't. I think it's best if we try to keep everything on the up-and-up, ma'am. But if you really don't feel you can go out, though, we can try something different."

It was a slippery slope, he warned himself. If he broke the rules for Miss Dorotka, he'd almost certainly get away with it. And then he'd break rules for other clients, and he'd fall back into his old habits. The rules he broke would get bigger and bigger until one day he got arrested again, and he'd lose everything he'd worked so hard to build. The new, heroic Porcupine Boy would once again be nothing more than a broken idiot who drunkenly shoved needles in his own face. That future loomed so clear and terrible in his mind that even if forging a script for her was purely a matter of kindness and efficiency … he couldn't justify it. Other patients depended on him, too.

She gave a heavy, rasping sigh, dry as a desert wind. "I do not want a nice boy like you to get in trouble. I will go to the appointment. But I need to find my things…."

He found her misplaced purse, aluminum walking cane and state ID—she hadn't been able to drive in many years—and then gripped her bony elbow and helped her totter out of the house and down the blacktop to his van. Once she was out in the light, Eddie realized that she was wearing a surgical mask under the heavy veil; he could barely see her eyes as shadowed caves beneath her painted-on eyebrows, and he couldn't see her mouth and nose at all beneath the green mask. The unpleasant smells that had worried him in the house clung to her strongly, and the light breeze did nothing to diffuse them. He first wondered if she'd spilled garbage on her clothes, but the dress looked clean enough. And then he worried that perhaps she had a wound or bed sore that had gone seriously bad. Nasty anaerobic bacteria *could* give off odors like these. And if that was the case, it was definitely for the best that they were going to the doctor.

"You should make sure to keep your doors locked," he said as he pulled out into the street. "I'm pretty sure junkies are squatting in the abandoned houses around here, and any of them could just stroll right in."

"I don't mind company," she replied lightly, shading her already deeply-shadowed eyes with a gloved hand. "They are welcome to stroll in if they like. I would make them tea."

Eddie paused, wondering if this was the fever talking, or if she were making a little joke. "These guys could really hurt you, ma'am."

He remembered all the shameful times he'd been high and threw rocks at people leaving snooty dinner clubs or broke uptown windows or started fights with prep school jocks just because his amphetamine-stoked anger at the world made it seem like the fun thing to do. Not just fun; it felt *justified*. There were so many rotten people living nice lives that they didn't deserve. So many rich people who'd rigged the system in their favor so that the heirlooms they stole and the families they ruined were just ledger entries to be handled by their accountants. Miss Dorotka was nothing like the spoiled plutocrats he'd hated when he was young and full of meth and Marxism … but anyone who had a house looked rich to someone homeless.

"They might not mean to," he said. "They might mean to but feel terrible about it once they sober up. But they could really, really hurt you."

She laughed, a dry rasp. "You speak as if I am but a girl, as if I haven't had to deal with violent young men my whole life. As if I never saw the treads of German tanks crush my neighbors' bodies into the cold winter mud."

Suddenly he felt acutely embarrassed. How could he have forgotten all that she'd gone through? Krystyna hadn't gone into a lot of details, but the whole *Hey, my great aunt survived the Nazis and went all over the Middle East on expeditions like Indiana Jones* should have been something he could keep in his mind. "I'm sorry, ma'am, I didn't mean to sound condescending. I'm just worried for you, that's all."

She patted his knee. Her hand felt like sticks inside the white cotton glove. "And I am touched by your concern. But I understand the addict's mind and I have no fear of it."

Her remark puzzled Eddie a little. What did she know about addiction? If she truly understood it the way he did, she *should* be afraid. But if he asked questions, he might only manage to

stick his foot further down his throat. It was more important
to him that she see him as an educated guy with a brain in his
head.

So he drove in silence, while she dozed beneath her veil,
and soon they arrived back at Dr. Shanahan's office. The waiting room was empty, and the white-toothed receptionist sat
playing Candy Crush on her phone behind the counter. After
Eddie got her attention, she quickly checked Miss Dorotka in
and escorted them to a small exam room in the back.

"Do you want me to stay with you?" Eddie asked as he
helped her onto the exam table. It was awkward with him being
a man, but some patients liked having someone they knew in
the room the first time they met with an unfamiliar doctor.

"I will be fine," she said. "I will call if I need you."

So Eddie went back out to the waiting room, settled in a
chair closest to the exam rooms, and started reading a copy
of *National Geographic*. He'd just gotten engrossed in an article
about the Saqqara necropolis in Egypt when he heard raised
voices.

"*Do diabła z tobą!*" Miss Dorotka shouted.

Oh, crap. If she was swearing in Polish, shit was getting real
back there. Eddie dropped his magazine and sprinted to the
exam room, the receptionist close behind him.

He pushed through the door … and he stopped dead in the
doorway, stunned into a scared-deer freeze at the mind-break-
ing impossibility of the scene before him. His brain flat rejected
what his eyes beheld. The receptionist pushed past him, then
gave a strangled gasp and stood stock-still, her cell phone clat-
tering to the grey parquet floor.

His brain started to assemble the impossible visual pieces.
Miss Dorotka stood very tall in the middle of the room. She'd
pushed her veil back and pulled her surgical mask down. She
had no eyes, no mouth, no nose. Just holes like bottomless tombs
carved into desert rocks. He'd seen coke addicts whose noses
had rotted off, and her face didn't look like that. They were dark
as collapsed stars, ragged bloodless skin opening into a vast,
empty void where flesh and bone should have been.

But *something* was spilling out of the dark *nothing*. Wriggling legless things like eels. Gleaming black and segmented like poisonous centipedes, or scorpions. Eddie's nose caught the sour insectoid stench from the house, and his skin shivered with goosebumps.

They were pouring out in dozens and dozens, cascading onto the doctor who had fallen to his knees at her feet. The strange vermin burrowing into his ears and eyes, filling his nose and mouth so he couldn't take a breath to make any noise louder than a strained grunting. The doctor clawed at his swarmed face, and the wrigglers burrowed into his flesh, stripping his hands and head skeletal in seconds.

The receptionist swore under her breath and out of the corner of his eye he saw her step back, try to flee, but the shiny wriggling dark swarmed over the floor and up her legs, and she didn't have time to make another sound before they were all over her face like iron filings on a magnet, clogging her nose and throat, the air filled with the papery rasp of hundreds of tiny maws devouring clothes and meat and bones.

This could not be. It *could not* be, but it was, and Eddie held his breath, waiting with clenched, sweating dread for the wrigglers to attack him, too … but they did not.

In fifty heartbeats, there was nothing left of the doctor but a pile of pens, pocket change, a belt buckle, the metal parts of a stethoscope, and his shoes. Nothing remained of the receptionist—whose name he belatedly realized he never even knew—except her shoes and her cell phone.

The mass of voracious vermin wriggled back to Miss Dorotka, swarmed up to her face and disappeared back into a mouth that was no longer a void hole but an actual mouth with soft pink lips and straight pearly teeth—

Eddie blinked. Old Miss Dorotka was now young Krystyna, lovely and mysterious as he remembered. She gazed at him gravely, her expression a mix of sadness and resignation.

"I am sorry this happened." She smoothed the front of the black dress and put her veil back into place. "And I am even sorrier you had to see it."

Eddie's mind still couldn't fully process what he'd just witnessed. A part of him was utterly horrified and wanted to run screaming ... but another, greater part of him was shivering with awe. This woman—was she really a woman?—was proof of the grand supernatural. She was proof that there was some greater power lurking in the seams of the universe. She was a tantalizing hint that he could find proof for all the eldritch things he'd heard rumors of.

Feeling dizzy and disconnected from his own body, Eddie stared down into the receptionist's shoes. They were perfectly empty.

"There's no blood," he blurted dumbly.

"The hungry host is thorough," she replied, a faint smile playing on her lips. "But it does not care for vinyl or steel. There will be no DNA, no evidence. If the police look for clues, it will be as if these people simply vanished."

"There could be hidden cameras," Eddie found himself saying. "They're not supposed to put them in exam rooms. It's a huge HIPAA violation. But some doctors are paranoid. Or pervs. Let me check."

He pulled on a pair of nitrile gloves from the box on the counter and started giving the room a thorough once-over, shining his cell phone flashlight around to try to catch the gleam of hidden lenses. More than anything, it was something practical to do while his mind settled. Two people were dead. *Murdered,* if she had any sort of conscious control over the hideous little monsters that had come out of her. But if there was no video— and he wasn't finding any cameras—then what would he say to the police even if he wanted to report what had happened? If he ran away, she could probably just track him down. He had no idea what she was capable of. If he ran away, he'd never know her secrets.

"You are helping me?" Krystyna sounded incredulous.

Act normal, he told himself.

"You're ... you're still my client," he said. "Protecting you from possible medical privacy violations is literally my job."

He ducked out into the hall to check the walls and ceiling and found nothing. "We should leave, ma'am, before anyone else comes."

Eddie plucked the check-in sheet that the receptionist hadn't yet processed off her desk, folded it, and stuck it in his back pocket. He'd burn it later.

His mind still turning the situation over and over like a Rubik's Cube he wasn't smart enough to solve, he escorted her out of the office, down the walk and put her in the passenger seat of his van.

As he was backing out of the space, the whole purpose of the visit came back to him. "Oh, crap. Your medication. I guess I'll just forge you a script."

"Well, I don't need it *now*," she replied. "I won't need it for … months. I hope. I'll start aging visibly, first. Then the fevers will come on. And then the rest of the unpleasantness."

Sighing, she pulled off the cotton gloves and removed the veil. "I didn't mean for this to happen. I thought that if I saw the doctor I could control it, but he was just so very unpleasant. The hunger was greater than my goodwill could bear."

"Were … were you born this way?" He pulled out onto the main road.

"Oh, no. I was born a perfectly ordinary child in Żoliborz in 1885. In 1903 I met a visiting British student named James Shruberry who was studying archaeology at the University of Warsaw. We married in 1907, and in 1910 I accompanied him on a dig in Egypt. The expedition leader thought he'd discovered the tomb of a pharaoh, full of untold mysteries and riches; it was, unfortunately, the tomb of a priest of Nyarlathotep."

She paused, rubbing her forehead as if she had a headache. "The black wind rose and each of us saw the god in a different form. It appeared as an indescribable monstrosity to my husband and the other scientists, and the experience utterly broke their minds. My husband died in a sanitarium right before the Great War.

"But the god appeared to me as a thin man seemingly carved from alabaster. And he told me he would give me a gift: eternal life. But of course it came at a dire cost."

"You have to kill to stay alive?" Eddie asked.

"No, I will live until the end of the universe. Even if they caught me and electrocuted me, if they drew and quartered me and burned me down to ashes, it would make no difference."

She sounded supremely frustrated. "The Nazis did that—burned me in the ovens without even knowing I'd destroyed fifty of them. The host emerged from their hellish plane and stitched my particles back together. I live, period. I must kill to stay *young*, to stay *beautiful*, to stay *sane*. And if I do not kill, the madness and disease overtakes me … and people die. And then I must live with the knowledge of what I've done."

"That sounds awful," Eddie replied.

"It simply *is*. I hoped this time that I could stave off the inevitable with the medication, but alas."

"Have you ever tried to lock yourself away? I mean, more than you have now."

She gave a short, bitter laugh. "Oh, of course I have. Many, many times. Somehow, I am always found. Often by a child. It's distressing."

"Why don't you kill people who need killing, then?" Eddie didn't like saying that out loud, but it was true: some folks were beyond redemption. And everybody had to die sooner or later.

"I don't know who needs killing," she protested. "I don't have the power to see into a man's soul!"

"What about the fifty Nazis you killed?"

"Nazis are purely rotten. One cannot regret killing a Nazi. But the rest of the world rallied together and annihilated them, as well they should have. I might as well wish to kill dodos."

Eddie blinked. "Do … do you not watch the news?"

"I haven't had a TV in years. Too many ads, too much hype. It's tiresome."

"What about the Internet?"

"I have heard it's for pornography." She shook her head. "I do not care for that."

"Well, I feel weird being the one to tell you this, but there are a lot of Nazis around these days. And skinheads, and Klan members … and maybe some of them are just dumb young guys, but plenty are grade-A scumbags."

"Really?" She looked startled. "I am frankly astonished that they exist in this enlightened age in such an advanced country."

"They've always been around, hiding like roaches," he replied, sneaking sideways glances at her to gauge her reaction.

"It's just they've gotten bolder recently. All those message boards and online echo chambers to get each other fired up. They feel ... justified."

The old shame washed through him again. He signaled left and turned onto her street.

"Their great-grandfathers would have fought the original Nazis." Krystyna twisted the gloves in her lap and gazed out the window. "The universe's dark humor never ceases to surprise me."

She paused, biting her lower lip thoughtfully. "So you can help me find some, when the time comes?"

"Oh, sure. I used to fight them all the time at punk clubs. I know where they hang out."

"Astonishing." She shook her head again.

Eddie shifted in his seat, shivering a little as he imagined the shiny black wrigglers spilling from her hollowed-out head again. "I had a question. When I came to your house this morning ... would the host have eaten me?"

She laughed with genuine merriment, and the sparkling sound thrilled him. "Oh, no. I chose you over all the other nurses and home health aides for a reason. You've marked yourself, so you're perfectly safe."

He side-eyed her as he pulled up into her driveway. "Marked myself? How do you mean?"

"The porcupine! You have a tattoo, yes? The host fears the porcupine spirit—I don't entirely know why, but I suppose everything has a nemesis."

"That's good to know." He smiled as he parked and turned off the van.

As they got out and stood stretching on the warm blacktop, he did some quick math in his head. "So you've been around for ... a hundred and thirty-four years?"

It was over one hundred years longer than he'd been alive. The age gap was as daunting as the Grand Canyon or the whole Atlantic Ocean. And yet he couldn't help but try to imagine ways to bridge it.

She blinked at him in the sunlight as if she hadn't considered her own age in quite some time. "That sounds right."

"So you've learned a thing or two, I'm guessing?"

Her expression darkened and she looked away. "Clearly I know a bit less than I thought."

He tried to think how to phrase his question as he walked her to the front door. "I mean … you know about the occult? You know about what's really possible, and what isn't?"

She smiled. "Yes, *that* I know a little something about."

"Would you teach me?" he blurted out. "I … I could take you out to dinner. Off the clock. Maybe we could go dancing. You probably know ballroom way better than I do, but if you don't, we could both learn—"

"Eddie." She turned and touched his cheek with a warm, soft hand. Her gaze was level and sad. "I will outlive you. By a very long time. I cannot have children. I would make you an accessory to many, many murders."

"I know. But, I mean … for you, I'm safe … no one in the history of my entire life has gotten attached to me. Not ever." The admission made a hot blush bloom in his cheeks and nearly made tears rise in his eyes, so he forced himself to smile. "But it's a great day to be alive, and so why not live? Why lock yourself away? You have so much more to offer the world than just killing a few Nazis every year. I'm *sure* of it."

As he said the words, he realized he believed every single one of them. Perhaps this was his truest calling: helping this woman who was so thoroughly cursed discover ways to use that dark power to aid humanity. And maybe he couldn't succeed in the face of so much primeval horror, but he felt deep in his heart that the *trying* mattered. The right thing to do was still the right thing to do whether he'd be remembered for it or not.

She gave him a crooked smile. "You're a strangely convincing man."

He grinned back. "So … dinner? Dancing? Maybe a trip to look at something really weird?"

Krystyna laughed, and he was thrilled anew. "Sure."

300 Down

By Keith Minnion

The first painting was still in Arthur's gallery backstock when he stumbled across the second.

Angela, his gallery manager, wrinkled her nose when he showed her. "My God, Arthur! Why on Earth did you buy that?"

He looked at it again. "Honestly? I don't know. It seemed… familiar."

"It should. It looks just like that other horrid little thing you bought a few months ago in Philadelphia. You know, the redhead in the green dress?" She clicked a few keys, swiped her thumb across the touchpad, then swung the screen so he could see. "Bottom row, near the center."

Then he did know. Christ.

He went to the basement backstock, found the painting in the high slots, where all his "maybes" and Angela's "oh my Gods" went after he returned from his buying trips, and pulled it out, into the hard light. "Shit," he said. Angela was right. They were the same painting, or, at least the same subject. Different hairstyle, different dress, and she smiled a bit more in the new one. But definitely her. Another crass, brassy redhead in a green dress.

Angela had followed him down. She looked over his shoulder, and clucked. "Told you."

Sally ran a tight ship at her Hanover Gallery in Georgetown but Arthur had heard the rumor
She met him at the back door."Back again so soon?"

"What, have I worn out my welcome?"

Sally gave him one of her signature belly laughs. No sincerity in it, but Arthur appreciated the effort. "Whenever I'm in D.C," he said, "you know yours is the first Georgetown gallery I visit. Anyway, I was talking to Sonya a few days ago and she let slip you have an uncatalogued Hopper."

"Sonya has a big mouth." Sally motioned with her chin. "I have some other new things in back. All offensively expensive, of course." As Arthur passed her she added, "You couldn't afford the Hopper."

"Very funny." Arthur dodged through a small jungle of pedestal sculpture. "I'm after portraits, anyway."

Behind him, following, Sally made an inopportune sound. "Portraits. Who buys portraits these days?"

Arthur stopped, turned. "Me, if it's the right one."

"Wait, didn't you recently purchase one from Aloysius in Philly—?"

"Al is another schmuck with a big mouth."

"Selling Arthur Wakefield a portrait is an event. Especially an Expressionist one. Word gets around."

"I'm sure. Anyway, it reminded me of something."

"Brilliant orange hair, crazy ice-blue eyes, blood-red lips, neon-green dress, yes? Horrid little thing."

"Those were my gallery manager's exact words."

"Angela has taste."

Arthur paused to look at a Linden Frederick, one of his little studies from 2009; he sighed, and dismissed it. "He charged me enough for it, as I recall."

Sally sniffed. "That one you could afford. Unlike…this."

They had stopped before the Hopper. It was one of his New York street scenes from the late 1920s. A prospective buyer came instantly to mind.

"Purchased from the original owner's family," Sally said. "It hung in her bedroom in Chelsea since the day she bought it in 1928. Never catalogued, never shown."

"How much are you asking?"

"Ah. Well."

"How *much*?"

Sally murmured a figure.

Arthur gave her another.

Sally blinked. "Jesus. You have actually surprised me." She stuck out her hand. "Sold." She regarded him. "You make me wish I had a portrait of a redhead in a green dress to sell."

"Do you?"

Sally shook her head. "But if I ever do, you're the first schmuck I'm calling."

Arthur entered the evening crowd on N Street like a fish in rapids, jostled along by the occasional bump or push as everyone headed for that after-work drink, or the Metro home. Just before reaching 34th, someone connected hard, shoulder to shoulder, and he staggered to keep his feet as he swung about. "Hey—!" he began, a rock in the river now, parting rapids, as the person who had struck him—a woman, red-haired, with a triumphant grin splitting her scarlet slash of a mouth—lost herself in the crowd. Beneath her coat, before she was totally gone: a flash of lurid green.

Then he remembered. Suddenly, like a screen switched on, flooding his brain with glaring images, he remembered.

"Marie!" But that was impossible, of course. Marie was dead. She was as dead as dead could be, and had been for twenty, no, twenty-*one* years.

Marie was dead.

A week later, returning from lunch, Angela saw the two paintings, neatly wrapped and leaning by the alley door. "It's starting to snow," she informed Arthur as she passed his open office door. Coat hung, on her way back, "Taking a few home?"

He looked up from his laptop. "The transport company took the big Stella from my apartment last night. The Chinese buyer is in a big hurry apparently." He returned his attention to the screen. "Freed up space on a wall."

"That's nice. So which ones are you taking? I'll make the entries."

He looked up again. "What?"

"Which two are you taking home? I'm assuming you haven't noted it in the database."

"Actually, I did."

Her expression was deadpan. "You're serious."

"As a heart attack."

"The Stella pickup, too?"

He smiled at her briefly, then returned to his work.

Five minutes later she was back at his doorway. "I can*not* believe you are taking those two ugly little redhead portraits home with you."

He spread his hands. "They've grown on me. We've had zero client interest, and anyway, you hate them."

"But..." She held a finger up, pointing at nothing and nowhere. "Wasn't that Stella in your bedroom?"

"Took up the entire north wall."

"So...these two are going into your bedroom."

He nodded. Before she could turn he asked, "How many inches?"

"How many inches what?"

"The snow. How deep?"

She shook her head as though to clear it. "They're expecting two or three."

"Lovely." He turned back to his laptop, "Snowfall in the city," and punched a key. "Just glad I don't have to drive in it."

Two of the three ceiling accent lights he had positioned for the big Stella protractor series piece were perfectly placed for the two portraits. Arthur sat at the end of his bed, gazing at them. The two redheads with their arresting blue eyes, red-slashed mouths and loud green dresses looked brazenly back at him.

"You're not her," he said, into the empty air. "You're not Marie."

Their smiles, each different, each distinct, shared one thing: they sneered.

He got up, went to the painting on the left, the more recently painted of the two ("That's the other thing," Angela had complained. "It's anonymous *and* new; nobody buys new-anonymous, Arthur.") and adjusted its level slightly. "You don't even really look like her," he said.

He crossed the sea of carpet to the patio doors and looked

out. "Three inches, my ass." The wind whipped across the wide expanse of glass, carrying curtains of snow on its shoulders. Below, three hundred feet down, children from the lower-floor condos were probably trying to build snowmen in the courtyard.

("You can relax, Arthur," his attorney had told him, two decades ago. "The Medical Examiner has ruled it an accidental death. She slipped, she fell, end of story. The district attorney has nothing, now. You're in the clear.")

He turned. "She slipped," he informed the portraits on the wall. "She fell. I'm innocent."

They sneered back at him.

"You have a visitor." Angela handed him his coffee as he passed her the next day. "In the conference room."

He stopped. "A visitor."

"In the conference room."

"Is this a game? Do I get three questions?"

"It's your wife."

Arthur paused his coffee halfway to his mouth. "My ex-wife."

Angela let out a long, calming breath. "Your ex-wife is in the conference room."

"Why didn't you put her in my office?"

"Because the last time I did that, you complained she 'fiddled' with your things. And anyway, she specifically asked for the conference room."

"Wonderful," he said.

The conference room was at the end of the short hall. He stopped in the doorway, "Sylvia!" testing a smile. "I'd offer you coffee, but I'm sure you're in a hurry."

Her returned smile was equally false. "I've sold the Amagansett house."

"Really." He took a seat opposite her. "I always thought you loved that place."

"I do, but I'm spending most of my time on the West Coast now. It just sits empty, even during the season."

"A pity. I always liked it."

Her false smile flashed again. "You hated it. Sand in the

carpet. The penthouse here in town is more your style, anyway."

She was right, of course. The east-side penthouse had been his before the marriage, and he had made damn sure it was still his after. "So…you came to tell me you sold the house out east. You could have emailed, texted, *phoned…*"

"Actually, I came in person to give you this." She reached under the table and lifted a flat rectangular package, a bit larger than one by two, and slid it across to him.

"A late Christmas present? I'm touched."

"I found it when the movers were packing." Her well-manicured nail tapped the brown paper wrapping. "There's no way in hell this was going to Santa Barbara with me."

He picked the package up. "If I remember the gory details of the settlement, you got both houses *and* all the contents in them."

"Not this." Her voice was flat, but her eyes flashed in sudden anger. "I don't want it, but I thought you might."

He began worrying at the packing tape. "You've got me curious. Should I open it now?"

"God no." She rose, and remembered perfume wafted across the table. "Wait till after I'm gone, please." She extended a hand. "If you're ever on the coast…"

He gave it a weak squeeze. "Always a pleasure, darling."

She gave the package a final venomous glare, then skirted the table for the door. "I'll see myself out. I hope you enjoy…it."

Angela appeared at the conference room door a few minutes later. "Don't forget your ten o'clock," she said. Then, "She gave you a painting?"

He stood it up in one of the chairs.

"Oh my God," she said, "not another one!"

A young woman in three-quarter view stared defiantly out of the canvas, a blue-eyed, scarlet-lipsticked redhead in a green dress.

"This one's different," he said.

"Well, smaller, but—"

"No. That's not it. I know who painted this one, and I know when. She was a young artist, fresh out of Cooper-Union. Her name was Maria Millard."

Angela shook her head slowly. "Not ringing any bells."

"She was before your time. She brought a portfolio to show me, hoping for representation, over twenty years ago. I…ended up not taking her on."

"Because she only painted redheads in green dresses?"

"Well, she did do this one, but she didn't do the other two."

Angela inspected it closely. "The technique and style is the same, even the brushstroke. This Maria Millard of yours must have done them all."

"Impossible. The other two are relatively recent—five, ten years old. Agreed?"

She nodded, her expression wary. "So?"

"So very shortly after Maria Millard painted this one, twenty-one years ago, she took her own life. Committed suicide." He turned away slightly. "Jumped off a penthouse patio."

"But—" Then realization dawned on her, and she put her hand to her lips. "Oh, *Arthur*…" She made a motion to go to him, but he raised his hand.

"It's old news," he said.

"So your wife—"

"Ex-wife."

"So your ex-wife had it and just now decided to give it back to you?"

"Sylvia didn't know about it. She knew about her, about Maria, but not the self-portrait. The movers, packing things up, must have unearthed it." He let his breath out. "She's selling the Amagansett house."

"Did you just say self-portrait?"

"Her hair was more auburn than red. And she rarely wore lipstick, never bright red. As for the dress…paint-stained jeans and tee shirts were more her style."

Angela looked at him, letting a few moments pass. Then, "Are you okay?"

He turned back to the painting. "I'm fine." He stood there for a long moment before rousing himself. "Cancel the ten o'clock." He picked the painting off the chair. "I'm taking this home."

His building was only three blocks east. It was snowing again, new snow over old. The pedestrian traffic was heavy, and the mix at this time of morning was about fifty-fifty commuter and tourist. Arthur found himself at the front of the crowd at the corner of 3rd. Contractor vans and taxis crowded the avenue, barreling south. He had put the little painting in a leather portfolio case, safe from the weather, and he held it securely under his arm, waiting with the unwashed masses for the light.

The shove came right between his shoulder blades, perfectly placed to push him completely off-balance. In that moment as he fell into the slushy gutter he saw two things, distinct and clear. The first was the woman who had pushed him, with bright red hair twirling about her shoulders as she worked herself back into the crowd…and the second was the oncoming taxi in the right-hand lane, accelerating through the intersection to beat the light.

I'm dead, he thought, at the end of that moment, closing his eyes as he fell heavily to the pavement, directly in the path of the oncoming taxi. *She did it. I'm dead.*

A screech of brakes combined with the sudden screams of people.

No contact. No hit. He opened his eyes, and saw the underside of a filthy bumper, dripping grey slush in his face. *Oh God.* The taxi had stopped in time. *Oh my God.*

The next few minutes were a blur of being pulled out from under by helping hands, voices yelling: "Don't move him!" and others: "The taxi didn't touch him!" and "I'm fine, really, I'm fine," realizing that was *his* voice, babbling as he was led to the curb, leaning against a pole, holding the painting—the portfolio case not mangled or torn, just scraped a bit—tight against him. When he heard someone say they had called 911, he straightened and steadied himself against the pole. Oh no; no police; no questions. No *way*. He shook off all remaining offers of help. "Really," he said, "I'm okay. I'm fine." Looking over his shoulder more than once, he crossed the avenue like a retreating soldier, with the light.

He took a long scalding shower, put on warm and comfortable clothes, and got the gas fireplace in the living room lit. Somehow, though, it wasn't enough to take the chill off he still felt inside. He raised the thermostat, and put on a sweater, but he still found himself shivering.

He started when the phone in his pocket rang. He pulled it out, stared at Angela's name on the screen, but still let it go five more rings before answering.

"So," she said, "where are you? Still home?"

"I have a good reason." He told her what had happened at the intersection, but left out the push. "I slipped," he said. "The curb was…icy."

"Holy crap, Arthur! Are you all right?"

"My shoulder hurts like hell, but I'll be fine. Probably just a bruise. I saved the painting anyway."

"Who gives a damn about that horrible little painting? As long as you're okay…"

"I'll be fine." He looked across the room at the portfolio case leaning up against the fireplace hearth ledge. "Good as new by tomorrow."

"Well, you only have the one o'clock scheduled for the afternoon anyway, with Harvey."

"Harvey can wait."

"Take a hot shower."

"Already did."

"Get that fireplace going."

"Crackling as we speak."

"Watch an old movie on that monster TV of yours. *Relax.*"

"On the agenda. Jimmy Stewart, I think. See you tomorrow."

He thumbed the phone, and dropped it back in his pocket. When he stood, the pain in his right shoulder was bright, but bearable. He crossed to the fireplace, took up the portfolio, and brought it into his bedroom. When he unzipped and opened it, he couldn't decide if he felt relieved or disappointed that the painting inside was untouched.

"You bitch," he said to the sneering redhead. "You tried to kill me. You *bitch.*"

He picked the painting up, and a sudden desire to slam the

canvas down on the nearby bedpost washed over him in a hot
wave. Up close, the blue eyes had laughter in them, the same
laughter he could see in the other two.

She knew. They all did.

The new painting needed wiring and framing, but he just
hung it on the wall bracket by the top stretcher bar. The align-
ment with the ceiling accent light wasn't ideal, but with his
shoulder there was no way he could move the light. It would do.

He stood back. There, all three paintings, side by side by
side.

"Fuck you," he said softly. "And you, and you."

His shoulder throbbed, and twisting his neck only prompted
the beginnings of a headache. His choices were either the left-
over pills from his summer ankle sprain, or the remaining two
inches of his favorite single malt. He chose the scotch. And after
that…

He awoke from his nap to someone knocking at the apartment
door. He heard three knocks in steady succession, a momentary
pause, then one more. He rolled onto his good side, favoring his
shoulder, burying his face in the pillow. There was a perfectly
good doorbell. Why didn't they—?

Four more knocks, in the same pattern as the first time.
Not loud either, not insistent. They were calm. Measured.
Knock-knock-knock…*knock*.

Afternoon sunlight slanted across the bedroom. The snow
was over. He squinted through the glare to his bedside clock.
Two-forty-three. Who the hell—?

Then a thin, crystal stiletto blade of fear pierced his chest,
and for a moment he couldn't breathe. *Oh my God*, he thought,
gasping, blinking in the light. He remembered the knock, the
pattern. It had been *her* knock; *her* pattern.

Silence. He waited for more knocks, but none came. The
silence lengthened.

He sat up slowly, realizing as he did so that he was shaking,
and panting like a frightened dog. The portraits looked at him
from the wall. Still laughing at him.

He eased out of bed and stood for a moment, listening, then

went out to the hallway to his wide, deep living room. The silence lengthened. The front door of his apartment was down the other short hallway, just out of sight from where he stood. The kitchen was that way as well, with the service door tucked away in the utility room beyond.

The service door.

He went quickly through the living room, shielding his eyes from the sun-glare off the patio snow, then through the kitchen to the utility room: washer, dryer, sink, folding table, closet… and the service door. He could take the fire stairs down to the next floor, then the elevator to the lobby. Then he could—

Knock, knock, knock…knock.

He staggered back, grabbing blindly. She was on the other side of this door now!

Knock, knock, knock…knock.

He ran back through the kitchen, into the entry hall to the living room. Behind him, from the front door:

Knock, knock, knock…knock.

The only other way out was the patio, the railing, and a drop to the courtyard.

He ran, stumbling, across the living room to the patio doors, fumbled with the locks, ignoring his shoulder as he wrenched the doors open. The cold air slapped him in the face, the snow like fire on his feet as he plowed across the patio to the railing. He grabbed it, flinging snow off to get a better grip, and looked down.

To the redhead in a green dress in the courtyard far below, looking back up at him.

The Dark Windmill

By Janet Joyce Holden

He was huddled inside a coffee shop on Wilshire, juggling projects and getting nowhere when he got the call—"Cheryl Oakley has agreed to see you."

His agent's words rendered him open-mouthed. "When?"

"Tomorrow morning. And Ben, I know it's short notice, but it's probably the only chance you'll get."

"I don't care. I'll cancel everything." He scribbled the time and place on the corner of a napkin, and afterward he stared at his laptop while his coffee grew cold. Five years of persuading silent filmmaker Chester Brack's granddaughter to grant an interview, and thus far nothing—until now.

He ordered another coffee and spent the next two hours pulling up research he'd amassed. Part way through, he panicked. He had so many questions, but how much time would she give him? How deep would he be allowed to dig? Incessantly, he tapped out notes until the battery on his laptop ran dry.

Back home, he skipped dinner and continued, until he realized he was being polite by asking about the film career, when what he really wanted was the scoop on another source of interest—mysticism, the occult, ceremonial black magic. It lay at odds with what had already been written about the man, but he'd picked up a whiff of dissonance here and there from the biographies of Brack's contemporaries, enough to pique his interest and inspire him to dig deeper. So, how about it, Mrs. Oakley? Was your grandfather secretly America's answer to Aleister Crowley? She would shut him down in seconds. Still...

The following morning he parked the car two streets from Beverly and walked to the agreed-upon restaurant. He was early and figured he had a good ten minutes to rehearse his opening gambit, only to discover that Cheryl Oakley had pre-empted him.

"I wanted to see you walk in," she said after a strong hand-shake. She was broad-shouldered, with a handsome face that bore traces of her grandfather when she smiled. She pushed the bread basket across the table as he sat down. "Try the cornbread muffins, they're delicious."

Stymied into silence, he flicked out his starched napkin and laid it across his lap. The restaurant was busy. She had chosen safe ground with plenty of visibility and distraction, should the interview go south. It's what he would have done. "Thank you for agreeing to see me."

"Your agent tells me you wanted something different, and I have to say, there are at least a dozen books out there already, gathering dust on everyone's shelves."

The waiter arrived. Ben ordered coffee and a vegetarian omelet, and watched her do the same. When they were alone once more, "I wanted to talk to you about his studies of mysticism. Everything I've read suggests it was a dalliance, a hobby, but I disagree." He expected an immediate brush-off. But after their brusque introduction he decided he was better off getting to the point.

"You want to know about the Magick." She leaned back in her seat and kept her eyes on him as their demitasses of coffee were presented.

He smiled. "Are you about to tell me to take a hike?"

"I've done it before."

"I'd still love to know. Although, I realize this might not be the best place—"

"Oh, I can assure you, Mr. Norman, anything of that nature will not be discussed over breakfast. I'm here to sound you out, nothing more."

While they ate, she insisted on his life story, and as they rose to say farewell, Ben realized he'd told her everything about himself—his not-so-stellar childhood, his failed marriage, the feast and famine of his career—and had gotten nothing in return.

"I'll be in touch with your agent," she said, and refused to take his business card.

He settled the bill and watched her walk away. Records told him she'd be in her late-seventies by now, but at the table she had appeared a good thirty years younger, and holy shit—some of the personal stuff he'd given her was way beyond his comfort zone. His shoulders tingled, as if she'd ripped off a layer of skin.

To get in the right mindset, he drove over to Los Feliz and parked outside the address of the old Brack mansion. There was no trace of the original house. The Spanish colonial had stood derelict for years, cordoned off and well guarded, until two years ago when a team of urban explorers had broken in. They'd been caught trespassing—the Brack family lawyer had gone after them like a pit bull—and they'd narrowly avoided jail time. Soon after, the house had been sold, torn down, and a blocky contemporary was now in its place.

Ben had, at great expense, managed to get a copy of the photographs the couple had taken. There had been no sign of the images online, no matter how hard he'd searched—the lawyer, he assumed. He'd also attempted to interview the husband and wife explorers, who didn't seem the type to be frightened off. According to their website, they risked life and limb rappelling off the side of old battleships in order to get the best shots, and yet they had been scared shitless of the Bracks. He'd tried to get them to talk, about whether they had been threatened or bought off, but the couple wouldn't elaborate and that was the end of it.

As for the images, they were beautifully composed. They depicted a house interior shorn of everything except torn drapes and the occasional stained carpet. In some rooms the weather had gotten in and rain water had partially collapsed the ceilings. The only exception to the lack of furniture—an ancient armchair that stood in what he assumed had been the living room. There was evidence of elaborate graffiti, and a significant scorch mark in one corner of that particular room, too, suggesting there had been a small fire at some point. Obviously, the explorers hadn't been the only break-ins. Someone had gotten in, sprayed gibberish on the walls, cooked dinner, and had almost torched the place.

However, there was little evidence of what Ben was really hoping to find. The house had been stripped clean and bore none of its heyday ambience. It was hard to imagine an auteur of Brack's stature, not to mention a black magic practitioner, dwelling within these forlorn walls. As for why the family had left the house rotting and neglected for so long, there were no estate battles on record, no family feuds. Only a single tragedy surrounding Brack's eldest daughter, Estella, who'd hanged herself from the hallway balcony, and that had been decades ago.

Back home, he cleared his desk, got to work, and he waited. Days passed by. He harangued his world-weary agent and waited some more. In the meantime, he spun a number of other plates and fought hard not to let Cheryl Oakley's reticence get to him. He wondered if she was toying with him, not realizing that during his checkered and occasionally illustrious career he'd dealt with threats, stonewalling, egos the size of Everest, and had still emerged triumphant. Three biographies, one of them a prestigious prizewinner, hundreds of articles—they had all arrived on his publishers' desks, despite the numerous roadblocks presented by their prickly subjects.

A frustrating two months later, his agent gave him the call he'd been waiting for. "You've been invited to the Laguna compound." Her tone suggested it was an honor.

Ben promised her a bottle of her favorite Merlot, and when the morning arrived, instead of the freeway he took the southbound Pacific Coast Highway in an attempt to chase away modernity and get into a bygone era. To his right, the sun shone, the ocean opened up; it whispered and gave him a yearning to fly, and despite the residence being difficult to find, he arrived in a beatific mood.

At the end of a narrow cul-de-sac there was no sign of his destination save for a brick-clad driveway, a locked gate, and beyond—steps leading down. Trees hid the view, while a camera bolted alongside the gate watched his every move.

The gate mechanism sprang to life. Cheryl Oakley was waiting at the base of the steps and he felt the familiar powerhouse grip as they shook hands. "We'd be grateful if you didn't use the camera on your phone, and before you start asking questions, you're not here to see me. You're here to meet my mother."

"But she—"

"—is old. Naturally."

He vowed to keep his mouth shut on that particular subject as he followed her into the house. By his reckoning, Oakley was either kidding, or the woman he was about to meet had celebrated her one hundredth birthday nearly ten years ago.

The house—a compound, his agent had called it—was built into the folds of the cliff, and after descending another flight of steps they emerged outside once more and approached a yellow-painted one-story building that bore window boxes of white geraniums.

Inside, floor-to-ceiling windows looked out toward the ocean. His interviewee was seated alongside them. He'd already studied the family tree and knew how to address her. "Mrs. Davisson."

She stood with the aid of a stick and held out her hand. "Ben, can I call you Ben? For pity's sake, call me Mary. Cheryl has told me all sorts of things about you."

He clasped hands with an ageless lady who appeared built of fine porcelain, and his well-rehearsed questions broke apart and circled like a flock of treacherous birds. Nothing of substance remained, so he went through the motions—"It's an honor, I didn't expect"—while he fumbled for grip.

Despite his earlier plans, he thought it only polite to delve into her father's film career, and luckily she didn't seem interested in going on at length. Maybe Cheryl had clued her in. It was just the two of them now, so after a reasonable preamble he gave it his best shot.

"Were you aware of his other interests?"

"Oh, yes." Her expression darkened. "Tell me, what kind of book do you want to write? You might not like what you find. I take it you are a fan of his work?"

"His films were a big part of my college thesis. *Realm of the Regent, The Ambassador*—"

"*House of Dreams*, you saw that?"

"What was left of it, yes."

"And what did you deduce?"

"That his work celebrated life, which is—"

"Ha." Her stick banged against the polished wood floor. "Some use art to give vent to their inner darkness. My father's work was a beatific mask. Beneath it, he was a monster, through and through."

In the silence that followed, he drew in a breath. "Can we talk about your sister, Estella?"

"No, not yet. Ask me something else."

"How about his relationship with T. Theodore Myers?"

Mary collected her cup and saucer. He expected the teacup to rattle. It didn't. She appeared steady as a rock. "What about it?" She sipped her tea.

"Records suggest they were longtime friends and business partners. And yet, in Polly Abel's autobiography, she advocates a darker, more competitive nature to their partnership."

"Polly was a straight talker, and paid dearly for it."

"I heard her descendants are living well on a considerable inheritance."

"You think money is a measure for the good things in life, Mr. Norman?"

Her voice hadn't shifted timbre, but her use of his surname told him he'd stepped over a line. He apologized and backtracked. "Were they fellow practitioners?"

"In the art? Most certainly. Theo was a benign investor in my father's films, but when it came to Magick, they were extremely competitive. No expense, and no depravity was spared."

"Depravity?"

"I asked you what kind of book you wanted to write."

"I won't shy away, but if there was any wrongdoing, I'll need proof. Iron-clad." He remembered the urban explorers' unease, and it underpinned his growing disquiet.

Mary Davisson rose and leaned on her stick. "Come. Let's dip our proverbial toes in the water, shall we?"

He followed attentively as she led him outside, along another section of the path that meandered along the cliff face. He could hear the crash of surf on the rocks as they approached a small cabin. Inside was a rich repository of film props, trunks, artifacts, and piled-high bookcases.

"You're the first non-family member to see this."

He approached a faded black-and-white photograph hanging on the wall opposite the door. Front and center was Brack, bearing his trademark narrow beard, accompanied by two sullen girls wearing pale dresses. Alongside him was a taller man. Ben recognized T. Theodore Myers, broad shouldered and stern, dressed in tweeds, his hand resting on the shoulder of one of the girls.

"My sister, Estella," Mary said.

The image made him feel uncomfortable. Myers' face bore a proprietary leer that was uncharacteristic of other photos he had seen of the man. Mentally, he filed it away, cleared his throat, and turned his attention to the props. "Is that what I think it is?"

"The cast-iron gate from *Song of the Storm*."

"Wow, and this?" He approached a heavy robe of dark velvet draped over a nearby chair.

"Not from the films."

His fingers sank into the lush fabric, regardless that he hadn't asked for permission to touch. The robe's edges were decorated with leaves of silver thread. A narrow section of the lining was visible. It had frayed at the seam, offering strong hints of the garment's age. He couldn't take his eyes off it.

"Have you heard of *The Dark Windmill*?" she asked.

"Ah, no, I'm sorry. One of his films?" Guiltily, he withdrew his hand from the robe, where his fingers had been busy, tracing the lines of embroidery.

"A film, an event—a ritual."

"If it's a Brack film, I'd love to see it, if there's a copy available."

"There's a copy, if you have the stomach for it."

He attempted to make light of it. "Not one of his best?" The old lady began to laugh, so hard he feared she might choke. "Mrs. Davisson—"

She waved him away. "Take as much time as you need." She turned and left him alone.

Regardless of Cheryl Oakley's request, he brought out his phone and immediately began taking pictures. One of the more compelling discoveries was a bookcase at the rear of the cabin, containing cloth and leather-bound volumes of necromancy and the occult. It was a library well kept, with no sign of dust. He assumed the books were old, and yet one or two appeared relatively new, as if Mary and her daughter were continuing to build on the filmmaker's collection.

Filling up the center of the cabin were more film props, an old bicycle, and a trunk bursting with neatly folded men's suits wrapped in tissue. Film posters adorned the walls. There was a filing cabinet crammed with yellowing papers, scripts and correspondence, and as he wandered through the collection he wished he'd had access to this treasure trove while writing his thesis.

He came across a banker's box of old photographs. He took a seat alongside the robe and balanced the box on his knees. Every photo was sepia-tinted with age. Landscapes, portraits of Brack and his cronies, or Brack and his family. But there were no clues regarding the man's esoteric interests. No masked figures gathered before an altar, no séances, and nothing of the afore-mentioned windmill. Nonetheless, he took copious notes and lost track of time, until hunger poked him in the belly and suggested it was late in the afternoon. He placed the photos back in the box.

Outside, the coastal path was bathed in pink light from a spectacular sunset. He returned to Mary's section of the house, where she and her daughter were in the midst of a heated conversation. Cheryl gave him a cold look and took off.

"She doesn't think I should have trusted you," Mary said.

"I returned everything to its rightful place, and I swear I didn't try on the robe."

"Anything of use?"

"I'd like to go through the filing cabinet and the photographs in greater detail. The bookcase, too."

"Naturally. We'll arrange more appointments. Cheryl will handle it." She rose. It was his cue to leave. "By the way," she added as they reached the stairway that led back to his car. "Something you won't find in the filing cabinet. T. Theodore Myers is Cheryl's father."

Back home, he uploaded his photos and lingered on the disturbing picture he'd seen on the cabin wall. The girls looked young, barely in their teens when the picture was taken, and Mary Davisson's last statement about Myers was still ringing in his ears. Had Brack pimped his daughters to his business partner? It was hard to ignore the guy's leer in the photo.

He did some digging on Myers, and searched for anything relating to Chester Brack and *The Dark Windmill*. He also reacquainted himself with stories of Mary's sister, Estella. Unlike Mary, who'd married twice and sank into anonymity, she had remained single and had been custodian of the Los Feliz house and her father's affairs. He remembered her name appearing on some of the documents he'd come across during earlier research.

As for Myers, he appeared to have been the consummate businessman who, despite the Brack connection, kept a low profile. No scandals or splashy divorces. Only opera singer Polly Abel's autobiography hinted at something darker—a secret affair between the two, and a mention of Myers returning from one of Brack's séances with *"blood on his hands"*.

He dug through his contacts and made a few calls, including a woman he knew at the Library of Congress, but no one had heard about *The Dark Windmill*.

His agent offered a different perspective. "What about location? There's a windmill in Solvang. Maybe there were more in Central Valley and a local historian could help you. Did Brack have any investments up there?"

"Not that I remember. But I'll check on Myers."

He discovered an address northwest of Bakersfield, a parcel of land that had been sold by Myers' estate in the Fifties, and the following afternoon he decided on a road trip. He left the L.A. Basin and joined a crawl of trucks on Interstate 5. Eventually, the mountains grew shallow in his rear view mirror and the land stretched out on all sides, flat as a board.

He blew by fields of cotton, and nut trees, beneath pale

bridges that bore cities of swallow's nests under their eaves. When the light began to fade he pulled in at a truck stop. The only room he could find was in a motel some way distant from its cousins, cloaked in a thick layer of agricultural darkness. Only two other vehicles were parked outside, and the *Open* sign flashed desultorily in the reception office window. The surrounding fields—a dark contrast with the L. A. sprawl and its myriad of lights—were beyond oppressive.

He slept fitfully, until the early morning brought vivid dreams of black ink and beating wings. He awoke to the distant roar of the nearby Interstate, and shook off his disquiet. He hadn't been this jumpy in a while—a city boy out of his comfort zone, he assumed. Suitable penance arrived post-shower, where the motel's threadbare towels tore into his hide.

Outside, he paused and breathed in air that bore a slight chill. Two heavy trucks rumbled by, heading inland from the highway and toward the east. They were soon swallowed by thin shafts of rising sunlight and dust. Ben took advantage of the complimentary coffee and pastries at reception. Behind the desk was the same guy who'd handed him his key the night before.

"Ever hear the name Myers in these parts? A farm, maybe?"

The man shrugged. "I've heard of the Myers Foundation. It's farther north, toward Fresno."

"Know anything about it?"

"Nope, but they do advertise." The man reached into a rack and handed Ben a tri-fold leaflet.

Back in the car, he chewed on a Danish pastry, checked out the leaflet, and re-configured his GPS. The Foundation appeared to be a quasi-religious retreat—well-tended brick buildings, smiling couples, a bucolic garden, and no windmill. Then again, Mary Davisson hadn't specified any details and he suspected he was on a wild goose chase.

He got gas, rejoined the line of traffic heading north, before turning off and driving further inland. He passed by silos and gateways to factory farms. He crossed a railroad and drove on, until citrus trees began to rise on either side, their boughs heavy with fruit.

Pale text on a sign posted at the side of the road announced The Myers Foundation. There was a narrow driveway, and now that he was here, he realized he had no idea what he was going to do. Turning off the road, he saw a gate directly ahead. He drove slow and stopped. The gate was padlocked. He got out, walked to the front of the car and stared at the buildings beyond. There were no vehicles, and no other evidence of anyone being at home.

He jumped the gate and approached the nearest building. It was brick, one story; its windows were shuttered. "Hello?" He braced himself and listened. Worst case, they'd have Dobermans, or some weird guy with a shotgun and he'd have to make a run for it. "Hello?"

Silence.

He took to wandering. Front and center, the formerly bucolic garden was overgrown. There were five other buildings surrounding it—a meeting hall or church, storage units, including one that appeared at odds with the rest, built high in corrugated steel. It had a roll-up door, currently shuttered. When he pressed his ear to the metal he thought he could hear the sound of a motor running. He spied another door at the side of the building which he promptly knocked upon. He rehearsed a couple of speeches, depending on who answered—*Hey, I'm looking for the Myers Foundation—Hey, I'm lost—*

The door was locked. The entire site appeared deserted. He rounded the corner, walked past the roll-up, and spied a security camera bolted beneath the roof. Its lens swiveled as he walked by and Ben cursed under his breath. Busted, he paused and waved, then decided to quit while he was ahead.

He leapt the gate, got back in the car and reversed it down the drive. At the entrance to the road he paused. His heart was hammering. The camera, he assumed. Back on the highway he headed home, having accomplished nothing. The sense of being watched, however, stayed with him.

The sun had dived behind the hills by the time he arrived home, and his answering machine was blinking. It was Cheryl Oakley, telling him to be at an address on Melrose the following morning. He returned her call but no one picked up.

South of Melrose, half a mile east of Paramount Studios, he found a cramped parking spot two blocks from his destination. The heat was already baking the sidewalk. Knotted power cables drew untidy lines above a forlorn neighborhood of industrial units and shabby apartments. He knocked on a scuffed door painted red, which was opened immediately by a younger man who didn't say a word and refused to look him in the eye. The guy led him along a narrow corridor, beyond a cramped projection room, and into a small screening area.

He took a seat in the middle row. The cushions had partially rotted. He sank deep and felt trapped. He expected Oakley to arrive but instead he was left alone, waiting in the dark, listening to the guy fumble with the projector.

Bubbles of light flashed and jumped onscreen, and the subsequent image—people walking along a dimly-lit road—jolted along. The camera panned for a moment and Ben identified the silhouette of the titular windmill. It was a grand, old Dutch model, which disappeared from view as the camera returned once more to the human parade—men, women, children—approaching the windmill's shadow.

He tried to relax, but there was no air-conditioning and the heat closed in and sank heavily onto his shoulders. The screen jumped to an interior shot. Figures silhouetted, they parted to reveal a spindly-legged calf and half a dozen chickens—one of the chicken's wings was flapping. Cut to a circular stone dais. Men were tying the animals to its surface. He caught sight of a porcelain baby doll being jostled amidst the fluttering and squirming. *Was it a doll?* Ben sat upright and leaned forward, but the film cut once more to an exterior shot of the windmill, its sails now turning, then once again, to a young girl's face. She appeared to be crying, or screaming. Dark vomit crusted her lips and a hand bearing a spoon was feeding her, pushing the bulky utensil inside her mouth. The image pulled back, revealing the windmill's inner mechanism—

"Jesus."

Struggling to rise, Ben's legs failed him and he fell forward. On his knees, he crawled between the rows of seats. His mouth felt full, his teeth bit down on something chewy that reeked of blood. The faint chatter of the projector had disappeared. In its place were the sounds of heavy grinding and the plop of blood and gristle as it flowed copiously into a shallow trough. As for the creature alongside it, Ben had managed one glimpse before his eyes had skittered away in terror. However, it continued to evolve in his mind's eye, regardless—hunger, anticipation, and desire—hair, horns, teeth, and tongue. It coalesced with a disturbing familiarity.

Once more he attempted to rise, but the theater seats were gone. Instead, he fought through a forest of dark-clad legs and pushed frantically to get away from the loaded, dripping spoon. *Please, no—I can't swallow any more!* Abruptly, he felt strong hands on his thighs. A heavy stench arrived, of sex, blood and slaughter. He felt a great weight descend upon him, and hot, intolerable breath against his cheek.

Ben vomited. Bile and sticky chunks added to the swill of dark fluid beneath his fingers. Flesh and heat slid between his buttocks. A vigorous aroma of sweat pushed like gauze over his face and he thought he heard someone laughing. His feet scrambled for grip and he stumbled past the projection room and out into the sun.

The projectionist was sitting on an upturned crate, smoking a cigarette. Calmly, he watched while Ben's stomach continued its revolt.

Blood spattered on concrete as he fought to pull himself together. His hands were dry, the awful stench was gone, and he realized he must have bitten his tongue. He shielded his eyes from the midday glare. "What the fuck was that?"

The guy stubbed out his cigarette, said nothing, and reentered the small theatre.

The wall alongside the door bore a narrow strip of shadow. Ben hunkered against it. The scent of cigarettes made his stomach roil. He wanted to go back inside and demand an explanation, but an explanation of what? The fight left him, the horror remained. Sweat had already stained the underarms of his shirt, and by the time he reached his car, it had spread to his chest and back, too.

When he returned home, the phone was ringing. "Did you keep your appointment?" Cheryl Oakley's voice sounded mocking.

He could barely speak. "Who—who's the girl in the film?"

"Depending on who you believe, it was either my mother or my aunt Estella. They argued about it for years."

"It wasn't real. None of it was real."

"Keep telling yourself that. It might help."

"Oh, sure—"

"We *did* ask you what kind of book you wanted to write." After an awkward silence she added, "Come down to Laguna tomorrow, and we'll talk."

Exhausted, he tried to get a nap. But when he closed his eyes, his mind dropped back inside the screening room and gave the horrors their cue. *The grinding of flesh and bone. Blood pouring through runnels, black as hell. The beast…* Again, he felt the sensation of someone standing close by, an observer to his every shallow breath.

With no other choice, he shook off his fatigue and began to reconfigure his outline for the book. He typed until his fingers were numb, until thoughts of going out and getting blind drunk forced him to stop. Worn out, he fell into bed, accompanied by scenes from *The Dark Windmill.* They stayed with him through-out the night, but they were grayed out and rendered into sil-houette, as if whomever was standing watch had taken pity on him and drawn a temporary curtain.

On this occasion the journey along the Pacific coast wasn't as carefree as the last. The sea was heavy as lead, the sky an oppres-sive blue. He didn't want to fly. Instead, he wanted to hide.

"Was it a test?"

"The test was whether or not you would come back here." Cheryl Oakley was sitting on a bench, looking out to sea from a narrow promontory on the property. A partially smoked ciga-rette was balanced elegantly in her fingers. Its Turkish aroma drifted toward him.

Ben thought he would have calmed down by now, but some images refused to stay hidden. "What I saw—the beast—"

"His name is Quozomal. Are you expecting an apology?" She stubbed out the cigarette. "This is just the beginning."

The view across the ocean was spectacular. Heat from the sun caressed his shoulders. He felt cold as ice. "You know what? Maybe this isn't for me."

"Are you quitting?"

"Yes."

Her laughter followed him as he headed toward the terracotta steps. "It's too late for that, Mr. Norman."

He stared at the piles of folders and notebooks on his desk. Together with the photographs and gigabytes of data, they represented years of work. Had he made the right choice? Regret tore at him, until he reminded himself that the two women were honest-to-goodness crazy and had fed him some kind of hallucinogen. Maybe this wasn't the end. If he—

He flinched as the doorbell rang. His teeth snapped on his tongue in the very same place he'd bitten it the day before, and the bell rang twice more before he answered. It was a FedEx deliveryman with an envelope. He had to sign for it.

The sender's address was a PO Box and the name was unfamiliar. Distracted, he pulled the tab and removed a torn section of newspaper. It was from the *Sacramento Bee*, dated almost two years ago. *Husband and wife urban explorers meet accidental deaths*—

He attempted to drop the newspaper clipping, but it stuck to his fingers and he had to peel it off. He powered up his laptop, and as he began a search on the accident, he brought the sticky fingers of his left hand subconsciously beneath his nose. A chemical smell drifted toward his sinuses. It wasn't unpleasant. In fact…

Tires on concrete, the hum of a vehicle engine,

"Are you awake? Ben?" Soft tapping on his shoulder. "Come on, sleepy-head."

He recognized the ensuing laughter, and his eyes opened to reveal the dim interior of a large sedan. He was in the rear passenger seat. His hands and feet were tied. Mary Davisson was sitting alongside him, wrapped neck to toe in the velvet cloak he'd admired at the cabin. He attempted to struggle, but he was still drugged and physically docile. "Where are we going?" It was black as pitch outside, no sign of street lighting, habitation, or any other vehicles.

"Somewhere you've already been. The windmill, of course."

"But I've never—"

"Oh, but you have. The cameras caught you snooping around. You failed to recognize it because the sails were removed decades ago. The mill itself is preserved and contained by the outer building whose exterior you were prowling. You're a curious bastard, Mr. Norman, which is why you'll prove useful."

Half-heartedly, he pulled at the bindings on his wrists; they scoured his flesh and he had to stop. "Let me go. I won't say anything."

"This is true. One way or another, your lips will be sealed. Let me enlighten you. In 1921, Theo and my father opened a door and discovered someone—"

Her words floated beyond his reach. Instead, light from outside the window caught his attention. It sailed by like a passing cruise ship—one of the factory farms he'd spotted during his jaunt through the Central Valley.

"—and the funniest thing, he wasn't interested in the men. Not in the slightest. All of my father's grand schemes, all of Theo's best-laid plans..."

"Let me go. Please." He reached for the door handle, but his bound hands were heavy as lead.

"So they used us—Estella and I. You saw him, didn't you? Felt him, too, I imagine."

The car was beginning to slow. He saw a squat line of citrus trees in the vehicle's headlights. "You're still practicing."

"Of course, we are. Quozomal survives on ritual and worship. He has some particularly base appetites. As for what he has to offer—wealth, longevity—" She laughed. "Humanity is so easily bought off, wouldn't you say?"

Ben's breath was shallow. His throat felt tight. "Did you kill the explorers?"

"They had no business in our house."

"It was empty."

"Was it? As a consequence we had to break into yours, and I'm sure you can imagine what we found."

"The photos—"

"The scribble on the walls in one of the rooms—it wasn't graffiti. Estella was quite careless in her later years."

The car edged by the gate and into the Foundation courtyard. The driver killed the vehicle lights, and illumination borne of naked flame danced across the brickwork and backlit a small crowd. The silver edges of their robes caught the light as they stared at the vehicle. "For the love of God—"

"He can't help you, now."

"What do you want?"

"There will be others, like the explorers, and we need you to search them out. Information travels so quickly nowadays, people have access to all manner of research technology and we need someone who is familiar with it."

The driver opened the rear passenger door, hauled on Ben's shoulders and dumped him on the ground. He recognized the guy—the silent projectionist.

"And if I refuse?"

Mary Davisson was being helped out of the vehicle. She approached him with the aid of her stick, while two young women fussed with the folds of her robe. She bore a smile on her face. "You become grist, Mr. Norman. Grist for our mill."

He began to struggle, but the drug still rendered him weak. The projectionist gathered him by his bound feet and dragged him across the ground. They joined a parade, heading toward the windmill, and while Davisson and her acolytes accompanied his pathetic, wriggling form, he saw the tall figure of Cheryl Oakley standing by the now-open roll-up door. Flickering torchlight offered bold strokes of a wooden-clad wall, enclosed by corrugated steel.

"It won't always be bad," Mary said, as they crossed the threshold.

He heard the low hum of a generator. A familiar stench hit his nostrils as he was dragged inside. A glimpse to his left offered him a view of the milling mechanism, and waiting beneath—

He began to scream.

A rare lightning storm played at sea. The clouds carried its reflection all the way across the San Fernando Valley, while a spec of light flashed incessantly inside his house, courtesy of his answering machine. The Myers Foundation had repaid his advances on other contracted work, and was in the process of cutting all of Ben's legal ties. But despite his countless emails, assuring her he was fine, his agent was having none of it and was insisting on a meeting, or at the very least, a phone call.

In the first few days after the ritual, he'd thought about picking up the phone when it rang and screaming for help, or calling 911, or jumping into his car and driving off the edge of a cliff. He'd entertained the notion that he could *escape*. Cheryl Oakley had also figured he might try something and had enclosed him in a net of monitoring equipment. But there was no need, for the shadow of the beast was with him, and had been since his first clueless visit to the windmill.

After an ungainly sip from a glass of water, he dabbed his chin with a napkin and examined his notes. Davisson had been right. There was a theatrical society digging up the history of Polly Abel's extracurricular activities for an article on their website, and a growers' collective looking to buy land from the Foundation, digging into County archives, hoping to find something to lever the price to their advantage. All of it was getting too close. All of it had to be shut down.

The answering machine was proving distracting, so he hit the button, played the most recent message, and erased the rest. His agent was playing casual. How about lunch?

"No can do," he attempted. His words came out muffled and incoherent, and he dabbed the ever-present napkin against his lips. A month ago he had pledged his silence and saved his own life. Quid pro quo, his medical insurance was top notch, his house in Sherman Oaks, fully paid off.

Naturally, once they had examined his phone and discovered the pictures he'd taken at the Laguna compound, there had been issues of trust, so as a warning against future betrayals they had offered him to Quozomal who, amongst other things, had ripped out his tongue.

It's in the Cards

By Elizabeth Massie

Bonnie Boone paid for a vendor table at the local science fiction convention, saved up the hefty $250 fee and sent in her check to secure her spot. Then she ordered 40 copies of her self-published novel and priced them at $20 each (tax included). If they all sold, she would come out $224 ahead. That kind of money would help her get some new supplies for her arts and crafts workshop and pay an overdue water bill. She also decided to save money during the convention by bringing her lunch and hiding it under the table since food wasn't allowed in the vendors' room.

She was so excited she was unable to sleep the night before. She just stared at the shadows on the ceiling and imagined various scenarios where people not only wanted her book and her autograph, but her photograph as well. And maybe somebody from the *Daily News-Bee* would come by, interview her, put it in the paper.

Oh, yeah!

Bonnie had attended the convention before, but always as a fan. This time, though, she was a genuine, flesh-and-blood author. *The Cosmic Arms of the Manetela Luda* was her pride and joy, a 578-page space fantasy with citizens of the planet Xetuh fighting citizens of the planet Binn, featuring a mysterious and powerful sorcerer, demonic spirits, a magical sword, tiny flying creatures that lived in characters' brain and taught them right from wrong, and a heroine named Dahina (of the Manetela Luda clan) who had four arms, scaly skin, and flowing blue hair. The cover was one Bonnie had designed herself from various stock photos. If featured stars, the moon, and a beautiful woman with blonde hair standing on a hillside and pointing a sword at the sky. She didn't look like Dahina (two arms, no scales), but that was a minor point. It was a damn good cover. Bonnie loved her book. Others would love it, too.

Setup in the vendors' room was scheduled to begin at 6:30 a.m., with the doors to the fans opening at 9:00. Bonnie arrived at 6:00 sharp, carrying her tote bag over her shoulder and pulling her wobbly-wheeled cart with her boxes of books. Other vendors were already there, crowded up against the door, talking, laughing with each other. She didn't know any of them but felt she was part of them. It was a glorious sensation.

When the guards unlocked the doors, Bonnie poured in with the rest, nearly tripping over a man who was wearing a pair of Zanti Misfit antennae and pulling a wagon filled with plastic bins. She circled the huge room until she found her table against a side wall, marked with an index card and her pseudonym, "Willow Starlance."

"This is my place," she whispered. "Oh, yes!"

She removed the index card and replaced it with a piece of black construction paper on which she'd written her name with a silver Sharpie. Then she stacked her books on the tabletop, adjusting them back and forth until they looked just right. As a final touch, she took out two yellow flowers from her garden that she'd encased in cubes of resin in her workshop and had labeled, "Space Flower from the Fields of the Manetela Luna." She put one flower cube on each side of the table. Then she sat. Folded her hands.

And watched.

And waited.

Within the hour, all the vendors had set up their displays. The vast room was transformed into a wonderland of flashing lights, bright colors, space music, and every kind of goodie a science fiction fan could want. Some vendors sold costumes, helmets, and exotic, alien headdresses. Others sold action figures and imitation futuristic weaponry of all kinds. Still others sold every science fiction film available to humankind (Blu-ray,

some DVDs) as well as posters and framed photos of science fiction stars. And then there were the authors. They were dressed
in science fiction wear—human-like aliens, robots, creatures,
interplanetary heroes, villains. All had large banners on the
wall behind their tables, banners featuring their photos as well
as those of their book covers. Their tables were decorated with
science fiction props as well as stacks of slick business cards.
One even had bowls offering free bite-sized Mars Bars and
Milky Ways.

And then there was Bonnie. Willow Starlance. No props, no
banners, no giveaways.

"It's okay," she told herself. "My book is so good I don't need
all that other stuff."

Bonnie sat, her feet crossing and uncrossing beneath her
table. If she leaned just right, she could see past the vendors in
the middle of the room to the main double doors. They were
closed, with security standing to either side. She looked at her
watch. 8:53. Looked at the door. Back at the watch. 8:55. Looked
at the door. Back at the watch. 8:57. She swallowed hard.

Three more minutes!

"And just what the hell is this?"

Bonnie looked from the door to the woman standing in
front of her table. The woman wore a black leather jumpsuit, a
silver sash, a spangled tiara with a sunburst at the crest, and a
nametag that read, "Melissa Anderson Wright, Award-Winning
Author." Melissa had her hands on her hip, chewing gum in her
teeth, and a smirk on her face.

"Huh?" asked Bonnie.

"This…this heap," said Melissa, waving her hand toward
Bonnie's stacks of books. "Where do you think you are, an elementary school book fair?"

"I…" began Bonnie.

"I mean, seriously? Haven't you ever been to a convention
before? This is, like, totally pathetic."

"I…" began Bonnie.

"Amateur cover on your book. Ugh. And just who are you,
anyway?" asked Melissa.

Bonnie pointed to her construction paper name card.

"Willow Starlance? Sounds like a porno name." The chewing gum snapped. "Where are your decorations? Your handouts? Your swag? Your business cards? Good Lord, girl. You got to draw people in with options. You have no options. Damn, but you're pathetic."

"I…" began Bonnie.

"And this?" Melissa picked up one of the resin cubes holding a yellow flower. "Space flower? What a joke. This is nothing but a common black-eyed Susan, a weed! You really think people will fall for this?"

But before Bonnie could think of a response, Melissa glanced at her phone and said, "Time for the fans! Good luck, Ms. Starfart!" She pranced back to her table, which was three down from Bonnie's.

The doors swung open. Fans pushed their way in and began making the rounds. Some clumped together at the tables that sold posters, costumes, and weapons. Others bee-lined it for their favorite writers. To Bonnie's right and left, readers oohed and aahed over new paperbacks and hardcovers, picking them up, flipping through the pages, and admiring the writers as if they were movie stars. Melissa Anderson Wright had quite a few fans, who immediately began snapping up her books as if they were pieces of gold and sliding them over for her to sign. Several people meandered over to Bonnie's table, looked at her books, said, "Hmmm," and kept moving. One heavyset man in a tight Star Trek sweatshirt with a coffee stain on the front picked up a resin-coated flower and asked how much. Bonnie said, "I'm not selling the flowers, just the books," and the man moved on.

A half-hour into the morning, two young women approached Bonnie's table. One said, "Hi! Tell us about your book." Bonnie sat up straight, smiled, and picked up a copy. "It's great. You'll love it. It's about love and war and magic and…"

"Hey!" shouted Melissa Anderson Wright from her table three down. She waved her hand at the women. "Don't waste your time over there. Self-published crap is what it is. Come on over here, I have a new book in my Time Raiders series! I'm sure you've heard of it!" The two women looked at Bonnie, shrugged, and walked away to see Melissa's newest novel.

Bonnie's jaw tightened. Her gut twisted. She watched as Melissa Anderson Wright charmed the two women out of a couple twenty-dollar bills, and then signed the books with a flourish and a purple pen.

"Not fair," she whispered. "Oh, so not fair."

The morning wore on. Whenever someone approached Bonnie's table, Melissa would either shout out that Bonnie was a hack, or she would send one of her fans over to tell them the same. Bonnie left her table once to go to the bathroom, and on her return, thought about asking one of the security guards to tell Melissa Anderson Wright to leave her alone. But she didn't have the courage. They would probably tell her to suck it up, tell her she didn't have what it took to be a writer selling books at a convention. And so she went back and sat behind her books and wished she were Dahina. Dahina would know what to do.

At noon, Melissa and several of her writer friends gathered to go out somewhere for lunch. They all placed "Be Back Soon!" sign on their tables, clustered and fluttered like a flock of herring gulls, and left the vendors' room.

At last Bonnie had a few moments of peace. She took her sandwich and can of warm Coke out of her tote bag, and carefully took bites and sips when the security guards weren't watching. When potential readers passed by, she smiled as wide she could without spewing bread. Several looked over sympathetically, but none stopped to check out *The Cosmic Arms of the Manetela Luda*. When she was done eating, she took the empty can and plastic wrap to the trashcan by the double doors, and then returned to her table.

And stopped.

And stared.

Hanging down at the front of her table, taped so subtly by one of Melissa Anderson Wright's minions when they'd swept past that Bonnie hadn't noticed, was a piece of paper on which was written in purple ink, "Beginner Writer. Don't Bother."

Bonnie pulled the sign off, balled it up, and threw it under the table. Heart pounding, she wormed her way through the crowd to Melissa Anderson Wright's table and when no one was looking, scooped up all the writer's business cards and crammed them into her jeans pocket. Then she sat down behind her table, tore the cards into little pieces, and dropped the pieces into her tote bag.

Melissa and her entourage returned from lunch and hour later. As they passed Bonnie's table, Melissa touched her sun-capped tiara and mouthed, "Loser."

The dealers' room closed at 6:00 p.m. As the convention would continue another three days, no one took down their displays, but rather covered them with light tarps or sheets of plastic. Fans slowly trickled out at the insistence of the guards. Bonnie had nothing to cover her books, so she put them back into the boxes until tomorrow. She had not sold a single copy. And one of her two Space Flowers had been swiped when she wasn't looking.

Bonnie shuffled across the parking lot to her car, her tote bag over one shoulder, her remaining resin-coated flower cube in hand. She squeezed it so hard that the sharp edge cut into her palm, but she didn't care. Her mouth was sour. Her stomach burned with the second Coke she'd drunk. Her head ached. It was all she could do to keep her legs under her and moving forward so she didn't crash to the pavement. She spotted an Audi nearby with a license plate reading, "IRITSF," and a bumper sticker that said, "Melissa Anderson Wright, Famous Author Inside This Car!" The bitch's vehicle.

"I can't go back tomorrow," Bonnie told herself as she unlocked the car and slid into the driver's seat.

"You have to," said the Dahina she wished she was. "Your books are back there. So is your pride."

"I can't face those people again," Bonnie said.

"You have to," said Dahina. "You have to go back and stand up to them with courage."

Bonnie put her forehead on the steering wheel and squeezed back furious tears. The world closed in around her like a heavy blanket. It felt as if the car rose and fell beneath her, shuddered and then rose again like a space ship launching off to a far planet. There was a rushing deep in her ears. The rushing became a humming. The humming grew louder and louder, until it was the sound of cheering. Cheering for her, for Dahina, who had raised her beautiful scaly arms and her mighty sword against the cruel Axiats, and had slashed her way to victory. Bonnie waved at her people, the Manetela Luda, thanking them for loving her, for celebrating her, for—

There was a banging on Bonnie's car door. She snapped awake. Standing close to the window, hands on hips, was Melissa Anderson Wright in her leather jumpsuit and sunburst tiara. She looked both pissed and chagrined. The rest of the parking lot had cleared and it was growing dark. Long shadows streaked the pavement with heavy, black fingers.

Bonnie hesitated then rolled the window down part way. She noticed that her door wasn't closed all the way. She was sure she'd closed it when she'd gotten in. Why was it now ajar? But before she could think about it further, Melissa said, "Okay, now just hear me out."

Bonnie nodded.

"First of all, you know I was, like, totally kidding in there, in the dealers' room, right?"

"I…" began Bonnie.

"I mean, come on," said Melissa. She rolled her eyes. "That was just an act. Okay? I mean, pfft, if you can't take a little joke how are you going to survive in this world, am I right? If you can't take a joke, you're pretty fucked up already."

"I…" began Bonnie.

"Anyway," said Melissa, hitching her thumb over her shoulder. "My front tire is flat. Totally flat like a fuckin' pancake. I think somebody slashed it. Who the hell would do that? But here's the thing. I left my cell in the dealers' room and it's locked and nobody will let me in to look for it. Fuck 'em, right? So listen, all I need you to do is let me use your cell to make a call."

"I don't have a cell."

"What the hell? You're kidding me, right?"

"No."

"Shit a brick! Okay, I need you to give me a ride to my friend Sallie's house. She's, like, two and a half miles from here. No biggie, right?"

Bonnie felt herself nod. Melissa trotted around the front of the car and tried the door. It was locked. "Hell-*oh*?" she said.

Bonnie unlocked the door. Melissa Anderson Wright slid in. "I bet you're thrilled to have an Amazon bestselling author riding with you, huh? Might rub off on you. Or maybe not."

Bonnie started the engine and drove out of the parking lot. And then she remembered the resin-coated flower sitting on the console beside her.

Sharp. Heavy.

Just right.

Melissa glanced out the window. Bonnie swung the cube.

She arrived almost two hours late to the convention the next morning. She'd had so much to do when she got home the night before. Find just the right tools for the messy, challenging task. Struggle with the heavy lifting and the initial crafting. Wash down the basement floor. Scrub out the pans. Locate two metal barbecue skewers to serve as stabilizers.

Luckily, there was just enough liquid resin in her workshop to finish the job.

Once the crafting was done and the space heater was running on high for a faster cure, Bonnie dug in the attic trunk and found her mother's old navy blue, gold-sequined evening gown. She cut it apart into strips that she would place over her vendor's table to create an outer space-like covering. She kept one small strip to fashion a sparkling sash for herself. The final touch consisted of black-eyed Susans from her yard, sewn together into a crown of Space Flowers for her hair.

The dealers' room was buzzing when Bonnie entered at 10:42 with her bulging tote bag over her shoulder. She marched to her table, past the vendors with their figurines, posters, flashing lights, and weaponry, past fans dressed like Iron Man and Wonder Woman, Wookiees and Trekkies. She pulled the cloth strips from her tote bag and spread them out on the table.

"That looks awesome," she told herself. "And I look awesome."

She arranged her books in two stacks. She placed the flower cube and a bowl of silver-wrapped Hershey Kisses (labeled "Kisses from the Outer Reaches") between the book stacks.

Then she carefully set her two newest, resin-coated creations on the front corners of the table—

a pair of lifelike arms standing erect with hands open and fingers grasping as if in an appeal to the Heavens. The scales on the arms caught and reflected the colorful lights of the vendors' displays across the way. At the base of each arm was a sign that read, "Reach High Into Deep Space With Dahina, Heroine of Willow Starlance's Newest Novel, *The Cosmic Arms of the Manetela Luda!*"

Fans were drawn in. They stared at the arms in awe as they munched on Hershey Kisses.

"Oh, my goodness!"

"These arm sculptures are gorgeous! So realistic!"

"Awesome!"

"You made these?"

"I did," said Bonnie.

"So you're a writer and an artist, both?"

"I am."

A woman reached out to touch.

"Please don't touch," said Bonnie.

"What are they made out of?"

"That's an artist's secret," said Bonnie.

"What about the scales? What are they made of? Wait, they look like torn pieces of business cards. Is that right?"

Bonnie smiled.

"I see! Clever! Waste not, want not, as my grandmother used to say."

"Nice! You're very talented."

"Thank you," said Bonnie.

Bonnie sold out of her novels by noon. Fans took note that Melissa Anderson Wright was absent from her table, and chalked it up to her slashed tire and that she'd probably show up before the day was over.

And Bonnie wondered what her next novel would be. Something with feet in the title, perhaps? Or the word "head"?

Nothing like having some options.

Roadkill

By Meryl Stenhouse

The air in the car is hot and humid, coming off the asphalt which is still baking even as the sun's last flare colours the western sky. Ceduna is behind them; Coorabie and Fowler's Bay just memories of wave-tossed rocks and glare. It's still five hours to Eucla and the South Australia-Western Australian border. They're not technically on the Nullarbor here, but the trees are low and sparse and there's really nothing between them and forever except a billion stars.

Rosie leans back against Andy, watching the trees disappear with the light. Her sister Norah is in the passenger seat, reading aloud from the Lonely Planet guidebook but her voice is drowned by the roar of the tyres. Lianna is driving, singing aloud to the radio. This trip was Lianna's idea and she's loving it. She turns to Rosie, just for a second, and Rosie remembers that glimpse of wild joy and windblown hair, untouchable youth.

There's a meaty thump under the front tyres and under the back a second later. They slide across the road, screaming tyres, grit and smoke. Rosie's head slams into Andy's chin and she hears the crunch. Everything swings and gravel bounces off the window. She wants to scream but she's too busy hanging on as the horizon lurches.

Then it's quiet except for the ticking of the engine and Lianna swearing in the front seat, fuck fuck fuck fuck, a shaky monotone.

Rosie tries to untangle herself from Andy. "What did we hit?"

"Kangaroo." Lianna's face in the dash lights is sickly. "Went right under the tyres." She struggles with the door and stumbles out into the night.

There's blood coming out of Andy's mouth and all down his chin. "Oh god. Are you all right?" His lip is split. "What did you hit?"

"You. You headbutted me."

When she prods her scalp her hair is bloody and there's a painful spot. Norah is already out of the car when Rosie manages to clamber out, her knees unsteady. Lianna is pacing in short, distressed circles, gripping her short pink hair. Her shadow jumps from tree to tree, huge and soft-edged. Rosie's worried about the sounds Lianna is making.

Lianna turns to face her, mouth twisted into a jagged line, and Rosie realises she's not the one making the sounds.

"It's still alive," Lianna whispers.

"Oh god." Rosie can't turn to look at what's behind them, but she does anyway, glancing at the shadow kicking and crying on the road. "What do we do?"

They huddle with their backs to the trauma, Norah frowning, Lianna tugging her hair like she might pull it out. They can't leave it here, injured, to starve to death or get attacked by dingoes or feral pigs.

"We'll have to put it out of its misery," says Andy.

This is what she likes about Andy. He takes charge. He's always in control.

"How?" says Norah.

Andy shrugs. "Hit it on the head?"

"With what?"

Lianna makes a choking sound and walks off the road into the dark.

Rosie hurries after her, puts an arm around her shoulders. "It wasn't your fault."

"Are you guys going to help, or not?" Andy's voice is over-loud in the darkness. Lianna follows her miserably back to the car. Rosie keeps her eyes averted, not wanting to see if the roo is still kicking, hoping desperately that it has died, feeling sick at herself. "What's the plan?"

In answer, Norah holds up the knife they packed, along with plastic plates and barbeque tools, with grand plans to cook a meal every night under the stars. It had taken one sticky, black-topped public barbeque at a roadstop before they'd unanimously decided to eat sandwiches the rest of the trip.

"We'll cut its throat," says Andy. "Norah's idea."

"It's the quickest and most humane way. I looked it up," says Norah. "Before we came. Just in case."

Rosie tries not to imagine Norah researching methods to dispose of injured animals. "So who's going to do it?" She knows it won't be Lianna, hunched and miserable. She hopes it's not her.

"Me, I guess," says Andy, holding out his hand for the knife.

Norah shifts it out of his reach. "Have you done this before?"

"Of course not."

"Then I'd better do it." And she marches behind the car, chin up, before they can do anything.

Andy gives her a glance with eyebrows raised. He doesn't know Norah. Andy didn't grow up with the three of them, her and Norah and their parents, with Lianna a more and more frequent visitor on their sofa bed. He didn't understand that Norah saw only what needed to be done.

Rosie's listening for a sound and trying not to. Everything is magnified; Lianna's short, sharp breaths, Andy's slow, even ones. A mopoke calls, low and lonely in the distance. Sound carries here, with no trees to disperse it, and something far away can sound like it's sitting on your shoulder.

Norah appears out of the darkness, from shadow to person in a few steps. "It's done." She holds up the knife, the blade bloody. Lianna makes a choking noise.

"Can you clean the knife?" says Rosie.

"Just throw it away," says Andy. "No one's going to use it now."

She glances back at the still form on the road, grateful to Norah for doing it in her precise way, saving them all from the awful task. She wants to say "well done", wants to say "thank you", but neither of those are appropriate.

Andy is also staring at the dark, still mound. "We should pull it off the road. So no one else hits it." It sounds like the decent thing to do, but she suspects that Andy is going to check that Norah really did it.

They climb back into the car. Rosie will have to drive; Lianna is curled up in the back seat, and after a significant glance from Rosie, Norah climbs in with her. That leaves the passenger seat free for Andy when he returns, holding his hands slightly away from his body. Napkins and cold water really don't do the job, and he sits awkwardly with his hands cupped in his lap.

They've hardly picked up any speed before a regular scraping and thumping comes from the front left wheel. Rosie pulls off the road. They've damaged something, though none of them are comfortable enough with the car to recognise what it is, let alone fix it. Norah wants to stop and investigate, but the rest of them just want to go on, even at a snail's pace.

"How far, do you think?" she asks Norah.

"We won't make Eucla until after midnight."

The scraping under the car sounds like nails on a chalkboard. Saltbush and banksia stretch out, grey in the beam of their headlights. Rosie glances through the windscreen. This is what she came out here for, but the stars have lost their allure. She doesn't know if she can do this for another five hours. And who's going to disagree? Norah would love to tinker about under the car, Lianna is a miserable lump in the back, her face turned into the seat. She's about to suggest to Andy that they stop when he says, "Are those lights?"

They crawl towards them. A building takes shape, an old motel, cinderblock-and-neon sign.

"Vacancy!" says Andy. "We can stay there and look at the car in the morning."

The tyres grind over gravel. Rosie pulls up at an angle, not sure where to park. It's getting cold now, a temperature they aren't prepared for after the baking-hot days. The lights in reception are low, and the carpet ancient. Andy dings the bell on the counter. They wait, and wait.

"It's been ages," says Andy. "I'm going to look for someone." He marches off through the door to the restaurant. Norah hesitates, then rings the bell again. Going looking for someone is off her list of comfortable actions.

Andy's back pretty quickly. "No one there, and I don't think they use it. Any sign?"

Rosie shakes her head. They end up splitting up and going around the motel. Rosie goes through the disused restaurant and out the back. A fibro cottage squats behind the motel, the front all shadows and pale walls. Two old galvanised water tanks take up one side of the house. The only lights are in the motel. She crunches across the bare soil but she's pretty sure nobody's home.

"Who leaves their motel unattended?" says Andy, when they meet again in reception.

"I guess they didn't have any bookings? Maybe they'll be back later." But how much later is unknown, and they're tired and cold.

"How much are the rooms?"

"Fifty-five dollars a night," says Norah. "It was on the sign." Of course Norah would notice.

"Well, let's pay them in the morning." Andy slips behind the counter and picks up three keys. He tosses one to Lianna, who fumbles it.

Norah doesn't even try to catch hers. "I don't want to stay here. I don't like it."

"There isn't anywhere else." Rosie picks up the dropped key. The keyring is a scrap of animal fur, dry and curled. Maybe it's supposed to be kitschy, but the fur isn't soft, it's stiff and clumped. A scrap of card warns her not to leave her room without the key.

"We should go on to Eucla," said Norah.

"It's hours away. Come on, let's have a look at the rooms and you might change your mind." Rosie doesn't know why she says that. When Norah gets that look on her face, nothing will move her. But Rosie's holding on to the vain hope that Norah will change her mind, just this once.

The rooms are functional and dated, peach walls and cream bedspreads. "It smells," says Norah.

Rosie sniffs. There is a smell, faint, like old dust. "They probably don't get many people here. It's musty, that's all. It will be fine, Norah."

Norah stands outside the doorway, picking at a chip in the cinderblock.

Andy gives her a glance, and Rosie hopes Norah doesn't see it. "We're staying?"

Lianna nods. Rosie's pretty sure nothing will get her back on the road tonight. "You and Lianna can share," she says to Norah.

"I'm going to sleep in the car."

Rosie glances at Lianna. She knows she should offer to stay with her, that Lianna is feeling like crap. But so is Rosie, and she just wants to curl up with Andy. She's mad at Norah for messing up her plans. "You all right on your own?" she says to Lianna.

"Yeah, sure." Lianna smiles, but Rosie feels like the heel she is. She turns her back on her friend and goes into the room.

"Do you want the bathroom first?" says Andy.

"Thanks."

In her room, Lianna sits on the edge of the bed, hands resting between her knees, staring at the horrible carpet. Rosie hurries past. The shower room is shadowy, even with the bare fluorescent bulb that flickers and hums. The shower is just a rectangle of cinderblock, painted pea green with an old rose head that sprays tepid water no matter what she does with the taps. It smells, too; artesian water probably, drawn up from the basin far below. An oversized drain takes up one corner. Warm, fetid air comes up from it, making her think of mold and disease. She tries to keep away from standing on the grill. It's big enough that she could fall in if the grill gave way, and it gives her vertigo.

While Andy showers, she takes the cover from the second bed in Lianna's room and goes to check on Norah. She's on her phone, with a packet of chips in one hand, and looks comfortable enough. "What is it you don't like? About the motel?"

"There's too many walls," she says.

That's a new one, and Rosie files it under "things Norah doesn't like".

Rosie wakes stiff and cold. The darkness is broken only by a rectangle of light—the neon motel sign coming through the thin curtains. Andy snores beside her. In the quiet darkness thoughts come crowding in, but she shies away from the immediate ones: Lianna and the roo. This trip was Lianna's idea. A break before final year for Rosie, a break between school and university for Norah. A madcap adventure between jobs for Lianna's wild spirit.

Andy is Rosie's addition. Six months of intense relationship were not to be interrupted for the three weeks they planned to be on the road. And this was a way to let them get to know each other more. This is a test of a different sort. To see if they can all fit together.

Something moves outside. Was that what had woken her? She gets up, feeling bruises twinge and peers out into the night. Beyond the narrow concrete verandah there's nothing but a stretch of gravel between them and the Eyre highway running from horizon to horizon. Beyond that, the dark shapes of low vegetation and the stars. Empty, except for the four of them in this old motel.

She has to shift to the other side of the window to see the car. Is Norah all right? She smiles in the dark. Too many walls. If anything, the motel has too few, a shoebox of flat-roofed compartments.

Gravel crunches. Rosie squints into the pre-dawn gloom. Drag-crunch. Drag-crunch. A shadow stretches out over the rolling scrub, formless and soft-edged.

A kangaroo crawls out of the scrub and Rosie's chest constricts. It's hauling itself along with its front paws. Its back legs drag uselessly behind the crushed and broken back. An animalistic cry of pain, long and low, shudders against the glass. The roo examines the car, head sweeping from side to side, sniffing the air.

When it moves it's a blur, body bumping behind it, gravel crunching beneath. It slams into the side of the car.

Rosie screams. The roo crawls up across the bonnet. Light flicks on in the car. Rosie has one glimpse of Norah's shocked face before the roo crawls up over the windscreen.

Rosie doesn't think, just throws herself through the door, screaming for Andy to help.

The car is gone. Rosie stumbles to a halt. The night is empty and quiet, only the distant call of the curlew echoing over the plain. She turns in a slow circle. Norah must have driven off.

There's a crunching sound to her left, down toward the shower block. Rosie backs up slowly until she can feel the wall at her back. The area in front of the motel is lit by the sign, but down that end there are only shadows. She fumbles for the doorknob.

It's locked. She tries it both ways. "Andy?" Her voice is strangled. Surely he would have woken up when she ran out.

"Yeah? What?" says Andy, short and grumpy.

She rests her forehead on the door. "Norah's driven off. And there's—there's an injured roo…"

"What? Hang on." She hears him stumbling about. "Why'd she drive off?"

How to describe what she'd seen? She was beginning to wonder if she'd been dreaming. But the nightmare lingered, in the way her shoulders tightened every time she heard a sound coming from the shower block. "Let me in. Something attacked the car."

"Shit. Okay, I'm coming, hang on." Footsteps approach the door and she steps back.

Silence. She waits, presses her ear to the door. There's no sound coming from the room.

But there's a dragging, slithering noise coming from the shadows. She turns as a shape forms in the shadow near the wall.

Her legs take off without any thought on her part and she bolts down the verandah toward reception. She can't tell if anything is following her, her heart is pounding too loudly. She dives into reception and pulls the doors shut.

The doors shudder, as if something hit them from the other side. She backs away toward the reception desk. Something sniffs, loudly, on the other side.

She's in trackpants and a t-shirt. She doesn't have her phone—it's in the room with Andy, and reception is patchy out here anyway. She climbs up on the desk, not sure if that will be any help, but it makes her feel better.

A dog yaps on the other side of the door, and scratches like it wants to come in. Rosie can't believe she's run from a dog, and a small one by the sound of it. Still, she's careful when she approaches the door, wary of remembered shadows. There's a white, shaggy terrier outside, sniffing under the door.

Feeling like a fool, Rosie cracks the door open and lets it in. "Hey, buddy, where are your owners? This—"

The dog looks up at her and the words die in her throat. One of the dog's eyes is hanging out of its skull, the jaw broken and swinging. The white fur in front has been torn away, gravel embedded in the raw flesh.

Rosie backs away. She knows this dog. It's Lianna's dog. The one her father bought for her, an apology for the state of her mother. Misty was its name.

But Misty is dead. Misty was hit by a car, years ago. Rosie backs away as Misty comes toward her, tail wagging, tongue hanging flaccidly from the open mouth.

She runs.

Visits from Lianna became visits from Lianna and Misty. They'd hear the happy bark and Rosie or Norah would run to open the door. Rosie's dad would frown, and peer out the window, then march down the road to see if Lianna's mum needed to go to the hospital. Rosie remembered her mother staring out the window after him, always worried that one day he'd be the one at the mercy of Davo's fists.

But Davo only ever hit his wife, and Marla wouldn't leave him. All they could do was give Lianna a warm bed and a glimpse of stability.

Rosie was home from school early that day, eager to sneak the car out while her parents were at work. Someone must have left the gate open at Lianna's place. It wasn't Rosie's fault, not really.

She couldn't believe that hitting something so small could sound so loud. She jumped out of the car, ran back to look at the little form on the road, knowing she was in trouble, hoping it wasn't too bad. They could afford the vet bills, even if Lianna's family couldn't.

But Misty was dying, torn and broken, gasping through bloody froth. No one was around. No one had seen. She jumped back in the car, put it away, ran back to Misty's still form, pulled out her phone, hands shaking, to tell Lianna that her beloved Misty had been hit by a car.

The school let Lianna come straight home. Rosie helped her wrap Misty in a blanket and carry her home—not to the mess that was Lianna's house, but to the only place she had found love.

Rosie meant to confess, she really did. But a few days later Davo put Marla's head through a window, severing an artery in her neck and Lianna's home broke for good.

After that there was no way Rosie could tell her that she had been the one to kill Misty. She'd tried, later, penning letters, writing emails, going to tell her face to face, but always at the last minute the desire had failed in the face of fear.

She told herself she was protecting Lianna, but in reality she was protecting herself.

She crouches behind an old trestle table, listens to the dead dog scratching at the door until the light blazes through the windows, until the sounds of the dog fade away, replaced by the shrill song of the grasshoppers.

Reception is still empty and so is the carpark and the road. No dog, no broken kangaroo, no Norah. What she does see is Andy, coming out of their room, frowning, looking around.

Looking for her.

She throws herself into his arms with a cry, and tries to explain, through her sobs, about Norah and the roo and Misty. Andy helps her into the room and makes coffee while she cries. As she calms down she hears what she's saying, and it sounds crazy. She doesn't want to sound crazy to Andy, but the shaky feeling won't go away.

He sits down next to her and hands her a coffee. "Okay, the roo I get, after last night, but how does the dog tie into it? Minnie?"

"Misty." She sips her coffee, but it's boiling. "She was Lianna's dog. I—she got hit by a car. Just before Lianna's mother died."

"Harsh." Andy leans in and puts an arm around her. "No wonder you were upset."

She leans into his warmth, and knows that she's never going to tell anyone about Misty.

"That was some dream."

"Yes." In the light she's willing to accept that explanation, but can't make herself believe it. "But what about Norah?"

"She said last night she wanted to go on. Maybe she did."

"Maybe." It's not like Norah though. Independent and single-minded she is, but Rosie can't imagine her abandoning them. "I'm worried about her though. And how are we going to go any-where without a car?" She rubs her face. This is easier to focus on.

There's a frantic knock on the door, and Rosie sloshes hot cof-fee over her legs. Andy jumps up and opens the door.

There's no one there. He frowns and looks up and down the verandah, then closes the door. "Okay, that—"

"Rosie!"

"Norah!" She jumps up and shoves past Andy, throwing the door open.

Nothing comes through except the chittering of the grass-hoppers under the scrub. "Norah?"

Andy comes up behind her. "Where did she go?"

"I don't know."

"Not the best time to joke around."

"Norah does not joke around. Ever." She looks down the verandah to the shower room. It's dark and shadowy, even in the daylight, and she shivers. "I don't get it."

"Neither do I." They go back in the room. As soon as the door is closed, Norah's voice comes through.

"Rosie, please—"

"Norah! I'm here, where are you?"

"I'm outside your room."

"You're not. We just checked."

"Open the door."

"I just did." She opens it again. There's no one there. She closes it, and looks at Andy. "Am I going crazy?"

She'd believe it, after last night, except Andy's looking just as confused as she is.

Norah's voice is strained. "You've got to get out of there. It's a ruin, Rosie. Abandoned. I can't get to you. I don't know where you are. I've climbed all over and there's no way in. And that thing is still out there, in the scrub. I can hear it crawling around. I think it's underneath."

"The...the roo?"

"Yeah. I think it followed us here." Her voice goes soft. "Or maybe this is where it always is. I don't know. Don't go any-where. Don't go outside. I've got to think."

There's silence. "Norah?" Rosie opens the door, not believing Norah can't be out there. But the verandah is empty. She closes the door and turns to Andy. "What do you think?"

He chews on his lip. "Honestly? I'd think we were going crazy. But you know, evidence of the eyes and all that." His face creases into a grin. "Unless this bore water is sending us crazy. Maybe we shouldn't drink it anymore."

"Maybe." She sinks onto the bed. "What do we do now? Just wait?" Her stomach growls. "All the food is in the car."

"Shit, what about Lianna?" says Andy. "I forgot about her. We should get her in here with us." He looks guilty.

Rosie jumps up. "Great idea." She feels even more guilty. Lianna is her friend, she should have remembered before Andy. But on the other hand, Andy didn't spend the night hiding from a dead dog. She takes a few steps to Lianna's room and knocks on the door.

The door swings open. The room beyond is empty, Lianna's gear scattered around.

Maybe she's taking a shower. There aren't many other options. But the shower room is empty, too. It's cooler in here and dim, despite the blazing sunlight outside. She's just about to leave when she hears a gasp, the sort of gasp you make when you've been crying a long time.

"Lianna?"

"I'm sorry, Mummy. I'm sorry."

The words are high, childlike, and too close to an uncom-fortable past for Rosie's liking. "Where are you?"

"I don't know." She sounds both close and far away. "I'm sorry. Don't be mad."

The grate sighs, sending hot, metal-scented air into the shower.

Lianna's sobs echo softly in the drain. Rosie lies on her stomach and peers down. At first it's all gloom, but as her eyes adjust she sees a pale round shape of Lianna's face. She hears a sound. A *drag-thump.*

Lianna's sobs break off in a gasp. "Can you hear that?"

"It's okay. It's okay. Just climb up here."

"How? It's dark. Help me, Rosie."

"I'm trying. But you've got to climb up here." Rosie scrabbles at the edge of the grate with her fingers. It isn't flush to the floor, isn't tight at all. She lifts it up. Long strings of slime hang from the bottom of it, leaving grey smears on the tiles as she pushes it away. She lies on her belly and peers into the darkness below. Air rushes up into her face—hot, stinking of water and metal and something else.

The drain is wide enough for someone to fit inside it. The walls are brick at the top, but farther down she can see dirt. She reaches down as far as she can. The *drag-thump* is getting louder, still slow, a muted noise just on the edge of hearing, but Rosie remembers the injured roo rushing at the car, remembers dead Misty and knows it wasn't a dream.

"Mummy?"

Lianna's mother is dead, too, and Rosie hopes that she's not crawling down there with Lianna. She bites her knuckles. "Please climb up. Please. We can talk up here. It's going to be all right."

Lianna screams, down in the darkness. Rosie screams too, at the noise and the crunch and the thump. She leaps up and runs out, and thumps into a solid body.

"Rosie! Rosie, what's wrong?"

She knows she rambling and it makes no sense, but Andy listens anyway and doesn't tell her she's crazy.

"How did she get down the drain?"

"I don't know. But we have to get her out. Something attacked her."

Andy sighed and looked around. "And it's just us. All right. Really makes you miss the city, doesn't it?" He leads her back to the room. She wipes her face on her towel.

"So what happened with Lianna's mum? I didn't quite understand you."

"Her father killed her. He was always hitting her, and then one night it went too far."

"Wow. Shit. And Lianna is okay?"

She wanted to say yes, but the real answer was not really. Lianna was personable and got jobs easily. She struggled to hold them though, because the darkness would always come back and she'd quit and go off the rails for a while. She'd been the impetus for this trip, after throwing in her job. Rosie should have seen the signs.

"Rosie? You there?"

"Norah. Listen." She tells her about Lianna. "We're going to try to get her out."

"Shit. Okay, wait. Let me have a look."

They wait, staring at each other. She reaches for his hand and he takes it. "I'm so glad I've got you." And she is. This feels right. He's the sort of person she can rely on.

Norah's back quickly. "Okay, I looked. It's a big sort of crack in the ground, but it runs north and opens out into a gully. You might be able to get out that way."

"And then what?"

There's a pause. "I don't know. I'm looking, but…I'm scared, Rosie. Every time I go into the scrub I hear that thing. But I'll figure out a way to get to you. Okay? Come back to the room."

"I will." She wishes she could see her before they go. "We'll come back."

They break into the house. It's clear from the inside that it's been abandoned and is slowly falling into ruin. Rosie breathes shallowly, trying not to think about old dust and Norah and the ruins of a motel. Somehow they will get back. But first they have to find Lianna.

They find an old clothesline and a rusty knife, the blade sharpened so many times it's bowed like a banana.

In the shower room, Andy lies on his stomach, like she had, and shouts Lianna's name down into the dark. His voice echoes back. "No way she could climb down there without a rope. Wish we had a torch." It was something they'd been unable to find. They had their phones now, and torches were about all they were good for, but the batteries wouldn't last long. Andy shines his down into the hole, his arm at full stretch. "I think I can see the bottom."

They tie the clothesline around the window bars. "I'll go first," says Andy, and she doesn't even try to dissuade him. He scrambles into the hole. "It's easy Rosie. You can prop against the side." She hangs over the edge and watches him, flicking her light on now and then to check his progress. When he is a dim shadow, he shouts, "Found the bottom! Come down."

She sits on the edge, hanging over the dark, stinking hole, thinking of a broken body sliding quickly across the soil. But she's alone up here, even if that thing is down the hole, so are the only people around. She pushes off. Andy was right, it is relatively easy to go down with her feet braced on one side and her back on the other.

"Rosie, I can hear Lianna."

She tries to look between her feet, but everything is black. "Andy?" Her voice echoes. She waits, the earth against her back cold through her t-shirt. Has he run off and left her? Deep breath. It can't be much further. She can get down on her own. It's just that it's so dark, hot, and slimy. She tries to hurry and her feet slip on the walls. The rope jerks, hurting her hand. Her foot slams into the ground and she falls into cold mud.

She struggles to her feet, wiping her hands on her shorts, and fumbles for her phone. The shaky beam illuminates a narrow, earth-lined tunnel sloping down. A channel shows where water had flowed, digging away at the soil. Red-brown algae lies in long strings on the soil.

"Andy?" She listens for his reply, for any sound, but the underground muffles all, like her ears are full of cotton wool. She tells herself not to be stupid, that there is only one way Andy could have gone, and sets off down the tunnel, feeling her way along. She doesn't dare use her phone too much, or risk using up all the battery.

Andy's nowhere to be found. The tunnel ahead of her is empty. What can she do, but go forward?

She can't believe he left her.

A sound comes down the tunnel, a distressed cry, scrabbling, and the fall of dirt. She hurries on. That must be him. The crying gets louder, a pain-filled wail. She hurries forward. In the narrow beam of light from her phone, something writhes on the ground.

It's Lianna. Rosie runs to her but stops, frozen, because Lianna is dragging herself along by her arms. Her back legs are twisted and useless behind her, and she's wailing in pain and distress.

Rosie backs away. This is too much. She should go to her, help her, get her to a hospital, but Lianna is no longer human, she is broken flesh dying on the road.

A shadow jumps up the wall behind her and Rosie sees the shape of the dead roo. She backs away.

Lianna scrabbles after her, dragging herself along by her hands. Rosie bolts, away from the shadow and Lianna, on into the dark. The tunnel narrows until the dirt is gripping her shirt, tearing her skin. She squeezes on, mouth dry. She can't go back. There's dirt in her mouth and she thinks she might die here, down in the dark all alone.

She's stuck, pressed in on both sides by wet soil and slime. She scratches at the dirt, feels her nails tear away as she forces herself forward. Then she's through and there's sky above her and bright light. She climbs, between a crack in the rock, her fingers stinging and bloody.

She comes out on the plain, surrounded by scrub. She stops to breathe, shaking, but there's a hiss in the undergrowth and she keeps moving, forces herself through the brush which catches her hair and tears her skin.

She bursts out into a clearing and stumbles to a halt. There's the motel, just as they left it. Andy is standing in front. He spots her and runs over. She falls into his arms. She's out of there. Lianna is dead. But they tried. They tried to save her.

"Where did you go?"

She's too tired to talk. Too hurt inside. Andy helps her to the room and they fall through the door.

"Rosie?"

Rosie goes to the window, leaves a bloody smear on the glass. She can see Norah standing outside the door. It's the only place she can see Norah. Through the window.

She picks up the lamp, lifts it, smashes open the window. They climb out. Norah is there. When she turns back, she sees what Norah sees. The motel is fallen down, just walls left, and the door, leaning crazily between broken walls.

"Too many walls."

Norah nods. Andy walks along the frontage, shaking his head.

Rosie is done with it. She limps toward the car. Norah walks beside her. "Lianna?"

Rosie shakes her head. She can't talk about that yet. She just wants to go.

"I'll start the car." Norah hurries off. Rosie turns to call Andy. The shadow of the roo climbs the wall behind Andy. He hasn't seen it. She draws in a breath to warn him.

But if she does, it will hear her. And it's a long way to the car.

Lovely, kind, supportive Andy. She mourns him even as she turns and runs. Norah screams, but it's too late for Andy. She dives into the car, and Norah slams it into reverse.

They get back on the highway, heading west. Rosie sinks down into the seat. Norah is crying, but Rosie can't find any tears. She'd left him to die. She'd made a choice to run and left him to die. What kind of a person did that?

"We should turn around. Go home. Tell…someone," said Norah.

Rosie stared out the window at the rolling scrub. A kite screamed, high up on the wind. "Just keep driving."

Ahead of them, a little white shape trotted out onto the road.

The Bone Arena

By Jeffrey Thomas

The Demon named Naberius wore only a loincloth of gold material, his beautiful onyx muscles on display for all the crowd, delineated with his glaze of sweat. A diadem of black metal, decorated with three canine heads with rubies for eyes, was bolted into his skull. He was a striking figure, but he had lost one of his great raven-like wings to a powerful blow from his opponent, and it lay in the sand behind him. He had also taken several deep lacerations, one across his left pectoral and a worse one across the top of his right thigh, a gaping crevice that sent a constant flow of red blood pulsing down his leg. Naberius tracked his own gore around as he bobbed and weaved, swung at the other combatant with his long, straight-bladed sword, also of black metal.

The other Demon, named Furcas, was of a different Demonic race. Though he was taller and bulkier than Naberius, he had the appearance of an old man, with flowing white hair and beard, but hollow pink skull sockets in place of eyes. He was granted vision by a single orb, twice the size of a human eye, that hovered just above his head. He carried a long weapon that sported a trident at one end, an axe-like halberd blade at the other. It gave him a greater reach, and this plus his superior strength had put Naberius at a disadvantage.

"Fight!" Furcas bellowed at his adversary, spittle flying. "You look like you're about to faint, you fool! Fight as if you mean to kill me!"

"I do mean to kill you!" Naberius panted, dancing black and

forth, looking for an opening as Furcas slowly spun his double-headed weapon in front of him. As much a flourish for the audience as a means of keeping Naberius uncertain which end would come for him.

"That's the spirit!" Furcas snarled. Then he lunged.

Naberius swung his sword, but Furcas trapped the blade between two tines of his pitchfork and turned it aside. He followed through by spinning his body around—allowing the redirected blade to slide out from between the barbed prongs—and swinging the axe blade toward his foe.

Up until fifteen minutes ago (if an earthly reckoning of time could be utilized in the netherworld), Naberius would have been able to jump back or duck under the halberd, maybe drop his sword and catch the staff in both hands. He was weak from blood loss, however. Though stronger than human beings, with greater healing abilities, Demons could be wounded...injured... and mortally so, because they had no souls, and were thus not immortal like the humans who in death had gone on to Hades as the Damned, or to Paradise as Angels. Unlike these former mortals, Demons could truly die. They were the real mortals.

And so, the halberd chopped sideways through the front of Naberius' face, at the level of his eyes, slicing through both orbits. With that one stroke, the beautiful Naberius was made a crude copy of the older Demon. He cried out, stumbled back, fell onto his remaining wing at a bad angle. Furcas heard the crack of bone. Blood poured from the upturned vessels that had a second ago housed Naberius' eyes.

"I'm sorry, brother," Furcas grunted, and he stepped forward, twirling his weapon around, cocking it back in both hands to plunge the tines into the fallen Demon's chest in a merciful coup de grâce—which in these games was known as Charon's Blow.

A klaxon's bleat, like the deep-chested roar of some gigantic animal, filled the arena...almost causing its walls to shiver. A single, circular wall, actually—a titanic, seamless cup of bone. In this way the amphitheater itself was like a skull socket. This ivory-tinted, glossy material was the same illusory bone that made up the skeletons of the Demons, and the Damned, and the Angels, and the Celestials—who were the equivalent of the Demons, but servitors to the Angels rather than tormentors of the Damned. Every form of matter, even in the mortal world, was simply another type of illusion than this. The Creator was an artist Who worked in multiple media.

At this blast of sound, which rumbled in his chest, Furcas turned his body and swiveled his floating eye to face toward the box centered in the lowermost tier of seats, wherein sat the highest-ranking Angels in this considerable group, that had journeyed here to Hades to enjoy these games.

Behind him, Furcas heard Naberius moan, "Will you kill me, Furcas? *Kill me!*" Yet Furcas remained focused on the occupants of that box, it too seamlessly a part of this bone coliseum.

The box held a handful of Angelic high officials, and their retinue, which included of course a squad of armed Celestial guards. From here Furcas saw a number of women and children in the party, draped in white robes, as were the officials and every other Angel seated in this arena. From his gold miter, Furcas could tell one of these visiting officials had been a Roman Catholic bishop in his mortal life. He'd overheard that another of them had been a prominent Southern Baptist minister and a spiritual advisor to a string of American presidents. Furcas knew nothing about the others; he understood he was only an ant contemplating the world of dinosaurs.

Then again, not an apt comparison. Though he had never visited the mortal plane, he knew that dinosaurs had long ago gone extinct, while ants still thrived. And he and his kind— Demonic races that had been patterned along anthropomorphic lines—were scheduled for extinction themselves. It was the very reason he stood here, waiting for the orders of his masters.

And they were soon forthcoming. An amplified voice, following the deafening bleat, solemnly boomed, "Stay your hand and hold your place, Damnatus Furcas. Charon's Blow will be delivered by the guest of an eminent visitor from Paradise."

At this announcement, a tsunami wave of wild applause reared up all around Furcas, filling the arena's bowl. It almost drowned out Naberius' desperate groaning words just behind him. "*No!* I don't want to die by some pampered Angel's hand,

Furcas! Kill me! Are you afraid of them? You're soon to die in this arena yourself…it can't be much longer."

Furcas didn't respond, instead scanned the faces stacked above him in the arena's sweeping curve, feeling their collective gaze weighing on him, crushing him immobile. The arena could accommodate 50,000 spectators, but for this current set of games there were only about 30,000 Angels in attendance—bussed in from Paradise, figuratively speaking—all seated in the stadium's lowest three tiers. Many wore white conical hats, though many others wore only attached cowls instead, and most of these let their cowls hang behind them. The majority, no doubt, under their robes wore "street clothes" of the type they had favored in life and wore in their native realm of Paradise.

In the fourth and top tier of seats, with the most distant view of the games, sat local Demonic officials, their immediate entourage, and a few thousand of their troops. These newer breeds of Demons had been designed not to look so much like human beings, such as the earlier forms of Demons that had presided over the torments of the Damned for so many centuries. From down here, in their ranks Furcas discerned large numbers of insect-like beings. Bird-beaked figures. Tentacled creatures. Entities for which there was no terrestrial counterpart. The Demonic officers, of course, were themselves nonanthropomorphic: regal, oversized, wildly and excessively nonhuman monstrosities. The *former* officials of this region of Hades had been the first to go—executed with much ceremony, in tribute to their former service. Despite this bloated show of respect, several of them had resisted—as if to prove the very need for the elimination of the old guard—and these embarrassing ingrates had been among the first to die in these gladiatorial games.

Above the uppermost tier, the sky seemed to cap the top of the bone area with a ceiling of restless but unbroken black clouds, hiding the inverted sea of molten rock behind it. The heavy cloud cover and his inability to see anything beyond the high surrounding wall of the amphitheater caused Furcas to feel fatalistic. There was indeed nothing more than this space, this bloody dance. His existence, his service of hundreds of years, was near its end. His former duties as an overseer and torturer of the Damned had been replaced with his current role as entertainer for those Demons that had come from the infernal factories to replace him. And, more importantly, entertainer for visiting Angels—eating mock hotdogs and drinking illusory beer in the stands.

A door opened in the base of the wall just under the box in which the Angelic officials were seated, and out into the arena stepped two Celestials, with platinum-blond hair and unblinking blue eyes, maybe male or maybe female or maybe no sex at all, wearing togas and carrying assault rifles. Furcas didn't understand enough about such things to know if these guns were identical to any particular model on the mortal plane. On the sandaled heels of the Celestial guards emerged an adult Angel, garbed in white robe and conical hat. He represented the pinnacle of the Creator's handiwork: white, pot-bellied, bespectacled, with a thick graying mustache. Beside him walked a boy of about ten, the hood of his robe hanging loose behind him. Short sandy hair, face rounded with a vestige of baby fat. Two more Celestials followed, then the door closed. The little party walked straight toward Furcas, and the applause gradually died down, replaced with murmurs of anticipation, as the group reached the two blood-slathered Damnati.

The official in the conical hat nodded at Furcas, in a minor gesture of respect for his performance, but made a little brushing gesture with his hand for the triumphant Demon to step aside. Furcas complied without a word. Then, the Angel turned to one of the Celestials and motioned toward the short sword carried in a scabbard on its belt. The Celestial transferred its rifle to one hand so as to draw the sword and carefully pass it to the esteemed visitor.

In turn, this man handed over the sword to the boy. In what Furcas had come to know as a southern accent, over centuries of handling the Damned—and in a rehearsed lofty tone besides—the Angel said, "'Smite with thine hand,' William. You will never become a man in body, for your body is no more, but your soul will become the soul of a man. With Demons such as these—Demons of human guise—in recent times sympathizing with those Damned that rise up in rebellion against the

Creator's order, you may in the future be called upon to take up arms against them in earnest, to help destroy the last of them."

Furcas wanted to protest. Though indeed great numbers of the Damned had finally begun fighting back against their Demonic overlords, and troops of Angels and Celestials had come to Hades in an effort to help contain the uprising, he himself had never sided with the Damned as a good number of his Demonic brethren had done. It was said that these Demons sympathized with the former mortals because they shared a similar form, but he felt this was an unfair generalization. He believed he knew the other Demons held in the outer buildings of the arena, awaiting their own gladiatorial service, well enough to say that the majority of them still maintained their loyalty to the Creator's plan. Furcas felt this damning of every anthropomorphic race of Demon, after thousands of years of loyalty, was a monstrous injustice. And on top of that, this final indignation: so many of them now being imprisoned and forced to execute one another in an arena in which, in the past, only the Damned had fought as Damnati.

The Angel went on, condensing biblical text to suit his purpose, "'The evil abominations shall fall by the sword.'"

"Where should I stab him, John?" the boy asked.

"*No!*" Naberius sobbed loudly, wagging his blind head, spattering blood onto the sand. He had heard the boy's voice. "Don't let me be killed by a child, Furcas! *Damn you*, Furcas! Kill me before they have a child kill me as a *game!*" He began propping himself up on his elbows, but two of the Celestials stepped forward quickly and hammered him back down with blows from their rifle butts. One blow opened a gash on his left eyebrow and he fell onto his back again, moaning.

"Silence, Devil!" the Angel snarled at Naberius as he was being subdued. "Die with dignity, for the love of the Creator." He then looked down at the boy and said, "You won't stab him, William." He rested a hand on the boy's back, ran it up and down in what was almost a romantic caress, and Furcas finally registered that the boy hadn't called the Angel "father." He wondered at the full nature of their relationship. The Angel went on, "You will strike him across the throat."

"Ohhh..." Naberius moaned. "Furcas..."

A Celestial handed its gun over to one of its comrades, knelt in the sand and grasped Naberius' head in both hands to hold it still. At the other end of him, another Celestial knelt to hold down his legs.

The Angel helped position the boy, like a baseball coach teaching a child how to cock back his bat. The boy looked up at the man with eyes and twitching smile agleam, and then he looked down at the wounded Demon and swung the short sword.

Furcas flinched, as if the blade had bit into his own illusory flesh. He wanted to close his eyes, but then he only had the one floating eye, and it had no lids—and besides, he wouldn't really have hid his face from the death of his fellow Demon in any case. It would be another kind of disrespect.

The first blow gouged the sand as much as it did Naberius' neck. The Angel urged the boy to strike again, and this chop struck Naberius on the chin instead, cracking bone.

"Bastard!" Naberius gurgled. "Cowardly pet!" At this, he spat out a mouthful of blood. The boy tried to lurch back but the hem of his white robe was splattered.

Die with dignity, Naberius, Furcas thought, echoing the Angel's words. *Die like a good warrior...*

But then, Furcas thought, as he watched the boy chop again... and again...and again, until Naberius finally writhed and moaned no more, his neck and lower face a pulped mess, he *had* died as a warrior, hadn't he? Defiant until his defiance had been smashed beyond recognition.

The various barracks the demonic Damnati dwelt in between games, outside the arena, were heavily guarded, not only by newer breeds of Demons, but by a contingent of Celestials— owing to the proximity of Angels visiting Hades for the games, housed in much finer accommodations not too distant. A minute ago one of these Celestials had unbolted this particular structure's metal door and stepped into the threshold, eyeing the Demons who sat on the edges of their bunks in low conversation. At first, Furcas thought the being—though wordless, as all Celestials were apparently—would gesture for them to be silent and get into their bunks for their rest period, but its flat blue eyes only took them in for a moment before it stepped outside again, and they heard the heavy bolt squeal back into place.

"They're just mindless machines, their lot," a Demon named Pithius whispered, as if the beautiful, blank-faced entity might be lurking beyond the door eavesdropping. "But we were given minds, and one might argue hearts, if not eternal souls. Why would the Creator have wanted us to be this way, if we would only end up being condemned for it?"

"Mortals have minds, and hearts," another Demon seated nearby, named Sabnock, argued. He had a noble hooked nose, and a pair of long corkscrewed horns like those of an antelope. "And they're punished when they err. Why do you make it sound like we alone are being persecuted?"

Pithius had pearly white flesh, bat-like wings collapsed tightly at his back. Hunched forward on his cot, he wagged his head and murmured, "They call those of us who are fighting alongside the Damned traitors. Maybe so. But to me, they are also traitors."

"Who is 'they'?" asked Sabnock. "Our new demonic leaders? The Angels? The Creator? Is the Creator a traitor, Pithius? You're skirting blasphemy."

"Who really knows the mind of the Creator? I'm leaving Him out of this. But do you not feel betrayed?"

"It's regrettable what is taking place, but I must retain my honor."

"You said 'err.' But how have I erred? I haven't aided a single Damned, in any way whatsoever, in regard to their rebellion. Though now, I swear, I wish I had."

"Fool," Sabnock said. "Even saying that, you prove our over-lords correct in their actions."

"So be it!" Pithius snarled through gritted teeth. "So be it, my self-hating friend! My defeated friend!"

"Defeated? I will die with head held high, Pithius. It will be my *honor* to give my life for the greater good, as it is for any soldier."

"Your life was never yours to give, Sabnock. But it could be yours to *take*."

"Bah!" the long-horned Demon laughed, looking around to

see who else felt as he did. Some of the Demons housed in this room grinned or chuckled. Others only watched him stonily.

Furcas didn't insert himself into their conversation; not then, in any case. Later, however, when Sabnock had stretched out on his cot and Pithius had wandered into a hallway between barracks rooms, to stand peering out through a narrow barred window, Furcas came beside him and said in a lowered voice, "I too feel betrayed, Pithius."

"I have seen that in your face, Furcas," Pithius said. He turned to face the taller, bulkier, more ancient Demon. "I'm not sure of our exact number in these barracks, but there are many of us. At the start of the next series of games, they'll parade all of us into the arena, as they always do—all the Demons and Damned that will fight in that program. Can you imagine, Furcas, if all of us agreed beforehand to fight back as one? Demons and Damned together? Of course, we couldn't communicate our plan to the Damned beforehand—they being in their own barracks—but when they saw what was happening I have no doubt all of them would be inspired to join in. Why wouldn't they? They have less to lose than we—they can't die a second time!"

"What would we do?" Furcas said in a hush.

"Spring up into the box where the Angel officials sit," Pithius said, his grin a harsh slice in his face, revealing his elongated canines. "Climb up there on each other's bodies if we have to, to reach them. Then we'll drag them down into the arena and tear them to shreds. Shrieking in agony. Screaming for mercy. We'll give that audience a show they never counted on."

"They'll just regenerate later," Furcas said, though the image blazed in his imagination.

"Of course they will."

"And the Celestials and the new Demons will mow us down with their guns."

"Of course they will! But we're going to die *anyway*, Furcas!"

"We would die in disgrace."

"In disgrace in the eyes of the new Demons. In the eyes of the Angels. Yes, and even the Creator." He took a step closer to Furcas and hissed, "But not in disgrace for *us*."

In the room behind them, they heard that metal door open again—slam open this time. A commotion of movement; the two Demons standing at the window turned toward the sound, and a second later two demonic guards stepped into the short hallway. One had a sleek-feathered head with a long, thin beak like a hummingbird's, and four thin red limbs like the legs of a stork. The other Demon had the appearance of a giant, greenish tick, standing on one pair of limbs and cradling an assault rifle in its uppermost limbs, as did its comrade. Both Demons immediately opened fire. In the enclosed space, the sound of their fully automatic weapons was punishing.

Furcas flinched back involuntarily, but it was Pithius who was hammered by both weapons. He flew back against the wall, his white flesh pitted by bullets. He then slumped to the floor, one wing half unfolding, its membranes punctured, holes chiseled in the wall where rounds had drilled straight through him.

Then the two Demons swiveled their guns at Furcas, and he threw up his hands, waited to be spiked through with holes himself. But the guns only smoked, and in a strange high-pitched voice the bird-like Demon said, "We heard your stupid friend, talking by the window. You don't hold his delusional views, do you, old one? You were only listening...you were not swayed...*were* you?"

How much had the guards outside overheard? Had they heard him say, at the start of the conversation, that he too felt betrayed?

"Yes...I was only listening to him," Furcas said, ashamed at his own words. At the shakiness of his words. He was soon to die...so why was he afraid to die sooner than that? "I was only curious...about what he was thinking."

"Would you have reported him for his treason?"

Furcas hesitated. So far he hadn't really lied. He didn't want to lie...

The bird-faced Demon laughed, a horrible twittering sound, and thankfully spared him from answering, by saying, "Let this be a lesson to you, old one." It turned to address the Demons who had gathered at the doorway through which the pair of guards had come, cautiously peering into the hallway to see what had happened. "Let this be a lesson to *all* of you. Don't die like this. Die with a sword in your hand."

They slung their weapons, by their straps, over their shoulders. No one moved forward to overpower the guards, though they were greatly outnumbered, and seize their weapons. The human-like Demons only watched, and parted to make way, as the two guards took hold of Pithius' corpse and dragged him from the room.

Furcas stared at the swath of blood left on the floor in Pithius' wake. He heard the heavy door clang shut, the bolt driven home. He shifted his gaze to the chiseled wall, and reached to touch the bloody smear where Pithius' body had slid down. He looked at the blood on his fingertips, as if he meant to write something with it, some defiant slogan on the wall, but then he only let his hand drop to his side.

All the present Damnati—Demon and Damned alike—had paraded through the arena, under the eyes of the Angels and the next-generation Demons. Obediently, cowed, they had all remained in formation. Not a one of them had broken rank to lunge toward the stands. The cyclops Furcas, in marching, had only stared ahead with his single hovering eyeball.

Then, the next program of games had commenced. From where he waited in the suffocating bone labyrinth beneath the tiers of seats, Furcas couldn't see the duels that preceded his own, but he heard the clash of metal weapons, the abrupt cries of pain, the vast cheers of the crowd.

At length, he and another Demon were called forth, pushed by their handlers out into the light. Their appearance was greeted by hoots and whistles of hungry eagerness. Furcas saw he had been paired against a Demon he had long known, and worked alongside: Gamigin, who was built on a heroic scale rather like himself. Like Furcas, Gamigin was without wings. His face was long and almost equine, his ears pointed, a Mohawk cresting his head and running halfway down his bare back. He carried a bow, a quiver of arrows slung behind him. Furcas himself had been handed an oblong shield and a gladius with a two-foot blade.

As they walked toward the center of the arena, Gamigin looked to Furcas and said, "Give me all you have, old friend."

"That and more…count on it," Furcas told him.

Gamigin smiled. "I would expect no less from you. I promise, though, to kill you as painlessly as possible."

"Ha," Furcas said. "My friend Gamigin, always the dreamer."

"If I were a dreamer," Gamigin said, "I would dream that right now you and I were lying in the grass beside a gentle stream of blood, drinking flasks of wine."

"Those times are gone forever, aren't they?" Furcas said.

They had reached the heart of the arena. A klaxon sounded, vibrating their bones. Without another word, without hesitation and no longer smiling, the two Demons sprang at each other.

Furcas had expected Gamigin to backpedal to put distance between them, so he could notch his first arrow. No doubt aware that Furcas would expect this, Gamigin had instead turned his bow in both hands and thrust one end of it at Furcas' levitating eye. Furcas jerked his head to one side, saving his eye from being crushed or punctured, but the tip of the bow still grazed the orb's side. Furcas shouted a curse at the pain, angry for having taken a hit immediately, and he was the one who backed off—swinging his sword wildly to cover his retreat.

Now that Gamigin had put some space between them, though not in the way Furcas had anticipated, he swiftly drew an arrow from his quiver, notched it, pulled back on his bowstring and launched it. Furcas raised his shield just in time: the arrow lodged into it. Furcas knew he had to close up that space again, before more arrows flew. He dove forward, but too late: a second arrow twanged through the air. Its tip struck him under the left cheekbone, raked across the row of his teeth. The arrowhead emerged at the back of his jaw, below his ear, the arrow's shaft having skewered through his face, but it had only injured flesh, and mock flesh at that.

Not squandering even a second to yank free the arrow projecting from his face, Furcas leapt and swung his gladius in one movement. He hacked Gamigin just below the nose, splitting his upper lip and his lower jaw, straight through the chin. With no time to notch his third arrow, instead Gamigin grasped it by its shaft and thrust it up under the ribs on Furcas' left side. It went deep.

They had collided into a kind of embrace. Panting. Bleeding. Both hurting badly.

His words distorted by his bifurcated jaw and mouthful of blood, Gamigin said close to Furcas' ear, "We're too good at this, old friend. We can't prolong things for them for long."

"Good," Furcas said. "It's time this all ended. At least for us."

"I love you, my brother."

Furcas cocked his head, cocked his blurred and smarting eye, and chuckled mirthlessly. "*Love*, brother?"

"Why not?" Gamigin said. "We have nothing more to lose. We can love."

Furcas shoved Gamigin back, and snarled, "Then, I love you!" And he drove the point of his gladius up behind Gamigin's breastbone.

The ancient Demon Gamigin staggered backwards, glancing down at his pouring wound, then grinned bloodily up at Furcas and said, "Thanks, you bastard, for making me look so incompetent."

"I'm sorry, my brother," Furcas said, "but why extend our humiliation?" He drew back his arm to chop at the side of his friend's neck. It was time to put an end to this sad farce.

The klaxon again. It seemed to ring through the length of Furcas' blade, making it a tuning fork. The sound froze his arm, fixing him in place like a dramatically posed statue.

An amplified voice, following the deafening bleat, solemnly boomed, "Stay your hand and hold your place, Damnatus Furcas. Charon's Blow will be delivered by the guest of an eminent visitor from Paradise."

"Oh Creator, no," Gamigin muttered. He sank to his knees. Furcas reached forward to take his arm, to help ease him into a kneeling position. Gamigin looked up at him, his halved mouth managing a grin, and said, "Allow me to take a moment to say fuck you, old friend."

A door opened in the base of the wall just under the box in which the Angelic officials were seated, and out into the arena stepped two Celestials, with platinum-blond hair and unblinking blue eyes, maybe male or maybe female or maybe no sex at all, wearing togas and carrying assault rifles. On the sandaled heels of the Celestial guards emerged an adult Angel, garbed in a white robe and a tall gold miter: that former Roman Catholic bishop. Beside him walked a boy of about twelve, the hood of his robe hanging loose behind him. Thick dirty-blond hair, too-pale skin and too-pink lips, his far-spaced blue eyes almost as dead as those of the two additional Celestials who brought up the rear. The door closed behind them, and the little party walked straight toward Furcas. The applause of the audience gradually died down, replaced with murmurs of anticipation, as the group reached the two blood-slathered Damnati.

"Well done, Demon," the bishop said to Furcas. He then motioned for one of the Celestials to pass him a sword.

Furcas found himself grateful that the Angel had not asked for his own blood-slicked gladius.

The bishop in turn passed the Celestial's sword to the child beside him. He rested one hand on the boy's back, and Furcas intuited it was not the first time the Angel had touched the boy so tenderly. The bishop said in a loud, grand tone, paraphrasing the Bible, "Duke, our swords are appointed for slaughter at all the gates of the rebellious Demons, so that their hearts may melt and stumble. Yes! Your sword is ready to flash like lightning; it is drawn for slaughter. Dispatch this traitor, and become a warrior! Become a *man!*"

The boy, whom the bishop had called Duke, accepted the sword with a smile just as bright and cold as its blade. He turned to face Gamigin. Gamigin stared back at him, blood from his bisected jaw streaming down the front of his bare, scar-crossed chest. *A mighty Demon*, Furcas, thought, *brought low. Too low.*

"What are you waiting for, little *boy?*" Gamigin said. "Kill me."

"Shut up, freak," the eternal child said, winding his arm back. Furcas figured he was already an expert at killing Demons—from having done so in video games, in life, many times before.

Before the child's blow could descend—in that moment when he hesitated, drawing out the suspense for the crowd, drawing out his triumphance—Furcas took only a single step forward, swung his own sword, and chopped it through the exact center of the boy's head.

The crowd of 30,000 roared as one. It was not the sound any of them had expected they'd make.

"Uh!" Duke said, blinking dumfoundedly, shocked with pain, as Furcas jerked his blade free. The child collapsed to the sand in front of Gamigin, who still rested on his knees.

"Kill me," Furcas saw Gamigin's lips mouth, though he couldn't hear him over the furor.

Furcas swooshed his arm sideways, cleaving Gamigin across the throat. He followed through with his blow, not taking the time to watch his friend pitch forward onto his face. Furcas slashed the bishop in two great blows, marking a terrible X. One diagonal blow not only sliced the old man's face into halves, the lower half sliding away from the upper, but badly dented his gold miter and sent it tumbling away.

The four Celestials came for him, suddenly and from all sides.

Oh, the boy would regenerate. His icy beauty would be restored. It would outlast the dying of every star in the universe. But so would his memory of the pain he had felt, at having a Demon's blade buried in his skull. So would his humiliation.

Furcas hacked this way and that, meeting this Celestial and then another, spinning, grinning, even laughing, with Gamigin's two arrows still poking from his body. He, who had never truly lived in the corporeal sense, felt *alive* perhaps for the very first time.

He flat-out killed two of the Celestials, who because they too possessed no mortal soul could also be killed in the realest way. He critically wounded the other two.

Finally, it was bullets from assault rifles—he didn't see who was shooting them, couldn't tell if it were Celestials or Demons— that dropped the Demon Furcas to the sand beside the body of his friend Gamigin, and the body of the Angel child named Duke, who was already beginning to heal.

But the healing process was agonizing, and the child wailed for his mother, and it was the sweetest music the Demon Furcas could have hoped to die to.

...and puppy dog tails

By P. D. Cacek

Everyone in the country sees it, either during the Breaking News segment of the Five O'Clock News or on later news recaps, a bus so engulfed by thick black clouds of smoke that, for a few seconds, it's just another traffic accident, tragic but not all that important, until the smoke parts suddenly and there is a quick flash of yellow-orange and everyone knows what they just saw weren't flames. They know because they remember the color.

And then the country can't look away, stopping whatever they were doing a moment before to watch and hold their collective breaths and hope they're wrong...watching as first two, then three Fire and Rescue Units battle back the flames and smoke until there is no doubt. A school bus in flames, a school bus on fire...children trapped inside, a reporter's disembodied voice—the normal, calm, perfect Mid-American unaccented voice—tight now with emotion as it describes the scene and cause: an SUV, blind hill, going too fast, failing brakes, head-on collision, broken gas lines, electrical short, fire.

The unidentified SUV driver dead on the scene.

Firefighters trying to get the situation under control.

The children still trapped inside—

"Wait!"

The voice stops as the emergency doors at the back of the bus are wrenched open and children spill out.

It's hard to see through the smoke and water spray, through the tangle of firefighters and EMTs who rush forward, through the helicopter-mounted camera's attempts to focus, but finally the children come into view. Most are crying, some need to be carried, some dragged silent and stone-faced, in shock, to the waiting ambulances. There are dark smudges on their faces and hair and school uniforms and they're soaking wet from the spray of the fire hoses. They are traumatized and scared but they are alive.

The children are alive and as that fact settles in, something else—taller and wearing what looks like a black sweater and mask—falls through the clouds of smoke pouring from the bus and onto the street.

It lays there without moving and the camera switches back to the news station just as two EMTs rush toward it.

"We'll have more information on the crash as it becomes available," the anchor promises. "Now let's take a look at the second game of the World Series."

The country goes back to their lives in progress and later that night the information is delivered as promised.

There'd been fifteen children on the bus, all students at Simon Woods Elementary in Bywood, Maine, along with their driver, Ellen (Ms. Elly) Bascombe. With the exception of Ms. Bascombe, 43, who suffered second-degree burns to both hands and arms and was being held overnight at Bywood Memorial Hospital for observation, the majority of children, ages six to ten, suffered only minor injuries and were released to their families after being treated for smoke inhalation.

There was one fatality: Jackson (Jax) John Premmer, age 9.

A miracle, considering how much worse it could have been.

Everyone said so.

"Ms. Bascombe?"

Ellen opened her eyes and automatically glanced at the wall clock over the room's hand sink. 7:43. This time her feigned sleep had managed to keep them away for thirty-seven minutes.

A record.

Before that, almost from the moment she'd been wheeled into the E.R., in pain and drifting in and out of consciousness from the head wound she'd received falling out of the bus, they'd averaged one or two every fifteen minutes.

Police, reporters, firefighters, parents...her union rep...and strangers—people she didn't know but who had seen the crash on the news and come, some from as far as Greenville and Little Squaw, just to thank her or bless her or bring her flowers.

There were already so many bouquets scattered around that they made Ellen think of a florist shop.

Or a mortuary's viewing room.

They called her a hero, all of them, even her union rep.

"Can I talk to you for a minute?"

Ellen shifted her eyes from the clock to the pale yellow wall and waited until the reverse-color afterimage faded before looking at her newest visitor. A man, roughly around her age, give or take a few years; sandy hair that would simply fade as he got older but never go gray, cut a little long over the ears; clear, hazel eyes framed by gold Harry Potter glasses; thin lips, straight nose. A good face, just short of handsome.

He hadn't brought flowers.

Feeling every bruise, every burn, Ellen inched her bandaged forearms and hands off her belly and to her sides where (she hoped) they'd be less noticeable. Behind the round lenses, the man's eyes followed the movement before returning to her face.

He offered her a sad smile.

"Unless you'd rather not," he said. "I can't even begin to imagine how you're feeling right now."

Maybe he was handsome, after all.

"S'kay." Ellen sat up and returned the smile as far as the thick bandage covering the entire left side of her face let her. Talking was problematic. Her throat felt like raw meat from the superheated smoke she'd inhaled and the initial impact had fractured her left cheekbone while the fall had split open her bottom lip. Thanks to the pain meds they finally gave her after making sure she didn't have a concussion or cranial bleed, nothing really hurt, but she couldn't stop herself from running her tongue over the thirty-eight tiny stitches they'd needed to sew up her lip.

The plastic surgeon told her the scar should be minimal.

And thanked her.

"Thank you and I promise I won't stay long." Still smiling,

he pulled a small card from the inside pocket of his suit jacket: dark blue with a cream-colored shirt and harvest-gold tie. Ellen smiled back. She'd misjudged him, he was very good-looking. "Ms. Bascombe, my name's Brendan Moss—"

Brendan Moss. Ellen Moss. Mrs. Ellen Moss. Mr. and Mrs. Brendan Moss.

"—of Moss, Jenner and Reeves and I'd like to offer you our services."

Ellen stopped smiling and tried to focus on the card he was holding out to her. "Wha?"

"To prepare your defense should Mr. and Mrs. Premmer decide to include you in a wrongful death claim on behalf of their son Jackson."

Ellen felt her heart begin to pound against her ribcage.

She was wrong. Brendan Moss was ugly as sin.

His sad smile faded as he laid the card on her beside tray. "Of course the primary claim will undoubtedly be against the SUV driver's estate, but, even though we know you were not in any way culpable in their son's death, the Premmers are understandably upset and might hold you partially accountable, along with the school district's transportation department. So, my first question is, was there any possibility that you could have saved this boy but didn't?"

"What the hell?"

Brendan Moss turned as he stepped back from the bed which gave Ellen a clear view of the room's doorway where her friend and fellow driver, Gail Whitmore, stood, hands on hips and glaring bullets.

All she needed was a cape fluttering out behind her to complete the image.

"Hello," he said, reaching for another card, "I'm—"

"I don't care who the hell you are. Out."

"Let me explain. I represent Moss, Jenner and—"

Her friend took a step closer, stopping him in mid-pitch.

"Fine." He cleared his throat. "But in cases like these it's always best to have a contingency plan. Look, I understand—"

"You don't understand anything," Her friend walked to the end of the bed and reached down, gently squeezing Ellen's leg.

I got this, the touch said. "Which apparently includes common English. I said, out...that means leave. Ms. Bascombe has been through hell and the last thing she needs is to have some pencil-necked shyster accusing her of anything."

That seemed to upset him, although Ellen wasn't sure if it was the label or that he'd been caught.

"I didn't. I was just attempting to—"

"Drain her bank account. We're in a hospital...go find yourself another ambulance to chase."

"How dare you? That's defamation of character and I could—"

Ellen watched the woman she'd known for almost ten years suddenly turn into Captain Whitmore, USMC, retired.

"Out," she said and pointed to the door. "Now."

He left without another word.

"'anks."

Gail waved the comment away and picked up the card he'd left. "Shh, don't give him another thought. It sounds like a fishing expedition, to me...a preemptive one at that. I mean, it just happened and the kid's parents are already trying to—" Shaking her head, she picked up the card and tore it in half. "Just rest and get better. I'll talk to another friend of mine, a lawyer, a good one. You have nothing to worry about."

Ellen tried not to flinch when Gail squeezed her shoulder gently.

"You're a hero, Elly, and everyone except that dickweed knows it. Hell, when people hear about this... Sorry." She exhaled and Ellen watched her friend deflate back to the sweet middle-aged woman who loved to bake and teach '70s songs to her middle-school riders. "I'm proud of you, Elly. You saved those kids, you got them out; and I know if there'd been anything you could have done you would have saved him, too."

Ellen kept her face very still and looked back at the clock.

Ellen left the hospital the next afternoon with three prescriptions—one for a non-opioid pain reliever, one for a stool softener, just in case, and one for anxiety—and the name of a grief and trauma therapist.

She left by wheelchair pushed by a student nurse, while Gail carried two plastic bags: one of hospital swag—a plastic puce vomit tray with matching tub, a box of wood pulp tissues, pink gripper socks, and a notepad and pen both imprinted with the hospital's name and 24-hour emergency number—and the other containing the few personal items she'd had with her the day before: her cell phone which had been in the pocket of her vest and survived the fall with only a small crack, the gold cross and chain her mother had given her, and her shoes, minus socks.

Her purse and jacket, stored in the small space behind her seat, went up with the bus and her jeans and sweater, soaked, scorched and cut off her in the E.R, had been disposed of along with the other medical waste.

Gail had stopped by her place before coming to the hospital and brought her a change of clothes.

As they road down in the elevator, Gail entertained them, Ellen and the giggling student nurse, with the story about her recent field trip to the Rockfield Pumpkin Patch.

"Second and third graders," she said as they dropped toward the lobby, "I don't know what it is with those particular age groups, and it's not like they haven't gone out to pick pumpkins each and every season, but the minute…the minute I opened the doors it was like something out of a horror movie. They howled, I swear to God, they freakin' howled. They wouldn't quiet down and I had teachers and parent volunteers…bet they don't do that again…trying to control them. I left the bus and walked over to Bill, you know, the guy who drives the hay wagon out to the field, and told him to run. He didn't, brave man. The teachers finally got the kids settled down enough to get off the bus and line up but you'll never believe what happened next. This one third grader—"

The elevator reached the lobby and doors whooshed open and suddenly lights began exploding in Ellen's face.

"What the—"

"Ellen! Look this way!"

"Hey, Elly!"

"Ms. Bascombe? I'm with *The Bywood Post* and we'd love to interview—"

"Over here, Elly!"
"Hey!"
"Look this way!"
"MOVE!"
Gail hip-checked the startled student nurse out of the way and, grabbing the handles, yelled another warning before using the wheelchair as a makeshift battering ram. Reporters and cameramen scattered before them like leaves caught in a windstorm, only to instantly regroup.
"Hey, Elly, look over here!"
"Hang on," Gail yelled and raced for the automatic doors.
There were others waiting for her in the late afternoon chill outside the hospital. They lined both sides of the sidewalk, children holding bright yellow Happy Face balloons in the front, adults—parents, teachers, other drivers, members of the School Board—holding posters over their heads that filled the spaces between the balloons.
THANK YOU, MS. ELLY!
YOU ARE A GAURDIAN ANGEL
BYWOOD'S OWN HEROINE
BLESS YOU FOREVER
WE LOVE YOU!
Ellen recognized the children who rode her bus, all the children who'd ridden her bus over the years.
The reporters stopped and began taking pictures.
"Look at this," Gail said as if Ellen had somehow missed it. "And, before you ask, I had nothing to do with it."
The crowd was silent, the only voices from the reporters, until they reached the halfway spot between the hospital and the PATIENT PICK UP space where Gail's truck was parked; then, as if on cue, the children who'd been in the accident rushed forward...surrounding her, engulfing her.
The same ones who had cried when Ellen pushed them through the smoke toward the back of the bus, away from the flames, were crying now. Their wet cheeks glistened in the glow of the hospital sign and their eyes were all but swollen shut and she wondered, as she accepted their bear hugs and damp kisses and touches, if they had ever stopped crying since the accident.

"It's okay," she told them, over and over again until their parents came to drag them away and offer their own words of admiration and thanks. "It's going to be okay. I'm going to be okay, everything's going to be okay."

Ellen wasn't aware that Gail had left her until she saw her standing next to the truck's open passenger-side door. When she turned to look over her shoulder, the President of the District School Board smiled and patted her shoulder.

"We're all proud of you, Ellen," he told her as he pushed her forward. "It could have been…" He cleared his throat and when he spoke again his voice was strained. "We lost a child and we're not trying to gloss over that, but you saved fourteen others and that's what you have to focus on, Ellen. That's what we all have to focus on. There are fourteen children still alive because of you."

He squeezed her shoulder again, then helped her out of the wheelchair and into the truck. Before he closed the door, as Gail ran around to the driver's side, he leaned in and smiled.

"We'd like you to come in when you feel up to it," he said. "Just an informal meeting, nothing to get upset about, okay? And don't worry about your job; you'll still have it when you're healed, okay?"

He waited until she nodded. "Good. Now go home and get some rest. Rest and heal, Ellen. God bless."

Gail didn't say anything on the ride home, just let the town's soft-rock station fill the space between them.

And Ellen blessed her for that.

The school board meeting was as informal as she'd been given to believe.

Four days after leaving the hospital, midmorning on a Tuesday, the board sent a car to pick her up because the burns on her hands were still raw and seeping. Dressed in their normal workday clothes, the board members turned when she walked into the library's multi-purpose room that served as their office and smiled, nodded their heads as the president himself escorted her to the chair at one end of the long table directly opposite his.

There were coffee and fresh pastries, small ones she could pick up between her bandaged hands, and the four men and three women were gently understanding and sympathetic. Before opening her laptop to record the minutes, the board secretary, a mother of three, took a tissue from her purse and dabbed her eyes.

The president asked her to tell them what happened in her own words.

So she did.

After dropping off the Freestone twins (grade 4), she proceeded to the four-way stop at Nelson Mill Road and Route 14, stopped the bus ("Yes, a full stop.") and had just accelerated into the blind intersection when the SUV struck the front of the bus and sent it careening sideways into a tree.

"Can you tell us where it hit?"

"The right side, near the door."

"Did you see the impact?"

"No, I didn't."

Ellen touched the bandage that covered her cheek and explained how she'd been thrown against the side window at the initial impact and against the steering wheel when they hit the tree but that she'd never lost consciousness. Yes, she was wearing her seatbelt. No, her hands weren't burned then.

Not then.

"Go on."

The children screamed. The bus filled with smoke. The fire started.

"Where was the Premmer boy?"

"In the first seat on the right-hand side. He always sat there."

"Always?"

"Yes." *He wouldn't let anyone else sit there. He once told a second grader he'd pull her head off if she didn't move. And said he'd do the same to me if I told.* "He liked to watch the road and...talk to me."

"Was he talking to you before the accident?"

"They're freaks...the Freestone Freaks. I hate them...run them over...squish 'em together. Make 'em one person like they're 'posed to be. Kill 'em."

"Yes."

"Do you think he might have distracted you? Children can be very loud and distracting."

"Why didn't you kill them? Nobody'd care. You're a freak, just like them. Ms. Elly jelly belly. Freak. Freaky freak."

"No, not Jax. He was always very quiet. He'd only whisper."

"You tell, Ms. Elly Jelly Belly, and I'll get you."

"Alright. Go on."

And she told them that she'd yelled at the children to move to the back of the bus, run, to leave their backpacks and just run to the back of the bus. She said she hadn't noticed the Premmer boy wasn't there until the children were being taken off the bus. That was when she ran back, but there was nothing she could do. The tree they'd hit had crushed in the side of the bus just behind the door and fused the front seat where Jax Premmer had been sitting into the stairwell divider.

By the time she reached him, the flames had broken through the cracked windshield and spilled over the dashboard onto the driver's seat and into the stairwell.

The seat was hot and it burned her hands when she tried to pull it off him. But she tried, even after the flames jumped the barrier she kept trying, and the sleeves of her sweater began to smolder...and that's when she heard something beneath the roar of the fire, a soft, wet sound like when you snap a stalk of celery in half.

That's when she let go, had to let go...

The board president stopped her and thanked her, then apologized for making her go through it all again. They gave her the box of pastries and the president drove her home himself.

"Try to put this behind you, Ellen," he told her as he walked her to her front door. "And get better soon."

Ellen promised she would, waved goodbye as he drove away, then walked to the kitchen and threw the pastries in the trash.

They wouldn't go well with her dinner plans.

Stopping just long enough to change from the "nice" sweater and pull-on slacks she'd worn to the meeting to a pair of sweatpants and matching over-the-head hoodie, Ellen walked to the kitchen, muscled the vodka from the freezer, carried it to her bedroom and drank straight from the bottle until she passed out.

It started like it always did, from the moment he got on the bus.

"Jelly belly Elly. Smelly Elly jelly belly. Smelly Elly…that's what you are. Everyone knows that's why you're not married. You smell."

And just like every other day—except weekends, holidays and summer vacations—he kept his voice low, whispering so the other children wouldn't hear him and tattle. Not that they would, they were all afraid of him, so much so that they never sat closer than four rows back, sometimes cramming three into a seat until he left the bus and they could move. His was the fourth-to-last stop and by then there were only six or seven riders, but the bus always felt lighter when he got off.

"Ms. Smelly Jelly Belly Elly. My mom says you drive a school bus 'cause that's the only thing you can do 'cause you're too stupid to do anything else. Is that true, Smelly Elly? Are you too stupid to do anything else?"

It wasn't anything new, his repertoire seldom varied unless it was to comment on a favorite sweater or blouse she'd worn and loved—

"That color looks like puke, did you puke on yourself, Ms. Smelly? The sweater makes you look fat like a pig. Jelly belly smelly pig."

—until that moment.

She hadn't been any more stressed than usual. Of course she'd prayed that morning, as she did every school day, that he'd be out sick, but when he wasn't, she took a deep breath and accepted it.

There'd been nothing out of the ordinary that day, except the accident.

And that she'd killed him.

If there'd been a choice she would have left him to burn. It would have been so much easier to just let the fire take him.

Every other time he whispered but now he was screaming and someone, a firefighter or EMT, would have heard him and tried to save him. She didn't have a choice.

The other children had screamed, too, but his screams were different. His screams weren't ones of fear or pain.

He was angry.

He was furious.

"Get me out of here!"

The collision had thrown him to the floor between the seat and divider, then folded the crushed side of the bus around him. All she could see was his head poking up through the narrow gap in the twisted metal and seat cushion.

He glared up at her through the swirling smoke.

"You'd better get me out! Right now! Or I'm gonna tell!"

Ellen grabbed the back of the seat, her fingers tightening on the plastic upholstery that was already was beginning to soften in the heat. The seat moved in her hands, the impact had broken it free from the floor-mount brackets.

"Help me!"

It was an order, not a plea. There wasn't the smallest hint of fear in his voice or on his face. She had to help him.

He smirked at her.

Ellen shoved the seat forward, pushing hard even after she heard his neck break (…a soft, wet sound like when you snap a stalk of celery in half…) and she was sure he was dead, only letting go and backing away when her sleeves caught on fire.

It's over, she thought as she backed away, *it's finally ov—*

And the darkness giggled. "N'uh."

At first it looked like just another misshapen shadow in the corner of the room, but then the shadow broke away and Ellen pushed herself backward across the mattress. When the headboard hit the wall with a hollow thud, she knew she was awake and not having a nightmare.

His head lolled against his right shoulder, rocking slowly back and forth on the broken stem of his neck with each slow, shambling step he took. His face was a scorched mask, his eyes the consistency and color of boiled eggs.

He stopped when he reached the end of the bed and Ellen watched a charred piece of his right cheek slip from the scorched skull beneath to land, soft as ash, on the bed.

The boiled eyes shifted downward as what had once been a hand reached out and poked at it. "Gross."

Ellen made a sound so small she wasn't sure she'd even heard it...but he did and those eyes shifted back toward her.

"You killed me."

"It was an accident."

"Liar."

"I—I wanted to..." *Liar.* "...but I couldn't. You—you were trapped...I couldn't get you out. There wasn't enough time. You would have burned to death if I hadn't..."

"Liar," he whispered. After everything that had happened he was still whispering so no one else could hear.

So no one else would know what he was.

Except her.

The alcohol haze suddenly cleared and she was stone-cold sober.

"You really are a monster."

His smile grew, cracking fissures lengthways along the cindered flesh that had been his face.

"That's what you are but what am I?"

Ellen threw the bottle. Missed. "You deserved it."

He lunged at her and tried to grab her legs with the twisted knobs of his hands, but Ellen kicked and caught him below the jaw with her left foot.

There was nothing wet about the sound this time. His head snapped back with a dry, burnt-wood crack, and his body shuttered as carbonized bits of flesh and bone flew from it. But he glared at her even as he stumbled back a step, arms pinwheeling to keep his balance...he glared and—

Knock. Knock. Knock.

It took three tries before Ellen was able to open her eyes, and when she did, it took another minute for her to remember where she was. The room was dark, which didn't help, but as her eyes adjusted, she could just make out the vague—but still remarkably fuzzy—outlines of the entertainment unit and wingback chairs her mother had given her.

She was in the living room, semi-conscious on the couch,

what remained of the almost-full vodka bottle sealed and cradled lovingly in her arms.

Only a small part of her remembered passing out.

"I really should have eaten something," she said to the darkness.

And the darkness answered.

—knock—knock—knock—

Blinking, she pushed the hair away from her face with her bandaged right forearm and, after letting the bottle slip from her grasp, somehow managed to stand up, turn on the lights and make it to the front door without colliding with the walls.

Or floor.

The night air brushed around her, clearing her head enough to let her focus on the middle-aged woman standing on her front stoop.

Ellen recognized her, even though she'd only seen the woman at the bus stop and, more recently, on the nightly news. Jax's mother had never ridden her bus as a field trip volunteer but Ellen didn't hold that against her. Volunteering was a younger woman's job and Jax's mother was at least a decade older than most of the other mothers on her route.

If not more.

"I'm not disturbing you, am I?" Mrs. Premmer asked, whispering, her voice so much like her son's that it sent a chill down Ellen's spine.

Yes, you are. Go away. "No, no of course not." Stepping back, Ellen pulled the door open with both hands. "Please come in."

The woman ducked her head and kept it down as she walked just far enough into the living room to allow Ellen to close the door.

"I'm..."

"I know who you are, Mrs. Pemmer," Ellen said, still at the door, afraid to move but more afraid not to. Whatever happened, whatever the woman planned to do to her, she deserved it. "Won't you sit down?"

"No, thank you. I won't stay long," the woman said and finally lifted her head to meet Ellen's eyes. "I just wanted to thank you for what you did for Jax."

Ellen felt her breath catch in her throat. It would have been better, much better if the woman had struck her across the face. It would have hurt less.

"I..." *killed him* "...didn't do anything."

"Yes, you did," Jax's mother said, "you let him die."

The chill deepened inside her. "No, I—"

Jax's mother rubbed her own arms, as if she felt the coldness.

"It's all right, I know you tried, but it's better this way. If he hadn't died, he would have grown up and... He was a monster, Ms. Elly. My husband and I didn't think we could have children, we tried for so long, but then I got pregnant and we thought... We thought he was a miracle, a blessing until he got older. He did things, hurt things."

Jax's mother took a deep breath. "I knew but I wouldn't believe it, I couldn't let myself believe it. How could I, he was my baby, the only one I'd ever have. His father wasn't taken in, he knew and tried to tell me but...there was an accident and he died. The police said it was an accident...they'd been together, fishing, and the boat turned over. Jax was such a strong swimmer and...the police said John, my husband, must have hit his head on the boat when it turned over... It wasn't an accident, Ms. Elly, and I knew it."

Jax's mother suddenly closed the narrow distance between them and threw her arms around Ellen, hugging her tight.

"If it hadn't been for you, I would have had to do it...but he was still my baby, I wouldn't have been able to.... You saved us both. Thank you. Hurry up and get better, Ms. Elly, the children need you."

Jax's mother kissed Ellen on the cheek and let herself out.

Ellen couldn't move until the room stopped shifting under her feet, and when it did, she walked back into the living room, picked up the bottle and carried it to the kitchen where she threw it on top of the pastries.

Jax's mother was right, she had to get better.

There were other children who needed her.

A lot of other children.

The Exclusivity of Ravens

By David Nickle

Tom's wife Ellen wouldn't talk about the dream when they woke. She would not even meet his eyes when he described it.

"I saw you standing with this guy... I recognized him, he looked a bit like your brother but he had a thick beard. He was holding a champagne flute. You were laughing and touching his arm."

She slid her legs from underneath the duvet, and stepped over the laundry that'd spilled from the foot of the bed, then into the ensuite and shut the door. Tom rolled out, too, his feet dangling from the side of the bed.

"Can Ian even grow a beard?" he called. Ellen's brother had a decade on her, seven years on Tom, but from the beginning Ian's chin had been baby-smooth. He could hear the water running and perhaps that was why Ellen didn't reply.

"There was a band playing," he said, a little louder. "It was old-style, swing music. No singer. We were on a boat."

The water shut off and Ellen opened the door. She smiled at Tom and touched him on the shoulder, then sat down beside him on the bed. He wasn't certain she'd heard anything he'd told her, but then she surprised him.

"No singer?" she said, and Tom said that was right.

"You'd expect a singer," he said.

"Not necessarily. Maybe it was karaoke. Maybe they were just warming up the crowd."

"You don't do karaoke with a swing band."

"It's your dream."

"You have a machine," said Tom. He was getting anxious, although not, just then, precisely sure why. "A machine and a TV for karaoke. This was a swing band."

"It's your dream."

"You said that." Tom flopped back on the bed, crossed his hands over his stomach. "They were playing a funny song."

"Funny?"

"Funny haha."

Ellen drew her feet up on the bed and crossed her legs. "How do you know it was funny haha, if there wasn't a singer?"

"You were laughing. So was he."

"Aha," she said. "Think we have time for a bike ride before brunch?"

Tom looked at the clock. It was early, not yet nine. The curtains were drawn but bright, white-hot sunlight framed the edges of their bedroom window. Annette and her husband Peter were in Wentworth for the day, passing through, and meeting them at eleven down at the Fish House.

"We could just ride our bikes there," he said and Ellen laughed.

"Think you can make it back up the hill?"

"Of course."

"Full of coffee and Hollandaise?"

"It'll be a slog. But I'm up for it. We used to bike for miles."

"You and Annette biked for miles," said Ellen. "When you were little kids."

"We did, too," said Tom. "You and I."

"We did," she said. "We still do. Do you think they brought their bikes along? We could all go for a ride afterward."

They might well have. Annette and Peter were on holiday, driving the coast, and they might've packed bikes. That's something that he and Ellen would do, Tom thought, if they found themselves driving the coast.

"I don't know why they didn't just stay here," said Ellen. "Spare bedroom."

"Peter likes his privacy." Tom sat up, patted Ellen on the leg, then bent forward to scoop the socks and shirts that'd fallen on the floor. He gathered the clothes and sorted them to be put away. Ellen watched, smiling, and began to hum.

"What is that?" asked Tom. Ellen stopped and looked at him.

"What is what?"

"The melody. What's the melody?"

"I don't know."

"It's from the dream."

"It's not anything." Ellen stood and scooped up her clothes where Tom had sorted them, and arranged them in her drawer.

"It's the music from the dream," said Tom. "It played while you were laughing."

"With Ian."

"He *looked like* your brother." Tom picked up his clothes, and set them in his drawers, which were in a bureau on the opposite side of the bed to hers. "I didn't say he *was* your brother."

"What's going on, Tom?"

Tom took care to not slam the door shut and drew a breath. He shook his head.

"I'll put coffee on. You shower first."

The kitchen was a mess from the night before. It was Tom's responsibility to clean it up, but there'd been some wine and he was too sleepy in the end, so he figured he'd get to it in the morning, and here they were. He'd had the plates and glasses scraped and in the dishwasher, the stools tucked back under the breakfast counter, the bottles all stowed in the dead soldier bin by the time Ellen emerged. She kissed him with a cool breath of toothpaste-mint and told him that she'd finish up if he wanted a turn at the bathroom.

Then as he was stepping away, she said: "I had a different dream."

Tom turned and leaned on the sink. "Oh?"

"It was a bit of a nightmare," she said. "I was in a toy store. A big one. It had three floors and big atrium up the middle. There was a giant mobile."

"A phone?"

She gave him a look. "A *mobile*. Like you'd hang over a baby's crib. With stars and moons and maybe cutouts of ducks all dangling and balanced on sticks."

"Got it," said Tom.

"It was that kind of mobile. But big." She pressed the button on the coffee grinder and when it had finished, continued. "And here's the nightmare. It was hung with people."

"Hung?" Tom asked if what she was describing was a gallows.

She shook her head. "It wasn't a gallows. No one was dead. They were strapped in harnesses and then dangled by steel cords from big wooden beams."

Tom shut his eyes and found he could picture that: struts like railway ties, hung from a chain, balanced so that one end could dangle another strut, while the other held some fellow in a suit, or a woman dressed for a winter-morning jog… a child, in a harness made for an adult, his arms pushed high, face red and like the rest, softly weeping. He started, as Ellen touched his arm. She was standing next to him, a half-bemused smile on her face.

"Everything okay?" she said, and when he nodded she continued.

"They were crying," she said. "But I didn't help them. I couldn't help them, because I had to find something."

Tom nodded again. "The ball," he said, and she frowned and said, "That's right. It was a red and blue rubber ball… with a white stripe around the middle."

"Like we had when we were kids."

"That was a good guess," she said. "Yes."

"Did you find the ball?" he asked.

Ellen put her finger to her lip, as though she were shushing, then turned back to the coffee maker.

"Tom, why don't you get in the shower," she said.

Tom made his way back through the bedroom, stopping to strip off the briefs and T-shirt he'd worn to bed so that he stepped naked into the shower, still steamy and fragrant from Ellen's passage.

He lathered up under the hot sprays, and as shampoo drizzled down his forehead he shut his eyes against the sting. He scrunched his hair and dug his fingertips into his scalp. He hummed a tune and frowned, and as he ran his head under the shower stream he changed the tune and followed it. He opened his eyes, and turned his face into the water to wash the soap away. He turned away and drew a breath.

"How did you know about the ball?"

"I didn't hear you come in," said Tom. He shut off the water, wiped steam from the shower door. Ellen stood next to the vanity. She had changed into her bicycle shorts and the blue windbreaker. She had been staring into her coffee mug, and now she set it down and looked straight at Tom.

"How did you know about the fucking ball?"

Tom opened the door and pulled his towel from the rack. Ellen set her coffee mug down on the vanity as Tom wiped his face and shoulders and wrapped the towel around his waist. They looked at each other without speaking a moment. Tom had to make himself meet her eyes but Ellen seemed to have no trouble meeting his.

"*How?*"

"I was aware," said Tom. "I was aware of it."

"That's no explanation."

"I'm sorry."

Ellen lifted her mug and looked into it again. "It wasn't my brother you saw." She poured the rest of her coffee into the sink.

"What?"

"It wasn't my brother. At the concert. On the boat. And you've already forgotten the song that was playing."

Tom drew the towel tighter against his belly as Ellen whistled, three sharp notes, and then two more.

"If he wasn't your brother," said Tom, "who was he?"

"Does it matter?"

Tom didn't answer for a moment.

Of course it mattered. She had lied to him after all; when they woke and he first broached the subject, she might have said then that it didn't matter—that she was with someone on the boat, laughing as he sipped champagne and the band played on, but it was someone Tom didn't know, not her brother... She might well have said something to acknowledge what he had seen with his own eyes. Unless, of course, she had reason to want to hide the man from Tom.

Ellen must have read his expression.

"I've never fucked anybody but you," she said.

Which is what Tom would have thought, at least until this moment. Given their long history, it was a very credible claim she made.

But at this moment, it did not seem credible at all. Ellen looked away as she said it, her voice flattened, and as though she seemed to realize it—how it looked, what it communicated—she turned the gesture around and looked back at him, meeting his gaze again with something other than her own.

"Is that why you followed me?" she said. "To see?"

"I didn't follow you," he said, and as she picked up her coffee mug and left, he called out: "I'm not following you!"

"Well we don't fuck," said Ellen.

"*We.*"

"We," she said. "If you must know, we travel around."

"The two of you."

"The two of us, Tom," she called from the bedroom, "yes."

"What's his name?"

She didn't answer, but when Tom followed her into the bedroom she had already left it, and shut the door behind her. Tom dropped the towel and rummaged through the clothes he'd piled on the bed for a fresh set of underwear and a shirt.

"Does he have a name?" he called again, as he finished dressing. Tom continued into the living room, through the kitchen, both of them empty, and at the door to the garage, which hung open a crack, he called:

"Ellen?"

There came in answer just a rattling sound, of the garage door moving along its tracks, and daylight glowed through the crack in the door.

"Ellen!" Tom pulled the door open and stepped through, shielding his eyes against the sun as it reflected from the windshield of their car.

"Are you in here?"

"She just left."

It was a man's voice, probably; deeper than Ellen's, certainly. Tom squinted into the shadows at the back of the garage, where they hung their bikes. There was only one there now: Tom's old racing bike. Leaning against the wall just next to it, Tom thought he spied the figure who'd spoken.

"Who's there?"

"I'll be leaving momentarily."

The figure pushed away from the wall, and turned to lay hold of the frame of Tom's bike.

"It's all right if I borrow this," he said, a statement and not a question, and he lifted the bike from its hook and set its wheels on the garage floor, bouncing it experimentally before wheeling it around the car and out of shadow.

He really did look a lot like Ian, Tom thought, but not precisely. Ian's hair was a dark blond, like Ellen's, and this one's hair was dark brown. Tom thought that his brother-in-law was taller by more than a couple of inches. But the man in Tom's garage was fitter... gym-rat muscles filled out the blue golf shirt and the yellow trousers. He was probably older than Ian, judging by the flecks of white in his black beard. It crept to his cheekbones, and down his neck.

Ian could not grow a beard like that.

"You're not taking my bike," said Tom.

"I'll bring it back," said the man. He threw his leg over the seat-post and kicked off toward the light.

Tom surprised himself then. He stepped into the light himself, stepped again, and then shouted. He felt his fingers close around the man's shoulder and then he pushed, and pulled back, with a great deal more force than Tom thought he would ever bring to such a thing. This was not a warning push, some trivial escalation... some empty display.

The man gasped and twisted the handlebar of Tom's bike, too far, and as Tom stepped back the bike was pulled over. Tom stepped back; the man sprawled on the concrete floor of the garage, his legs still tangled in the frame of the bike.

He pushed himself up with his arms and the bike frame clattered as he drew his legs from it. He rolled to his feet, and only as he stood to his full height did he look at Tom again, his gaze unperturbed. Tom looked away, and the man shook his head, with a small bemused smile.

"I saw you," he said finally. "Last night... earlier this morning. That's what you're wondering, isn't it?"

"No," said Tom. His fists were clenched at his side. "It isn't."

"Well, I did see you. You were at the bar. Hands in your pockets, no drink nearby. Hardly inconspicuous." The man bent and lifted Tom's bicycle and leaned it against the wall. "Now you tell me something. How did you know about the ball?"

At that, Tom found his voice. "What are you even doing here?"

"Answer me first. The ball, Tom. How did you know about it?"

Tom opened his fists and his fingers stretched out in fans.

"From our Ellen's dream."

"The ball she was looking for," said Tom. "In her dream."

He nodded and turned back around. "Were you there, Tom? Maybe dangling in the atrium? Hiding among the Damned?"

Tom shook his head.

"She doesn't want you in her dreams," said the man. He stepped toward Tom, and Tom stepped back.

"She was in mine!" Tom was disgusted to hear the sullen whine in his own voice. He drew a breath. "Who are you? You look like her brother."

The man smiled in an odd way: his mouth slightly open, but without a hint of teeth visible.

"I've been told there's a resemblance. You can call me William," he said. "Bill if you like."

"Bill."

"Now," said Bill, "about the ball."

"The ball," said Tom. He couldn't look away from Bill's mouth... a black void between parted lips. "All right. It was maybe a guess? Ellen had one when she was a girl. It was red on one half, blue on the other... with a white strip around its equator. If it were a world."

Bill nodded. "A planet," he said, and Tom said, "A planet."

Outside, a car drove by and a flash of sunlight reflected from its side window caught Tom's eye, like a lifeline thrown in the water. When it passed, Tom made a point of not looking back at this man... at Bill... who was presumably standing in his garage, getting ready to take off on his bike, in pursuit of Tom's wife. Bill was no dream.

"Bill," said Tom, "were you here all night?"

"I was travelling."

"Of course." Tom stepped outside, and looked either way down the road. There was no sign of Ellen. There was no sign of anyone in the hot morning sun. "Travelling with Ellen."

"Travelling with Ellen. That's right."

"Have you been travelling with Ellen for very long?"

"My whole life," said Bill.

"That's a long time."

"I don't know," said Bill, "it seems very short. Time goes quickly, spent with Ellen."

Tom didn't look back, but he was aware that Bill was stepping close behind him. He felt a hand on his shoulder—not grabbing hard, as Tom had taken hold of Bill. Tom started to turn, but stopped himself. He felt Bill's breath on his neck, and Bill started to hum, and then he began to sing. Lyrics that Tom thought might have been in French. He thought it might have been a love song because there was a tenderness to it. He thought he had heard it before, although he was sure it was not the song that he remembered from his dream. But he could no longer recall how that one went; so maybe it was that song. Tom couldn't say.

Bill patted his shoulder and stopped singing.

"You're crying," said Bill, and as he said it, Tom realized it was true.

Tears burned down his cheeks, and his mouth clamped shut against a sob. At that, he did turn and look back at the man in his garage—at Bill—as Bill himself stepped away and pulled the bicycle away from the wall. He threw his leg over the saddle and kicked off into the light.

Tom was too slow to stop him this time. He might have caught up with him in the car, but as he was halfway into it, he heard his phone ringing… back inside … another song, the song that played when it was Ellen. He found it, and swiped his thumb across the image of her smiling face to answer.

"Hi."

"Hi."

"You sound far away," he said. "Where did you go?"

"I'm at the Fish House. I'm outside. On the patio by the pier. Can you hear the birds?" Tom could. "I've got a table. I'm early."

Tom climbed onto one of the stools and turned it to lean on the counter.

"You ran off."

"Do you have Annette's number? I should give her a call, let her know."

"Just a minute."

Tom scrolled through his contacts for Annette's number. He read it off.

"Thanks, Tom."

"Before you go…" he said, and hesitated.

"Yes?"

Tom shut his eyes. He considered saying more. He considered letting her know that Bill might be coming. That there might need to be another seat at the table she picked, overlooking the harbour where the gulls reeled and the sailboats drifted. He thought about humming that song. Maybe putting lyrics to it…

Telling her about the ball.

"Are you still there, Tom?"

"It's fine," he said. "Call Annette."

"All right." Ellen waited for a heartbeat, then rang off.

Tom held the phone to his chest, and turned on the stool, around a full circle nearly, until he felt his knees touch the edge of the counter. He shifted, and turned again, and this time he did not stop… just kept turning, slowly but constant, under the power of nothing but inertia, suspended on a single thick twist of steel cable.

"Wait," he croaked.

No one was waiting. Alongside and above, the harnesses dangled unbuckled, turning in the light from the tall windows above the entryway to the store, against the empty shadows between shelving, cleared now in a hungry rush.

Had those shelves once been filled? With a monstrous stock of history, of memory?

Was there movement in the gloom? Was there something—someone waiting there for him, in this dream-space?

Tom thought he might wait there forever—but his phone played again, the ringtone an utterly unfamiliar melody, and he let his eyes open, and peered into the screen.

"Oh, Tom," Annette said when he answered, "I just got off the phone with her. I'm so sorry."

Thank You for Not Ignoring Me

By Violet LeVoit

"I have this idea for my thesis project," he said. "I'm going to draw these body outlines. Like, Philadelphia has, what, two hundred murders a year?"

"Three hundred and twenty four." She wasn't really paying attention. She was scribbling something on the corner of her newspaper. The steam rose from her hot chocolate.

"Really? That's crazy. Anyway. So what I do is figure out the body. Most victims are male. The average man is five-foot-ten. The average suit size is 38. That's a circumference measurement so I need to halve that. So 70 inches times 196 is 13,720. So 38 divided by 2 times 196 is 3,724. I need to draw a chalk outline for an imaginary man that's 1,143 feet tall and 310 feet across the chest and that will represent the amount of space all the murdered bodies account for together for one year. Think about it. Every city has a different chalk man." She stood up and sucked down the sweet dregs of her hot chocolate in one swallow. He watched her throat jump as he kept talking. "Fargo will have a little chalk man, just big enough to fit in a driveway. Detroit will have a chalk man big enough to cover several blocks. Where are you going?"

"To class."

He shuffled the stack of orange papers on the table. "But I have all the leaflets."

"I didn't know that was today. I can't document you today."

"But it's finally sunny."

"You have to text me or something. I can't just …" She set

her jaw. "I have the loom reserved. Final crits are in a week." She looked at him. "You shouldn't just do it. Get someone to document it."

"I'll just do it."

"No, come on. You really should. You have to document it or it's like it didn't happen."

"But that's what great about performance art. It just exists. It doesn't need physical detritus to matter. It's pure that way."

She crossed her arms. "I'm not getting into this argument again."

He went by himself anyway to the corner of 8th and Market where all the leaflet guys hang out. He'd watched those leaflet guys for a long time, how they'd perfected that urgent snap that said *you've got to take this*. Pizza places, tax places, strip clubs. He fumbled with the stack of orange paper leaflets in his hands. They said:

THANK YOU FOR NOT IGNORING ME

He thought about doing them in black and white, to have a stark, sharp minimalism:

THANK YOU

FOR NOT

IGNORING

ME

But that made them too precious, too self-conscious, too Bruce Nauman. Wasn't the point of a leaflet to be noticed? He shuffled the papers and practiced his snap. He tried to sink into the character: a guy who got paid by the leaflet, a guy who had no investment in the content of the paper in his hand, but his own excitement betrayed him.

Commuters passed him with practiced disregard. Some took the papers. He watched them crumple them and toss them away. Finally an enormous guy fumbling with his cigarette grabbed one in distraction, did a double take and circled back to him.

"Fuck is this?" he growled.

"It says thank you for not ignoring me," he said.

"Yeah, I read. You selling something?"

"No." His voice was starting to squeak. "It's a closed-loop system. You took it and I thanked you." The guy was still staring at him. Fear watered his mouth. "It subverts the paradigm of advertising—" he began, parroting back a phrase she'd spouted during a critique in the performance art class where he'd met her in the first place, where she'd kneeled on scrub brushes under one hot spotlight and crushed one orange after another into her teeth until her white linen shift was stained with tangerine gore and he'd watched as thoughtfully as he could. "It's a brilliant critique of gender roles," he said in the crit afterwards, trying not to see where the wet linen tented the hard thumbtacks of her naked nipples underneath.

The guy gave him a look that said *white boys are crazy* and walked away.

He tried the snap after that but the guy's dismissal took the wind went out of his sails. *It has succeeded as a piece*, he tried to convince himself. It would be different if she was here documenting this. He could hear her whine: *That's why I got out of performance.* There's nothing left at the end. But she and he would have this day, this moment, each other's testimony to take back to class. Well, just him, since she wasn't taking performance this semester. She spent all her time now bent over a loom in the fibers department, tossing the shuttle back and forth to make some rough-hewn stretch of greyish nubbly fabric. Every time he came to see her, the fabric had barely gained any length, splayed out in the white strings of its weft like the world's slowest-growing creeping mold.

"So all that repetitive action is performative?" he asked again and again, trying to get some clarification as to what she saw in the endless process, and she finally sighed and said, "No, some things are just hard and take time." And he said, "Well, you sure like things that are hard and take time," and she said, sotto voce, "You don't know the half of it, buster."

He checked his phone. She hadn't texted. The sun was getting a little oppressive. He felt stupid and silly and no one was getting the joke. "Fuck this," he muttered, and slunk back to the train.

On the train he decided to text her.

Hey so I have an idea that I read about this study that said symmetrical people are more sexually attractive so I'm going to build this device that's like that picture of two people's faces making a vase but the vase part will be a mirror and the people can strap it onto themselves and when they look at their bf/gf they'll see their face as symmetrical and they'll love each other longer

No answer.

He went to the fibers studio. She was there, the only one left. The lights were out and the wide warehouse windows showed the twilight skyline outside. She was bent over her loom, her grave face lit like a Joseph Wright of Derby painting by the gooseneck lamp, the soft threshing sound of warp and weft clicking out its *shh-clik-shh* rhythm.

"Hey," he said.

"Jesus Christ!" She jumped and put her hand to her heart. "I didn't hear you coming."

"That's a funny gesture," he said, sitting down on the weaver's bench. "Putting your hand to your heart. It's a gesture that a woman—a lady—would make sixty years ago if she were scared. It's like you saying something is 'the bee's knees'. It's really cute. Did you just start doing it or is it like some kind of ancestral memory gesture?"

"What do you want?"

"I want to tell you about the performance today. It went well."

"Mmm-hmm." She reached over him for the shuttle and tossed it back through the tent of threads.

"It was an interesting cross-class intertextual experiment. Most people ignored me but I did have one meaningful interaction—"

"Did you take photos?"

"No, what I thought would be even better would be this." He took her hands. "Let's do a performance action right now where I hold your hands and I imagine the experience and then you imagine the same experience and then you're going to come into class with me and we'll present two experiences, one real and one fictional, and then that will be the piece, and we won't tell anyone until the teacher asks—"

"I'm not going to class with you. I have to finish this."

"No, you don't have to come for the whole class. You can come just for three minutes. And then we can tell our competing narratives and then the class—"

"Jesus Christ!!" She yanked her hands away. "Don't you get it?" she screamed. "I'm actually *making* things." She started packing up. Something about the angry way she jammed her arms full of her belongings stirred his dormant anger.

"Yeah, a blanket out of a million little threads? The world is full of blankets and full of quicker ways to make them. You could be a brilliant artist with me and you're choosing *this*?"

"It's a tapestry. I'm sick and tired of being your witness! Get a fucking camera! I'm not your camera! I'm not proof that you exist!"

He suddenly saw it, nakedly, embarrassingly clearly. Peacocks have feathers. Elk have antlers. Useless ectomorphs from northern cities have performance art. He suddenly had a vision of blanketing the city with this poster: it would subvert the dominant paradigm and be self-reflexive and referential and maybe it would actually

work:

MY GOD IT'S LIKE YOU FINALLY GET THIS WORK OF ART AND ALL MY SOUL-CRUSHING LONELINESS IS OVER FOREVER.

He walked outside. It was dark now. He kicked stones in the parking lot. *What's the size of our dead romance?* He took a piece of chalk out of his pocket and did some calculations on the sidewalk. 5' 10" + 5' 4" = 11' 2". A 36 suit and a B cup. Or thereabouts. He paced out eleven feet and drew a chalk outline big enough for two. Then he lay down in the middle of it. Like how the feet of coma victims curl in on themselves, he found himself crumpling into a fetal ball. The air was cold and the sky was bright. *Someone should document this*, he thought for just one second, and then he took a deep breath and wished no one could see him at all.

Jacqueline Laughs Last
in the Gaslight

By Paula D. Ashe

Early July 1888

The young bride strides alongside her handsome deacon, her hand like painted porcelain nestled delicate and safe in the sanctuary of his forearm. The two are spectacles of health in Whitechapel's sprawling garden of steaming grime. They walk the Flower and Dean, mouths stiff but smiling as cutthroats and pickpockets threaten the woman with rape. Slatterns with pickled brains emphatically offer the Anglican a variety of slick and tight delights, flipping their ragged skirts at the pass of his shadow to give him a glimpse of their puckered and pestilent holes.

This is their honeymoon.

The Deacon insisted; his new wife complied. She loves her man more than she loves their God. The couple strolls through streets steaming with bodily waste, sermonizing to anyone who will listen until nervous police notice the setting sun and gathering crowds and insist they depart.

Safe in their cottage on the pristine grounds of St. Mary Matfelon, the Deacon and his wife remove their sodden, stinking clothes, set them aside for tomorrow's laundry. The church bells ring in the evening hour. A strange yet sacred custom; with rags soaked in lavender water they each take turns standing in a bucket while the other wipes away the filth of the day.

Outside the bed they pray to God, inside the bed they say a sort of prayer to each other. Warm and sated beneath her sleeping husband, Jacqueline smiles in the fragrant dark.

The next day, they brave the dogs of Dorset Street to share ale—safer to drink than the water—with troll-faced whores, urging them back into the ever-waiting arms of Christ. The blasphemous retorts in return: "May I charge 'im extra for that Second Coming in advance, then?", "Easier ways fer a man ta get nailed, love.", "Nah, got my own 'oly trinity; kettledrums, quim, 'n cooler. If ya'd care fer a bit of 'eaven, you, me, and your blushing missus can all 'ave a go."

It is that last invitation that sends Jacqueline storming from the public house and into the streets, ribald laughter at her heels. Quick as silver she is, their world washed away in her ocean of furious tears. She rushes past lewd laborers who whistle at her passing and will later recall her lavender while tupping a three-penny upright. Insides burnt black with humiliation, the Deacon yells her name and she ignores him, careens towards the cool, dark pocket of a crumbling alley. She watches her husband interrogate scoundrels and brigands, the fever of panic so bright in his eyes they flinch beneath his gaze. The alleyway smells of urine, excrement, spoiled food, and decay. Her stomach roils. She will not contribute to this collection of human filth. She spares him the indignation of retrieving her from the rubbish-lined passage and emerges into the grey sunlight. They say nothing to each other. He reaches her, takes her hand, and leads her from the slums.

The Deacon spends the night with his face buried between the pages of the Good Book. Staring at his back, she sighs with an impatience that uncharacteristically borders on irritation. She too has gospels. From a gentle Genesis to repeated Revelations, their lovemaking could—and has been—an entire Bible of experience. Jacqueline falls asleep alone and alone feels the first cracks of doom shear through the brickwork of their marriage.

She dreams of strange images coupled with stranger sensations. A river of visions heavy with prophecy: crumpled skirts, the gleam of a blade, snapped links of a cheap chain, an open palm, the torn skin of worn black boots, a star of silver, strings of bright hair stretched between fingers damp with angel's spit.

She wakes at the edge of dawn knowing scalding truths too horrid to forget; pink-cheeked urchins still bound in babyflesh know well the taste of sailor spunk, penniless widows offer their grieving cavities to wealthy sadists.

Despite the soft music of her husband's snoring and the peaceful rhythm of raindrops against their cottage, Jacqueline contemplates yet another truth: God is blind. Whether that blindness is the result of cowardice or shame, she cannot discern.

Sunday morning and St. Mary's is occupied by fifteen bodies; the Deacon and his wife, six ancient parishioners whom Jacqueline suspects reanimate every Sunday morning and return to dust at the setting of the sun. The remaining few are relatives: Jacqueline's kind uncle, aunt, and cousins. The Deacon's sermon is a flaccid embarrassment. Those impious whores have sucked the spirit from him. As his tongue trudges through tepid benedictions, Jacqueline remembers the exhilarating dictum from her dream: God is blind.

They have dinner with their family and return to the cottage. There is no lavender water, only quick prayers. The Deacon at least takes Jacqueline into his arms and kisses her forehead before turning over to sleep. He will die if he cannot save them. Whether the death is quick or wasting, his vitality depends upon his ability to spark salvation in souls soaked through with sin.

What could be the kindling to ignite their spirits? Reason was worthless; most of them were slaves to drink and even fouler vices while the others were slack-jawed simpletons. Their lives were without structure or order, chaos was the frothing sea they swam in. Agitated, Jacqueline turns over and stuffs her hands beneath her pillow. As far as she can understand, the lower classes are without fear; of arrest, of disease, of death, of God.

What, then, of the Devil? She'd seen even the most villainous blackguards shudder in rapt fascination at lurid showhouse retellings of Goethe's *Faust*. The deacon shifts beside her in his sleep and like a mischievous child caught reading by moon-light, she freezes. Her husband stills with an outstretched arm resting across her narrow hip.

What of the Devil, indeed.

On those few occasions when she and her Deacon were required to socialize with the other members of the diaconate, she met many men who wore thin robes of holiness, fabric easily singed by hellish depravities. Their cloth was merely costume. Jacqueline had been born to a family of actors and entertainers. Much of her love of the Church was the result of exchanging one sort of stage for another. If one could play at sanctity, could one not also play at villainy?

Jacqueline eases into her husband's somnolent embrace. Even then, his touch sends a trill of pleasure up her spine.

She will have him again.

Late August 1888

Mary Ann, the first, was practice. Rough work it was, marked by passion and fear. Protest. What else could be done to shut that shrieking bone box? A couple of sure swings from the gentleman's cane and her mouth shut up like a trap. A knife is to a body as a ship is to the sea. How does a vessel choose its path? So many possible routes, suggestions in the stars, half-remembered superstitions, promises in the wind, and above, a waning, half-lit moon.

Crisscross the ocean with that upright ironclad, set loose her estuary of secrets.

God's eye closing.

Early September 1888

The next one was a steadfast drunk and an occasional whore. What need had she for her womanhood? *The Star* called her, "a person in poor circumstances". Her friends called her 'Dark Annie', because of her foul moods and auburn hair. It did gleam in the gaslight, bright and quick, like a wick just after its flame has been extinguished. Freed from her mistreatments and ill-hygiene, things stuffed inside tumble out in rubbery spools. Blood blooms from her like a living shadow, splashes against the paling and the gentleman's shoes.

Later, her friend said, "I knowed her; I kissed her poor, cold face."

All that was left to kiss.

In twilight, while the Deacon snores, Jacqueline wipes the gallies clean with a damp rag, tosses the soiled cloth into the fireplace. Quietly, she opens the battered steamer trunk and places the boots back into their compartment beside the gentleman's carefully folded cloak, crumpled deer-stalker hat, and the fine swordstick, nestled in a long, narrow indentation lined with velvet. She lowers the lid and it latches shut with little more than a whisper. No need to lock it; the key probably rusted to dust in her dead father's moldering pocket. Her Deacon graciously allowed her the trunk and its contents as one bulky keepsake of her worldly life; as such, out of respect for her privacy, he will have nothing to do with it.

Thus, the secret keeps itself.

The act complete, sunlight slowly burns away the night's gloom as Jacqueline prepares breakfast.

Late September 1888

At the alms house, the Deacon evangelizes and Jacqueline passes out fresh-baked bread to the unfortunate. Some look upon her with pitiful eyes, others with glass-shard glares. The latter she stares down until they shudder and turn away. *God is blind*, she thinks, *but I am not.*

That Sunday, her beloved family is in attendance, along with the old dusties, and—miracle of miracles—four wretched women in the very last row, huddled together in rags, shivering for want of drink, eyeing the door but unmoving. Jacqueline smiles at them with a warmth that quiets the unkind whispers and stills shaking limbs. The Deacon flattens the light around him, condenses it into a shield to momentarily conceal the penetrating, promising glance he gives his wife. It is only for a sliver of a moment, but his spirit thrusts and swells in her every cell.

Jacqueline bites her lip, presses her thighs together beneath a skirt of satin and silk.

The work she has done in the lonely hours before dawn has brought him back to her. The warm, wet work of salvation. The sharp, stinking work of charity. In the nascent months of their marriage, a blessing has been his deep, dreamless, and sinless sleep.

After the service the pair blushes through hurried apologies to eager relatives and their solicitations to dinner. The door to the cottage is barely closed before the good Deacon, still clothed in the finery of his sanctity, shoves away fevered silk for a taste of his wife's velvet.

Sonorous and seductive, the tolling carillons ring in the evening hour. This is the magic of Whitechapel; at sun's fall a spark of liminal alchemy ignites the ruinous city. Even the ditch-diggers feel it. A change, a turn, a transformation. The brutish depravities of the day are lulled to a decadent limerence. In daylight, cut knuckles and bruised bones are evidence of wounding. In candlelight, every injury is an invitation.

The air in Dutfield's Yard is as damp as a whore's last breath on a rheumatic autumn night. She had been pretty once, this one. Before disease, drink, and malnutrition had taken several of her teeth. Strange, melancholy music from a distant beer hall dances through the dark, wraps the two of them in dulcet, burnished notes. Sizzles of cold along the cherry-red ridges of her split throat. Cachous in her hand.

Her last breath had been sweet.

And then, the blind god delivered the happy gentleman another.

The dying girl was still bleeding when he heard the new one sing. Swaddled in a childlike joy. Enraptured, dazzled, awakened. Carve the shadow from her face. Who is she beneath that shuddering mask? Who could she be? Marvelous garlands of shit-smeared intestines loosed in jovial loops. The grizzled nubs of her teeth peek out like pale mushrooms in rubicund loam.

Early November 1888

In the common houses, Jacqueline learns the necessary work has inspired others. Newspapers report about "Saucy Jacky" and a letter addressed "from Hell". She smiles while the drunkards slobber out their mad theories.

"Mailed off an ear, then fried up her kidney?"

"It wassat Jew! Leather Apron!"

"Sawed out 'er womb, as I 'eard, it!"

"No, a butcher, hungry to crawl back up into his old mum's runny slum!"

"Bollocks! It was that dumb pollack with the burned face!"

Ladies of ill-repute looked at in ways they had forgotten existed. Kindness. Concern. Sympathy. The Deacon and his wife greeted by grave eyes, still tongues, hungry ears, open hearts. A different sort of passion warms those gathered near the hearth. Jacqueline sees it ignite beneath their sin-stained skin: hope. The thrashing animal hope that there is a place for them beyond the terminal purgatory of Spitalfield. The quiet and raw hope that there is a soft, warm love somewhere that aches for them, singularly.

No butcher, no baker, no canticle-maker.

Fair Emma, the worst and the last. A bonny girl. A laughing girl. Laughed at her, didn't she? Offered her 'holy trinity' to her and her husband. That dog of Dorset laughed at her. She, of course, invited the gentleman back to her scabrous room.

Spilt private colors on bedsheets sodden with cruelty.

A whore is nothing more than the sum of her parts; the parts alone are worthless.

Jacqueline leaves her in pieces.

Early April 1889

The Deacon and his wife meander along the newly posh Durward Street, each smoothed stone like an iced sweet-treat. From the polished storefronts of tidy shops and the open doorways of reputable gin palaces, gaslight, gay music, and laughter spill into the chill evening. The two pause at a corner as a large and loud grocer's carriage trots down the lane. The Deacon places gloved hands onto his Jacqueline's burgeoning belly, whispers something lewd and loving into her adored ear.

She laughs loudly into a sky the color of a bruise and briefly recalls the cries of the women she tore open.

Taking her husband's hand, the three of them cross the street for home, haloed in gaslight.

Adrenaline Junkies

By Ray Cluley

"Carpe the fucking diem."

I'm thinking about Suki when Cate pats my arm and gives me the thumb-to-forefinger okay. For a moment I think she means we're ready to jump but the door's still closed and everybody else in the plane is triple-checking their harnesses and packs, pockets, cameras. She means the sign as a question, I realise. I don't want her to think I'm worried about the jump—I'm not—so I smile, and return the sign with a nod. She gives me a thumbs-up, grinning. She's excited, adrenaline already working its magic. This is her first freefall, no static line, and I can't be looking sad when I know she's probably as nervous as she is excited. She doesn't know much about Suki yet, just the little she's heard from the others and maybe a tiny bit more from a well-meaning Kit. I'll give her my version after we've landed. Or tonight. I'll tell her tonight.

"You okay, pretty lady?" Todd shouts. We're flying in a tiny prop and the cabin is loud with its noise. I have no okay sign or thumbs-up for him, just a middle finger, and he laughs. He's called me 'pretty lady' ever since Quintana Roo where one of the barmen kept trying his luck, complimenting my dress, my hair, no gaydar whatsoever. Cate had joked I should kiss her so he'd get the hint and a few tequilas later I did, but it wasn't for the barman's benefit. I'm not sure what I was trying to prove. Or who I was trying to prove it to.

There'd been tequilas last night as well, and a morning wake-up so early that we may as well have not gone to bed. It had left most of us silent at breakfast, even though it was jump day. For the other stuff, the climbing and kayaking, we'd fill up on oatmeal and protein snacks, but a jump day breakfast was whatever you wanted it to be. I opted for brown toast, scrambled egg, and half an avocado because that was what Suki used to have. Todd noticed, I could tell, so I stole a spoonful of baked beans from his fried breakfast and spread it over mine and he'd laughed, pretending to protest, and everything was okay.

"Come on, come on," Måns urges, sweeping his arms to bunch us together for a pre-jump selfie. He's got his phone on the end of a selfie stick. He actually owns a selfie stick. Maybe it's a Swedish thing. He leans into us, arm outstretched, and Todd rubs at Måns' bald head as the picture's taken. "Makes me more aerodynamic," Måns says, and although it's an old joke, we all laugh. We're all excited. Pumped.

Måns retrieves his phone. He's taken a good picture. Four of us huddled close, Måns in our laps. Cate where Suki used to be, right beside me. She's made rabbit ears behind my head, fingers sprouting from my helmet. A sign for two. A sign for peace.

I wonder if the others feel Suki's absence as strongly as I do. There's a quiet moment after the picture when everyone's lost in their own thoughts, and I like to think they're all remembering her. But maybe they're not. Maybe they're just suffering what's left of their hangovers, or thinking about the jump, running through a mental list of everything they've done in preparation.

Måns is flicking through the pictures on his phone. They're old ones. He stops at one of him and Suki; she's in profile, a curve of glitter garish around one eye, planting a big kiss on his painted cheek as he grins at the camera. A club in Rio, almost two years ago. Måns notices I'm looking and turns the phone so I can see better and I smile at both of them.

"Okay," says Todd. "Okay, okay, this is it. We ready?"

"Yeah!"

"I said, are we ready?"

"Yeah!"

"Wieslander. Helmet."

Måns reaches to Kit and she slings it to him. He straps it on, knocks the top of it with one fist, and Kit copies. We all copy.

Even Cate, who hasn't been told, realises the ritual of it and does the same. I catch her exhale a few hard breaths, looking at the door, then Todd yanks it open and the wind tears in.

Nothing wakes you up or blows away a hangover like squatting in the back of a light aircraft with the slipstream rushing in around you. I do my best to take slow, deep breaths. Kit crouches in the opening. She's flexing her knees, rocking on the spot, pulling and pushing at the doorway, back and forth, back and forth. Todd crouches beside her, looking down, then he pats her on the shoulder three times—go-go-go—and she's gone.

Måns is next. He stands long enough to put his head to Todd's and they bump, then he squats and rolls forward out of the plane in one quick movement.

"Cate."

Todd beckons her and she shuffles to him, squatting. I follow her. She glances up at where she would normally hook onto a static line and then she looks at me. I sign the okay, nodding. She puffs out another breath then Todd's patting her, go-go-go, and she's gone.

It's a good clean exit. We've timed the jump especially for dawn and the light is breaking out over the jungle below. I can see her as she falls. She's holding a stable position, her body open like a giant starfish, arching into the force of the wind.

"She's all right," Todd yells.

I can't see anything of his expression behind his face shield, but I can see his eyes and they are like mine. I know what he really means and yeah. She's all right.

"You ready?"

I give him a nod. He gives it back to me.

I bend my knees to crouch lower. Hold the sides of the door. The wind tugs at me from the front, pushes at me from the back, and passing below is the vast green carpet of jungle canopy. Between me and that is 13,000 feet of sky.

"Carpe the fucking diem!" Todd shouts, then he's slapping at my shoulder: go-go-go!

And I'm gone. Plucked out into a sky Suki never got to see.

I first saw Suki in a waiting room. Not my practice, a colleague's.

And as important as that meeting was, as striking as she'd been, sitting there in one of those god-awful plastic chairs, the memory that always comes first when I think of how we met, my preferred memory, is of her walking a slackline at Malham Cove. We were meeting there to climb Upper Terrace, but I was late thanks to some unavoidable overtime, and when I'd arrived at the site there was something of a low-key party already in progress. Nothing too wild; a night of drinking before jumping out of a plane isn't genius but the night before a climb it's a definite no-no, even if the climb is supposed to be an easy one. Low-key party meant only a couple of drinks, a bit of a smoke (courtesy of Kit), and some music (courtesy of Måns). Someone had strung up a rope between two trees. Suki was barefoot, toes scrunched around the line as she walked a metre above the ground, arms out for balance. She had a line of stars tattooed on her foot, I noticed, and she'd changed her hair since I'd last seen her, her head shaved on one side while the rest of her hair swept over in a deep purple wave. This is how I always see her first when I remember her, balanced between a beginning and an end. Laughing, and giving Todd shit about something he'd said. My heart had expanded into a feeling far more intense than the attraction I'd felt in the waiting room, turning into something far more powerful and needy. I wanted to be with her, and belong to her, and all of that happened right there and then while she balanced on a taut tightrope.

"You'll never make it," Todd said. He turned to Kit and said, "She'll never make it." He called over to Måns, "What do you think, Wieslander?"

Suki raised one leg out to the side, oh so carefully, and brought it around slowly to the front. She did the same again with the other leg.

Without looking up from his guitar, Måns said, "She'll never make it."

Suki had her arms out to balance, but she made fists of her hands and turned them to raise a middle finger both sides, moving slowly forwards as the others laughed. That was when Måns looked up from his guitar and noticed me. He stopped playing to raise a hand in hello and the others noticed me too.

They were quiet, taking me in. Kit nodded hi and looked to Todd, smiling. Suki must have picked up on the mood change, or maybe just the new quiet, because she looked up from the rope to glance at them, left quick, right quick, and then at me. "Hey."

"I love your hair."

She wobbled on the rope, "Fuck," and adjusted her balance as the others made dramatic noises. She stepped quickly now, rushing to beat her fall, but even I could tell she'd never make it, much as I wanted to believe otherwise. She was moving too fast. She slipped from the rope about a metre away from the opposite tree.

The others laughed and clapped and cheered, and Todd declared, "Told you," to all who would listen, saving his grin for Suki who told him to fuck himself. She'd done better than anyone else.

"So far," said Kit, stepping up onto the rope and immediately stumbling off again on the other side, much to everyone's amusement. "That doesn't count!"

Suki came over to me and I had a moment of, oh shit, how do we do this, a hug, a handshake, what? She swept her hair back and exaggerated tossing it, a shampoo model, and said, "Part of my 'alternative' phase. You like it, then?"

"I love it."

I love.

"Sorry about that just now," I said. "I distracted you."

She put her hands on my arms, just below my shoulders. She looked at me for a moment, then came in to kiss me on each cheek. Afterwards she opened her arms to the group at the rope. "These are my friends," she said. "And Todd."

Todd smiled like she'd complimented him. "You must be the hot doctor lady."

I've often wondered what Suki'd said about me prior to that meeting, and Todd probably would've told me if I'd asked, but I never did.

"Yeah, Todd," said Suki, "thanks for that." But she barely looked embarrassed at all. "Come on, I'll introduce you properly."

She took my hand to lead me to her friends and she held it the whole time we exchanged hellos and little bits of background. She smiled with me, and laughed with me, and by the end of that night I was hers forever.

You don't jump out of a plane: you drop. You hold the doorway and somehow you convince your brain that it's okay to let go, to pull yourself out of a perfectly good, fully functional airplane. You tuck in tight. You plummet. There's no better word for it. You might even experience a few moments of sensory overload while the mind tries to figure out what the fuck has just happened, sorting through all these new sensations while the whine of the plane fades and wind rushes up and all around you. Some people even black out for a moment. But your brain figures it out soon enough and maybe you scream because you're scared or because it's fun, maybe both. The wind pushes at your clothes and at your face and if your mouth's open then it rushes into there as well and flaps your cheeks. Your thoughts roar with the sound of your falling.

I'm falling in silence this time, feeling the fullness of the rush downward and thinking it's apt, thinking this is how I've been feeling for nearly a year now. I'm waiting to stabilise so the chute can get a good clean wind when I open up, but I don't know if I'll ever stabilise. Don't know if I'll ever open up again.

Below me: Kit, Måns, Cate. Kit's rolling, knees tucked to her chest to spin around her own axis, head over heels. Måns is spread wide, looking left and right. He has a GoPro mounted on his helmet and he's catching as much of the experience as he can because memories are all anybody ever has, something I wish I'd realised a lot sooner. And there's Cate, her arms and legs open wide in an X that marks the spot. Somewhere safe to land, maybe. Or maybe she's just a shooting star, bright and brief like all of us are. Not much more than a kiss in a jumpsuit.

I could lean, if I wanted to. Could tilt forward, streamlining myself, and choose to fall faster. I could urge the winds to take me closer.

Instead, I pull the cord to release my chute and force a greater distance between us.

"So there I am, bungee-jumping over crocodile-infested waters—"

"They weren't crocodile-infested."

Todd was standing to tell his story, *grand*standing, you could say, for the benefit of the new group we'd joined for the night. He was lit from below by the campfire that cast classic eerie shadows up his face. We all saw him scowl at the interruption, though.

"They bloody well were crocodile-infested, mate."

Måns shook his head. He exhaled smoke and said, "The crocodiles live there."

"Like I said."

Kit passed the joint up to Todd as if to calm him. "He means if they live there then it's not infested."

Todd puffed once, twice, and said, "Whatever," with a tight voice. "Smart-arse."

Of all of us, Todd had travelled the most. He had a world map outlined on his back, and he added a flag to the tattoo for every place he visited. There were a lot of flags. He'd done it all, and done it almost everywhere, and he had plenty of stories to prove it. I think that's one of the things Suki loved so much about him. His eagerness to cram as much as he could into life. Carpe the fucking diem, as she put it to him once. They'd kayaked the Congo River together, at the turbulent low end, and they'd gone BASE-jumping in Hong Kong, leaping illegally from the International Finance Centre. The Grand Canyon was the one big one Todd still hadn't done, the flag he most wanted to add to that atlas on his back, but he was caught between desperately wanting to thru-hike the canyon to completely avoiding it as too touristy. Never mind that more people have walked on the moon than have thru-hiked the GC.

"So there I am, bungee jumping over this, fucking, crocodile *residential area*, right? Fucking, croc central..."

I'd heard the story before, so I tuned it out to focus on Suki. She was looking into the flames of the campfire and I doubted she heard Todd's story either.

"You okay?"

Suki smiled. It was one of the gentle ones I'd grown to hate, a token gesture rather than one of her typically vibrant smiles. The fire was bright in her eyes, but it was only reflected there. Used to be they lit up with a light all of their own. They drew you to her, those eyes. Pulled you along for whatever wild ride she had planned next. Before meeting her, the craziest thing I'd done was go trampolining with my nephew, but since Suki there'd been plenty, starting with that first climb at Malham Cove. There'd been abseiling, zip wires, hand-gliding, skydiving, an awful attempt at surfing, and the whole time I felt like I was trying to catch up. It was exhilarating. *She* was exhilarating. Or she used to be. Those days near the end, she spent a lot more time in her own head, and I couldn't blame her for that, though I still did. Just a little.

"You remember the first time I came back to yours?" I asked her quietly while the others listened to Todd. It worked; I saw a proper Suki Smile. She leaned into me. Nudged me.

"*Yeah*, I do."

She was referring to the sex, but for me it had been a much bigger step than that. No adrenaline rush has ever come close to what I felt that night, stepping into that private space where she lived. There had been ropes everywhere, loops of it draped over furniture or coiled on the floor, with metal clasps and caribiners and hooks. I made some terrible joke about her being kinky. Then I saw the mountain bike held on a wall mount, the collapsed sail of a windsurf board leaning beside it like a bright limp shark fin. There were skis and a snowboard. In the ceiling, sitting across the beams, was a kayak and paddle. She was a cooped-up city girl in a tiny flat surrounded by all the things she enjoyed going elsewhere to use. It was overwhelming, seeing so much of her so clearly on display, and not in some pretentious way for others to appreciate: this was what she loved. What was familiar to her, the equilibrium she moved about in, was to me an exciting presentation of her personality, and it brought with it a lightness to my stomach, a shortness of breath.

She took my hand and led me to her bedroom. There was a helmet on the dresser next to her vanity mirror, a headlamp attached. She draped a vest over it and switched the headlamp on, then went back to the other room to turn the main light off.

"Sorry about all the mess," she said. "Romantic, hey?"

It its own way, it really was. The light shone back out from the mirror at an angle that diffused it. The décor here, if you ignored the safety gear and the wetsuit draped over a chair, was a nod to her Indian culture that she otherwise ignored. And the bed looked very comfortable.

"It's very comfortable," she said. I laughed at her mind-reading, and with nervousness, and because I had clearly been staring and waiting, expecting. She laughed with me and pulled me to the bed, and to her.

Afterwards, hearts pounding, we'd talked about adrenaline.

Todd was trying to do the same now, in a roundabout way, but Todd's adrenaline-fuelled stories were always about Todd. Where he'd been, what he'd done, what he'd dared. Stories were what he told so he had something to hide behind.

"Look, do the crocodiles eat you in the end, or not?" someone asked.

"Hey, if you want stories about being eaten, you—"

"Don't you go there," Suki warned, and people laughed. I tried to, but I'd just seen my attempt to cheer her up surpassed by a crude joke.

Todd held up a hand to accept the warning. "Okay, where was I?"

"Heart hammering, blood pumping, something melodramatic like that."

Adrenaline does lead to an increased heart rate. There's an increase in blood pressure, too, thanks to the kidneys producing more renin, and the blood is redistributed to the muscles, increasing the power for muscular contraction and altering the body's metabolism to maximise glucose levels, all of it happening very quickly in anticipation of fight or flight. I remembered, when Suki and I had talked about it in bed, that I explained how fear was healthy in its own way, thinking I was being clever and talking about us, the excitement of a new relationship, but having no fucking clue what she was going through at the time and how scared she must have been.

"A lot of people think adrenaline is a kind of fear," she'd

said, "like there's a good kind of fear, right? But the adrenaline is what you get when you say 'fuck you' to fear. That's what it is for me, anyway."

She used to say fear was subjective, that you could choose whether to be scared or not, but thinking back, I realise she was scared all the time and did whatever she could to shift it elsewhere. Fight or flight. You couldn't fight what she had, not really, and there's no running from it either, though she tried for a while. Not so much flight as falling at high speed.

"You okay?"

She wasn't, but it would be a long time before she told me. In the meantime, she would distract me.

"Are *you* scared?" she asked.

"What?"

"It's just… How did you put it? The airways to the lungs expand." She leaned closer; quickened her hand. "Or, to put it in normal language, you're breathing heavy."

I smiled. "Because of what you're doing right now."

"And your pupils have dilated."

"Because you're so fucking beautiful."

"Yeah," she said, slipping away from me, farther down the bed, "keep saying things like that…"

I did. I said things like that all the time, through all of that night and all the others after. It's just that, as it turned out, there weren't as many of them as either of us would have liked.

Nylon and rope spews behind me, unravelling above, and suddenly the chute is forced full. On TV you'll see the body jerk upwards as if yanked by the parachute, but that's bullshit. I've seen it myself in some of Måns's films, but it's just the camera falling faster than what it's seeing. The slider slows the opening of the chute, and you get an intense deceleration, but that's it. A jolt. It's a little abrupt, but not severe.

Below me, one, two chutes blossom open. Three.

On TV, you also see people suspended gently beneath their parachutes, floating like fucking dandelion seeds in a breeze, but the truth is you're still falling and you're falling fast. You've got more control, and you're able to guide yourself by pulling on the toggles left and right, snaking long Ss in the sky, but you're still buffeted and tossed about by the wind. The lush green canopy of the jungle might look like some giant moth-eaten green blanket plumped up thick and soft, but it won't be. It'll be hard and sharp if we haven't timed this right, and we'll hit it with force. If we miss the clearing, we'll be shredded by the trees or jerked dead with a sudden neck-snap crack. We might all look pretty from down there, flowers falling slowly, but thousands of feet up it's a different story, and that's fine by all of us. That's the rush. The adrenaline. The reason why we do it. One of the reasons, anyway.

I can see a gap in the trees. And there, taking up most of the clearing, is a vast sinkhole. A cenote. Godzilla, we've been calling it, but it's Zotzil-aha or Zot-hilza, or something like that. Aligned with it, the ruins of a Mayan temple, a relatively new discovery far off the tourist trail. We'd all been to Chichén Itzá and marvelled at it, glad we'd missed the equinox when tourists descend on the place to watch the light snake its way down the pyramid, but it had still been a little too crowded for us. Godzilla was ideal. We'd look around the site then abseil down into the cenote. Todd had wanted to drop right into it, wipe away our primary sense for a moment, namely our sight, and plunge into sudden night for that extra rush. But there was daring and there was stupidity. We'd hit water in the dark and our next adrenaline rush would be trying not to drown in a tangle of parachute ropes.

I glance at Cate below, wondering how she'd liked her first proper freefall. At this altitude we had a whole sixty seconds of it. How's she feeling?

Is this how Suki used to feel, watching me?

The wind I'm falling in changes abruptly and a sharp riffle of the canopy overhead has me yanking hard left to compensate. Then the canopy flaps wildly as the wind suddenly drops and I plummet twenty feet faster than a moment ago before lurching into a steadier stream.

Todd falls past me. He twists around onto his back as he passes. His face shield is gone and he's so stricken with terror that I think I know what's happened, I'm sure I know: his chute has failed. And for a moment I see it's tangled around him somehow, and I'm thinking ditch it, cut it loose, pull your reserve, come on Todd. Except it's not his chute at all. Whatever it is wrapped around his legs, his waist, it slithers up and around him in a quick tight coil and a wing, a fucking *wing*, long and leathery and brightly feathered, unfurls from behind him briefly before snapping shut again against the wind.

"Todd!"

The wind snatches that away.

A head appears behind Todd, at the nape of his neck. I see only the squat shape of it, only for an instant. The dark colour. The open mouth. It snaps at him. Then a splash of something hot is on my face and I shut my eyes, twisting away. I wipe the blood away with my forearm as best as I can. Blink my eyes clear. I've arced away in my S shape but hurry to twist back and look behind, look down, look for where Todd falls. Something that's not his parachute unfolds around him, a mottled rainbow of colours spanning left and right, and just like that he's carried away out of sight on beating wings.

What the fuck? What the *fuck*? What the actual *FUCK*?

Coming in from the right, something too snake-like to be a bird, too bird-like to be a snake. It dives right into where Måns hangs suspended. Folds its wings away a moment before impact and strikes him like some scaly torpedo, disappearing beneath the canopy of his chute and snapping it sideways.

"Måns!"

He's carried away somewhere out of my sight. His chute has whipped free, some of the ropes severed, and drags behind him like a bright streamer.

There's no way he'll hear me, but I scream for him anyway.

Måns collected trinkets wherever we went. Kit collected postcards, sending them home to herself as mementos, Todd collected tattoos, and Suki would pick up a rock, or some sand, or a shell, something like that. She had jars filled with these bits and pieces. We all had our things. For Måns, it was the trinkets, and the local stories.

Two nights ago, we'd been sitting around the fire, listening to it pop and crackle, while behind it, somewhere in the dark, the sea hushed up the sand and washed it away. Måns had pulled a pendant out from under his shirt. He held it up to us, as much as the length of cord would allow, and said, "Look at this, eh?" before ducking out of the loop to pass the necklace around.

It was a wooden carving, impressively intricate, about the size of a pen. A nearly-naked man stood in front of a column or cylinder. He was wearing what I thought was a feathered headdress, wonderfully detailed, and part of it had a long beak coming down over the head. But I noticed, too, talons at either side of the figure's waist and turning the pendant saw a scaled tail running down from the head and snaking around the column. A very elaborate headdress, then, I thought. Or some weird lizard-bird thing standing behind him. In which case the beak wasn't decorative at all. It was coming down to scrape at the face and throat of the man, talons ready to rip at the stomach.

"What the hell, Måns?"

"Grim, huh? Bit weird."

"Just a bit." I passed it on.

"There were these Mayan heroes—"

"Oh, here we go," said Todd, settling back into the sand. "Story time."

"They were twins," Måns said. "These heroes. And they were put in a cave filled with bats."

"Why?"

Måns shrugged. "Punishment for something, probably."

"What were their names?" Cate asked. She was already pretty good with the banter. For some reason I liked her a little less for that. Or maybe I liked everyone else a little less for letting her fit in so easily. I don't know.

"Come on, guys, just let me tell it."

We pretended like we were doing him a favour, but the truth was if it wasn't for Måns our only local knowledge would be geographical and alcoholic, nothing cultural. He was the one who told us about Chaak and other gods, the Quetzalcoatl, the ancient Aztec sacrifices. All the fun stuff.

"These two brothers," he said, turning to Cate to add, "whose names I've forgotten because they're probably unpronounceable with lots of Qs and Xs and Zs, they were put in a cave with these creatures called Camazotz and—"

"I thought you said bats?"

"These are like bats. Camazotz are, like, bat creatures. Or bat-gods, or something."

"You remember that name, then?" Todd said.

Cate laughed. Måns gave them both the finger.

"They have these noses, these long snouts, like blades. Like a beak. And these giant leathery feathery wings. They're like birds and bats mixed together. Flying around in the dark of the cave."

Måns lunged at us all in turn around the fire and we humoured him with shrieks and flinches. I clutched playfully at Cate in mock-fright, and perhaps lingered longer than I should have afterwards. She felt good.

"So to get away from these Camazotz, the bat-things, these brothers hid inside their blowguns—"

"But—"

Måns silenced Todd with a warning glare, exaggerated into cartoon proportions. "They hid," he said again. "Inside their blowguns." He waited, but there were no more interruptions. "And the whole time, these creatures tried to attack them while they hid inside, all through the night, until, at dawn… nothing. Not a sound. So one of the brothers looked to see if it was safe."

Cate said, "I'm guessing it wasn't."

"As soon as he poked his head out…" Måns looked around, choosing someone, and lunged at me suddenly, clapping his hand together at my face. "No more head!"

"Well that *does* sound terrible."

Cate grinned at me. I smiled back, politely. Quick and then gone. I've never been very good at flirting, except with Suki. Suki was the queen of flirting, pursuing it with the same eagerness for new experience as she did her shots of adrenaline. It made me worry about losing her, the same way I worried about slipping off a cliff face and smashing myself on rocks, or the way I worried about drowning upside down in a capsized kayak. Which is to say, I was always careful to pay attention, just like she taught me. Never become blasé, because complacency could end everything. It was how accidents happened. "Always be, like, super aware of where you are and what you're doing at all times. Live in the moment," she told me, "be right there, in it, all the time." So that's what I did with her. Seized every moment I could until suddenly she was never there at all.

"It's hollow," said Kit. She was holding the pendant horizontally to the fire. She put it to her mouth.

"It's a whistle," Måns said.

"It's a blowgun." Kit mimed shooting it at him and he collapsed back into the sand.

"They've got a lot of bats here," Todd said. Kit feigned a blowgun shot at him as well and he clasped it to his chest with a groan of pain. "Makes sense that they'll tell stories about them. Southern Mexico, Bolivia, Brazil, Paraguay even, and Argentina. All these bats."

"Vampires?"

"Meat-eaters."

"When the fuck did you suddenly become David Attenborough?" It was the sort of thing Suki would've said, and I was glad to have said it because of how he laughed.

"I got to talking to some guy and he said as soon as the sun goes down, the whole sky around the Yucatán Peninsula comes alive with bats. Regular ones, vampire ones, these meat-eater ones. All of them out to feed. He was probably exaggerating, trying to sound smart or scary of something. He was probably coming on to me. But yeah. Lots of bats."

Måns had his pendant back. He gave it a long look and said, "Pretty fucked-up bat," and ducked into the loop of its leather cord, tucking the carving back under his shirt.

"Hey," said Kit, rummaging in her bag, "I've got one for you. Why did the Mexican push his wife off the cliff?" She produced a bottle for her punch line and we all cried, "Tequilla!" and cheered.

"Okay, I have a story," Cate said.

Everybody settled into quiet for her because, well, she was new. There was no getting around that fact, although we all did a pretty good job of pretending otherwise. I saw Kit and Todd share a look and I thought, don't fuck this up Cate. You've just volunteered for an early make-or-break moment, created an audition for yourself, and the spotlight is bright on you right now. We're all looking, and we're all listening. Don't try too hard, but do try.

"I got this from some tourist in—"

"Tourist? There are no tourists out this way, just people like us." Todd glanced at me and I knew right then he was judging her as hard as I was, and testing her a bit, but mainly hoping she'd pass. I think.

"Those are the tourists I mean. The extreme sports kind. Anyway, out here, tourist is just another word for foreigner, right?"

There was some agreement.

"Well, some of these people, they disappear. Nothing all that unusual, I suppose, when many of them are a little off the radar anyway, and doing crazy shit like jumping out of airplanes or swimming with crocodiles or whatever. People fall, they drown, get eaten."

"This is one of those cheery stories, yeah?" Kit said, passing the bottle.

"I can add kittens and lollipops if you like?"

She was doing well.

"Anyway, if they just disappeared, that would be one thing. But sometimes they'd turn up again in crazy places. The bodies of white-water rafters found in the treetops, miles from the river they disappeared from. Skydivers found years later in cenotes, their chutes still packed. Things like that. This one group, they were climbing, although fuck knows what because there aren't many mountains around here, maybe it was one of the ruins or something? Whatever. Three of them were climbing, one of them wasn't. The climbers all vanished. The one on the ground, he heard them scream but that was all. By the time he got to where they'd secured their lines, there was nothing, not even rope. They had a guide with them, some local boy, but all he could do was say, '¡Lo vi! ¡Lo vi!' I saw it! I saw it! Pointing up. But there was nothing. No one. They were all there one minute, and the next minute—" She clicked her fingers. "Gone. Just like that."

I knew exactly what she meant.

"There was a full-on search, but nobody found them for days. When the bodies eventually did turn up, they were ten miles away. And all of them were cut open."

"Cut open," Todd said.

Cate nodded. She made a slashing motion across her abdomen. "Same for all the others that turned up, the kayakers and the skydivers. Their kidneys, gone."

There was some groaning at this, a collective sigh of exhalation.

"The black market thing? Selling organs?" said Kit. "Basic urban myth stuff."

"I know, I know," Cate said, "but these weren't clean excisions or anything. More brutal. Ragged." She settled back, a little deflated. "From what I heard."

"Wieslander's bats got 'em," Todd said, and Måns swooped at her, screeching while we laughed.

"It's interesting," I said. "The kidneys are where you'll find the adrenal glands."

I suddenly had their full attention. They liked it when I went doctor on them. Sometimes because of the gruesome stories, sometimes for the more exotic ones, like how the parasite *toxoplasma gondi* can make its host take greater risks, they loved that one. Humans can catch it from cats, but cats pass it to each other through rats—an infected rat becomes reckless, daring, gets caught and eaten and that's that: toxo-cat. A cautionary tale if ever I heard one. They also liked to be reminded that as a doctor I could patch them up pretty good if I had to (and I often had to). But I wasn't looking to reassure them right now.

"Yeah," I said. "The adrenal medulla. And from the sounds of it, the victims all had one thing in common—apart from the missing kidneys…" I paused just enough to make it dramatic. "They were adrenaline junkies. Like us."

I watched as each glanced at the other, Todd eventually making an ominous *"oooh"* noise. Cate smiled her gratitude at me, but I hadn't really done anything. Whatever fixing her story needed had been achieved by Todd and Måns joking about bats. She was part of the group now, and she was smiling at me, and I was okay with that.

Below me, Cate is spinning. Whatever's happened to her, I missed it, but her chute is tattered and her body swings around beneath it. An occasional flash of colour suggests one of the things is on her, too, or close by; she doesn't seem to be entwined yet, but there's an irregularity to her spinning that suggests something more than momentum has her moving like that. One of the creature's wings is beating while the other is held upright, caught in the ropes of her partially ruined parachute. Some sort of tail lashes around as if to balance or steer and—

I'm hit hard in the chest. It knocks me swinging in a direction that deifies that of my falling. I feel a sharp line of pain in my thigh as something clawed takes hold there, and suddenly I'm wrapped about the leg. A muscular pulse and the coils spread upward, enveloping my abdomen. A head rises to look up at me from there. It is both snake-like and bat, squat-faced but with fangs, sabre-toothed and red-fleshed where its mouth opens. The fangs are so close together as to be almost one tooth, like a curve of beak. It tilts its head in an effort to sink these into the softest part of my body, uncoiling slightly to allow it more movement.

Somehow, I get my hands under its jaw. The flesh is scaled but it feels leathery, with ridges to hold onto as I try to redirect its attack, shoving its face away from my body. Two monstrous wings unfold and beat… beat… beat, controlling our descent. I flail with the sudden shift in direction and speed. With one leg still free, I kick at the creature wrapped around my other. With my elbow I smash at its puckered snout before grabbing at what I can find of the nearest wing. I slap at it, push at muscle and pull at scales, at feathers, but it constricts tighter. The wings fold around me with the smell of something wet and dark, and something snags at my back, yanks at the pack I wear.

This close to its body, I can smell meat, alley-meat, something spoiled. I'm too close to strike it now, arms crushed to my chest. But I can reach the cut-away. I yank at the handle on my harness and detach the main chute. I'm not thinking of how it might help, only that it has to.

And it does.

Whether it's caught in the main chute, or simply surprised

by the sudden change of circumstances, the creature parts from me at the same instant I jettison the main parachute, one claw raking a line of pain across my abdomen. I see the thing only in snatched glimpses as I spin, falling. Its wings are open at full span to arrest or maybe steer its descent as I plummet. My chute flutters away above us both.

I turn from the sight. Lean myself into a headfirst vertical arrow, streamlining my fall to get away. To get to Cate.

I can see someone else below me. Whoever it is, they're being tossed from one creature to another like a toy, parachute nothing more than a tangle of torn colours pulled after them. They spin spread-eagled, and even from this distance I see, or imagine I see, lashes of blood thrown out from the body. Because that's all they are, now. A body. That, or they've passed out.

I think it's Måns.

It is Måns. I recognise the colours of his jumpsuit.

The flying snake things with the bat faces, they're strikingly colourful from above. The wings are a combination of blue, red, orange, like twin skies at twilight. They're not beautiful, I've seen too much to think that, and the length of body that whips around denies them the majesty of birds. The sound they make is a high-pitched screech but short, like the quick scrape cutlery can make on a plate, only louder.

I don't dare look above to the one that had me moments ago. I've no doubt that it pursues, or readies itself to, spiralling in or diving on my fall. I'm flooded with adrenaline—seeing Todd, the attacks, falling without my chute—and I keep thinking of that story, that stupid fucking story, and I'm thinking that'll make me a tasty breakfast for them, all that adrenaline, and I'm thinking that's what we'll all be now, nameless victims in a tale told with beers around a fire, and I'm thinking I'm going to die, we're all going to die. Even as my heart tells me not yet, not right now.

I've got a reserve chute. I can control this descent.

I'm gaining on Cate. I am controlling this descent.

Above me, behind, something makes a series of shrill sounds. A shriek of noise. A stuttered *reek-reek-reek-reek*, each syllable louder than the last.

I'm not going to fucking die. I can't die. Not yet.

"You hear a lot of near-death experience stories doing the adrenaline-junkie stuff," Suki told me once. We were in bed, which was where we spent a lot of our time when we weren't pursuing some sort of outdoor adventure. Not always for the sex, you understand, but the intimacy. It was our private place, our safest space, where the rest of the world disappeared and there was only us.

"I bet," I said. "Near-death experience stories, and actual real-death experience stories, too, no doubt."

"Fair enough. That's true. But I'm talking about the whole, 'life flashing before your eyes' moment. You believe in those?"

"I'm not sure. You?"

For a moment, I had forgotten about her cancer. I was thinking of rock climbing and freefalling and BASE jumping and all the other crazy shit she'd done and continued to do. She could tell I'd forgotten, or rather she could tell as soon as I remembered—which was almost immediately—because she kissed my shoulder. "It's okay," she said.

"Suki."

She kissed my neck and then leaned over to kiss my mouth. She'd told me about the cancer a month or so prior to this conversation, but any time I tried to talk about it she kissed me to close the subject before it could begin. We were only allowed to talk about it on her terms, which had seemed fair at first but less so as time went by.

"When the doctor first told me," she said, "I had something like one of those near-death things, only instead of seeing my life so far flash before me in a series of snapshots or whatever, it was more like a flash forward. I saw every little thing I hadn't done yet, it felt like. Every part of the life I had left to live, if only I could've lived it. The things I could've done if I'd been brave enough. When I realised I was thinking in the past tense, like my life was over already, I decided, fuck it. I'll do it all."

"Carpe the fucking diem."

She nodded against me. "Damn right. Carpe the fucking diem. I started taking greater risks, travelling farther abroad to try things, racking up the credit card bills. But it changed the nature of it for me. I thought it would be like, I dunno, more of a 'fuck you' to death or something, right? But it was weird. First time I jumped out of a plane after getting the shitty news, I kept thinking of that Tom Petty song. Fucking, 'Free Fallin'' Just the chorus, over and over."

"I don't know it."

She sang, dramatically grabbing at the air above us and pulling it down to her face with, "Because I'm freeeeeee… Free fallllling."

I laughed a lot at the abruptness of that. The kind of laugh that leaves you breathless. She watched me, smiling.

"You know, that one."

"No, I don't know, you'll have to sing it again."

She pushed me lightly. "I felt it, you know? Free. Rushing towards something that would kill me, i.e. the ground, but having control enough to stop that from happening, right? Like, I'm the one that says, that's enough now, let's slow it down and live for a bit longer. Up in the clouds. Yank the cord and all is well." Her lip trembled. Her chin. "Except when I land I'll still have cancer."

"Baby."

"The ultimate fucking c-word, right?" she said, and she was crying now. "What a cunt of a disease."

"Baby, hey. I'm here."

"I *know*, and that makes it even worse, because now I've got so much more I want to live for, and it's not *fair*. I've only just met you."

I held her for a long time, and wiped away tears, kissed away others.

Eventually she settled, and the first thing she said was, "You know, it's fucked up, but if it wasn't for that c-word bitch fucker, I never would've even met you."

I was stroking her hair by this point, her beautiful now-blue hair, but I stopped at that.

"Yeah," she said, and sniffed. "Exactly. Fucked up, right?"

"God, then I wish you'd never met me."

She sat up then, suddenly, and said, "No. No fucking way, don't wish that. Not ever."

"Are you angry?"

"Yes I'm fucking angry. You're too fucking perfect for me to ever wish I never met you, okay? I'm so stupidly happy."

"I thought you were angry."

"Fuck off."

"I can't take your anger seriously when you're naked."

"Shut up, I'm trying to be serious. And you know what else? You're too perfect to be wasted on just me, so when I'm gone—"

"That's it, this conversation is over."

"No. When I'm gone—"

"Come here."

I tried to kiss her, pulling myself up to her, pulling her down to me, but she shook me off.

"I'm going to be gone, that's just medical fact, doc, and you need to find someone else quick before your beautiful body gets all old and decrepit."

"Suki—"

"I mean it." She relaxed, and she touched my cheek, and she said again, "I mean it. You're too good to go to waste. Someone else should get to experience you like I have. Fall for you. And you for her. Promise me."

"Suki, I'm not—"

"If you don't promise, I'll end things right now."

"No you won't."

She didn't say anything. She just held my stare. And I realised, with absolute certainty, that she wasn't kidding.

"All right. I promise."

"Okay," she said. "Okay. Good." She laid back down beside me. "That's good." She nestled close, resting one arm across my chest, and kissed my shoulder. My neck. My ear. "If she's too pretty, I'll haunt you."

I wanted to make her promise, but all I did was kiss her.

I'm hurtling towards Cate. It isn't going to be graceful, like with a team jump, gliding towards each other to hold hands. I don't even know if Cate's done one of those, and she won't have seen me coming anyway, so she can't prepare for it. Her chute's open, but only partially effective, damaged as it is. I'm heading right for her.

For all I know, there's something heading right for me, as well.

Closer, I can see the creature on Cate is as much caught around the ropes of her parachute as it is around her. One wing buffets them both back and forth, the other tugs and drags at the chute, claws it with talons.

Cate's conscious. She's kicking at the length of tail or scaled body that curls first one way and then the other, whipping around her as the thing struggles to free itself.

I tilt into a more horizontal position. Doing it slowly. I even sweep at the air like I'm swimming, for all the good that does. I'm only going to get one shot at this, and after that we're both on our own.

"Cate!"

It's pointless, but I scream it anyway.

She's still moving erratically, but for a moment it looks like I'm going to fall clear of her chute and manage to latch onto her. It doesn't go that way. I strike a taut edge of her canopy and am engulfed by it. Briefly. It whips over me with burning speed as I fall past, though I've collapsed it enough that Cate drops quicker for a moment. A suspension line slices the inside of my wrist and face but then I hit her and grab her, and grab something of the creature, too. I yank them with me before Cate's parachute takes a fuller shape again and by then I'm holding her suit, her harness, I think a handful of her skin as well. The creature slips away from her body, tearing as it goes. She screams. She tries to buck me off, too, still screaming, and panicked.

"It's me! It's me!"

Above, still caught in her ropes, shaking us around like marionettes, is the fucking Camazotz or Quetzalcoatl or whatever the hell is fighting to free its wing.

I grab at Cate's helmet, not too softly, and pull her to face me. "The cut-away!"

She screams again, this time in surprise, in recognition. Her eyes are cartoon-wide, pupils so dilated there's almost no colour, only blackness.

"Your cut-away! Pull it!"

She nods.

I tighten my already white-knuckled grip on her.

She pulls the cut-away and clutches at me simultaneously. The lines fly free of her, seem to whip up above us. I look up after them to see the creature become more tangled in its attempts to escape. But there's no joy to be felt in that: another is bearing down on us in a dive. Its serpentine body is straight. Its wings are folded back like dart-flights. It comes at us with its mouth open wide, twin fangs bared.

"Hold on to me!"

She's got handfuls of my clothing and harness like we're about to fight. I wrap my legs around her like we're about to do something else. "Don't let go!"

I pull my reserve chute. Immediately as it deploys, I'm freeing my hook-knife. I've never had to use it before. I pray it's sharp enough to do the job quickly; a reserve chute doesn't have a cut-away.

I slash at the lines just as the chute puffs full, setting it free to envelope the fucker coming at us. The thing streams past us like a fiery comet, a bulk of red nylon and a thrashing tail.

Cate and I are freefalling again. I'm holding onto her like my life depends on it because it really fucking does.

"You need to pull your reserve," I tell Cate, yelling into her ear, "but not yet."

She nods and reaches for it.

"Not yet!"

She nods again, just holds her hand ready. Her other is holding onto me. She's wrapped some of my harness into her fist. I still have my legs around her. I've got one arm around her, too, wedged between her back and her pack. The other I've forced under the harness at her front so that the straps cross my forearm and I'm able to hold a handful of her clothing. I can't be separated from her. Cate's reserve is all we have.

But she can't release it too soon. We're turning, rolling. She can't release the chute until we can hold a decent position. Also, releasing it will slow us down, make us easy targets. We'll need to alter our course, too, if we're going to make the clearing and not smash ourselves into the trees. That'll slow us down, as well. She needs to wait as late as possible.

I worry about the AAD; the Automatic Activation Device automatically opens the reserve chute at a pre-set altitude if the descent rate exceeds a certain pre-set speed. We must be nearing those parameters.

I catch glimpses all around us. Shapes in the air. Colours that are the bat-snake things, colours that are torn chutes and limp jumpsuits. My friends. Below, the lush green carpet of jungle, coming up at fast. The clearing, with its ancient stone. I want to point it out to Cate but with no chute of my own I'm too scared to let go for that kind of movement.

"As soon as we land, run for the rainforest!"

I can't tell if she's heard me.

"We'll get cover from the rainforest!"

The wind is trying to wrench us apart, whipping our hair around, ruffling our clothes, sharp and loud. Cate's hand, the one pressed closed to her chest for the release pull, finds mine and grips it hard without forcing it away from where it clutches at her. She nods at me.

Even hurtling towards the ground with weird monsters in pursuit, the world turning topsy-turvy around us, it's a strangely intimate moment. I think, yeah. I can do this again. I'm sorry, Suki. And thank you, Suki.

Then there's a *beep-beep-beep* and a sudden unravelling and Cate's reserve chute releases.

"Hold on!"

I'm not sure which of us yells it. I think maybe we both do.

Above, the parachute billows open and fills. It's a good, clean deployment. We're blind to any dangers directly above us, though.

Can't think about that.

Cate begins to guide us. No long, snaking S moves, but quick pulls that correct and re-correct our course in short circles. I can't tell if it's calculated or panicked. Sometimes there are trees beneath our feet. Sometimes the ruins. A short distance away I can see another gap in the trees and the dark open pit of the cenote.

Drifting across the jungle canopy, caught in a breeze, are the ragged remains of someone's parachute. It's snagged on something, or it's still tethered to someone, and before I can help myself I'm straining to see who, turning my head each time Cate changes our course, moving to see around her without lessening my grip. If there's a body, it's caught in the lower branches somewhere.

Above, the shrieking screech of one of the creatures coming at us from a blind spot. There's a moment I think I see it in silhouette through the chute.

The ruins are right there. Right fucking there.

The creature hits our parachute, claws it into a bunch of nylon and lines, and pulls us away with it. Yanks us off course at the last moment.

Cate gives a short scream. I'm wrenched along with her.

For an awful moment it looks like our legs are going to get dragged through the treetops, but they're not as close as that and suddenly the trees are gone altogether. We're still dropping fast.

"Oh, shit!"

We pass across the gaping hole of the cenote, then swing down into it. Collide into the side of the opening. Cate takes the brunt of it across her shoulders and grunts with the impact. We smash our heads together with the force of it, too, and I'm shaken loose. Thrown from Cate to grab at the ground's edge, at air, at nothing.

I'm falling again, this time into the dark gloom of the cavern. Cate's legs kick for a moment and are gone, dragged out of the light above, out of my sight.

Looking up, I tumble into icy water, back first. The sudden cold dark closes over me and pulls me down, farther down, settling over and around me and closing out everything else and this, I realise, is what death feels like.

We were going to go to China. That was the plan. A last trip together, climbing and caving, mostly.

"I'll show you Crown Cave, which is all handrails and elevators, now, probably, but after that we'll see some proper caves."

Suki had been excited about the trip. She'd been several times already, but she loved the place. China has a huge concentration of karst, which makes a decent playground of rock columns and sinkholes and rivers that just disappear into nothing, swallowed up by the ground. She wanted to show me The Stone Forest, a vast area of limestone eroded into a variety of column formations with beautiful names like 'stone singing praise to the sun' and 'tiger roaring at hawks', things like that. Geographical poetry.

"Karst areas hold loads of chi," Suki had told me. "You know, life energy."

Suki loved all that spiritual stuff. A lot of travellers do, I've noticed. Maybe they're more open to other possibilities, having seen more of the world and accepted their own very small part in it. Near the end, as the cancer took a firmer hold on her, tightening its skeletal grip around her organs, so she grasped harder at a range of religious beliefs. Some she'd been brought up with, others she'd picked up on her travels the same way Todd collected tattoos. She liked to point out that there was plenty of weird shit out there that no one knew or noticed, whatever my science might say. *My* science. She pulled away from me at the end, you see. Only a little, but it hurt. I understood it, though. I represented those who couldn't help her. And she didn't want me diagnosing her, seeing her only as someone to be cured. She didn't like that I would know how hopeless it all was, or that I would pretend otherwise for both of our sakes.

But China, with its wonderful caves and all its life force, all its glorious chi, never happened.

You know what they worship in Mexico? Death.

I see a light. A tunnel of dark, and a circle of light. I reach for it, pull at it. Chop my legs back and forth and sweep my arms to get to it. I pull. I kick. And with a sudden gasp of air, I'm there. Inhaling lungfuls of breath, sucking up my own echo, head back and arms splashing to stay above water.

The cenote is deep. The few I'd seen already were tourist spots, with steps carved into them, or laid with wooden boards and rope rails. This one, though, is natural and untampered. Above—far above—is a circle of morning light surrounded by stalactites. The walls around me are twisted thick with the roots of the surrounding rainforest.

I swim for them. I unclasp my harness and refasten it around one of the lower roots, freeing my hands so I can pat down my body, checking for injuries. The lacerations on my wrist and face are minor, but the gash across my abdomen feels serious. I fumble for my headlamp; the LED light will give me about 150 feet of clear sight. Only it doesn't work. I can feel that the helmet is cracked right through, too, probably from when Cate and I hit each other. I leave it on, though. If nothing else, it will help keep my hair out of the way.

I feel lightheaded, as if simply acknowledging the possibility of a head injury has created one, made me aware of a concussion.

I want to rest. Sleep.

"Can't, baby. You've gotta climb."

"Suki."

She's treading water, looking around at the walls. Looking for decent handholds. Suki used to free solo, climbing with nothing but rock shoes and a bag of chalk, daring the world to kill her. Something like this would be easy for her. I'd seen her dancing across rock faces, leaping from one outcrop to another like she's playing fucking hopscotch.

Not me, though.

"They used to throw people into these as sacrifices," I tell her.

"That's nice."

She turns a circle, looking for the easiest route.

"Cenotes were home to the ancient Mayan rain god, Chaak. Or Chuck, or someone. He was very important to the Mayan people because he was a rain god. He poured the rain from jars he smashed to make thunder. I don't know how I know this."

"Måns told you."

"Mm. That's right. He also told me that cenotes are entrances to the underworld."

She glances at me, but that's all.

"Yeah. An open mouth that devours the living, that was how he put it. And you know what else he said? He said, sometimes it spits out the dead."

"You believe that?"

I sigh. "There's some weird shit out there."

"Karstic rock, doc. It sucks the rain down to groundwater level. Cenotes are where the Mayans got their drinking water, that's all."

"Karstic. Like, with all the chi?"

"Exactly. Now come on, climb."

Sunlight angles in from above. It holds Suki like a spotlight.

"I just want to rest for a minute."

"You can't." She slicks her hair back in the water. "Come on. Jam your hand into whatever crack you can find."

I smile, remembering how she'd made that into an innuendo before. She doesn't smile back, though, not this time. She points up, and I remember the guy in the story, '*¡Lo vi! ¡Lo vi!* I saw it! I saw it!'

"You're not here. I'm seeing you, but you're not here. You left me."

"Did I?"

I've hit my head. That's what this is.

"Cate's up there, and she needs you."

But I'm already unclipping my harness from the root that had been supporting me. I pull myself upward with one arm and reach with the other. Taking hold.

"Yes. You can do it."

I look up at where the sunlight of a new day forms a circle far above me and I think, carpe diem. Carpe the fucking Diem. I try not to remember what happened when one of the twins poked their head out of the blowpipe.

And suddenly there's Suki, leaning out of the light, offering her hand.

Below me, the water of the cenote is empty, but I hear her voice down there. "She's pretty."

From above comes my name, and I look again to see it's not Suki silhouetted against the daylight but Cate. She's lowering the lines from her parachute.

I grab for handhold after handhold, eager to reach her.

Eager to climb out of the dark.

Contributor Biographies

Natasha Alterici is a writer and artist living in Tulsa, Oklahoma, with her fiancé and their two cats. Best known for her work on the queer viking fantasy comic *Heathen*, she has also contributed her writing and illustrations to projects such as *Dinosaur Project, Gotham Academy: Yearbook, Grayson Annual, The Lez Film Review, Mixed Signals, The Good Fight, Lovers and Other Strangers, Transcience, Moonshot, The Wilds* and more. When not drawing or writing, she tends her small garden and bakes a mean shortbread cookie.

Paula D. Ashe is a native Ohioan who lives in Indiana with her wife, their son, and too many pets. Her supernatural novella "Mater Nihil", was published by JWKFiction in the *Four Ghosts* anthology in 2013. Her award winning short fiction has been published in several anthologies. Most recently her work has appeared in the heavy metal horror collection, *Axes of Evil II* (2015), the third installment of the Horror World Press series, *Eulogies III* (2015), Trevor Kennedy's Phantasmagoria Present's *Gruesome Grotesques Vol. 1* (2017) and Burdizzo Books' *Visions from the Void* (2018). Her short stories "The Mother of All Monsters" and "Carry On, Carrion" were both recognized with honorable mentions in Ellen Datlow's *Best Horror of the Year Volumes 7 and 8.* She is an irregular contributor to the Ladies of Horror flash fiction project, compiled and edited by Nina D'Arcangela. Paula is one of seven contributing writers to *7 Magpies*, the first horror film anthology written and directed by African American women. She is completing a PhD in American Studies at Purdue University.

The winner of both a Bram Stoker and World Fantasy Award, P.D. Cacek has written over a hundred short stories, six plays, and six published novels. Her most recent novel, *Second Lives*, published by Flame Tree Publishing, is currently available from Amazon.com. Cacek holds a Bachelor's Degree in English/Creative Writing Option from the University of California at Long Beach and has been a guest lecturer at the Odyssey Writing Camp.

Ray Cluley's work has appeared in a various magazines and anthologies and has been reprinted in Ellen Datlow's Best Horror of the Year, Steve Berman's Wilde Stories: The Year's Best Gay Speculative Fiction, Johnny Mains's Best British Horror, and Benoît Domis's Ténèbres series. He has been translated into French, Polish, Hungarian, and Chinese. He won a British Fantasy Award for Best Short Story and has since been nominated for Best Novella and Best Collection. That collection, Probably Monsters, is available from ChiZine Press. He's currently working on too many things at once. You can find out more at probablymonsters.wordpress.com.

Brian Evenson is the author of a dozen books of fiction, most recently the story collection *Song for the Unraveling of the World* (2019). Other recent books include the story collection *A Collapse of Horses* (2016) and the novella *The Warren* (2016). He has been a finalist for the Shirley Jackson Award five times. His novel *Last Days* won the American Library Association's award for Best Horror Novel of 2009. His novel *The Open Curtain* (2006) was a finalist for an Edgar Award and an International Horror Guild Award. Other books include *The Wavering Knife* (which won the IHG Award for best story collection), *Dark Property*, and *Altmann's Tongue*. He is the recipient of three O. Henry Prizes as well as an NEA fellowship. In 2016 he received a Guggenheim Award. His work has been translated into Czech, French, Italian, Greek, Hungarian, Japanese, Persian, Russia, Spanish, Slovenian, and Turkish. He lives in Los Angeles and teaches in the Critical Studies Program at CalArts.

Catherine Grant is an author of weird fiction, editor with Lamplight Magazine, and Assistant Director of Core Programming for NecronomiCon Providence. She resides in Providence, Rhode Island.

Janet Joyce Holden is from the north of England and currently lives on the outskirts of Los Angeles. She is the author of the Origins of Blood vampire series, the novel Carousel and its sequel The Only Red Is Blood. Her short stories can be found in a number of anthologies.

Website: www.janetjoyceholden.com
Twitter: @janjoyceholden
Instagram: janetjoyceholden
Facebook: janetjoyceholden

Christopher Jones is the co-editor of *Eulogies II: Tales from the Cellar* and *Eulogies III* with Nanci Kalanta and Tony Tremblay. *The Porcupine Boy and other Anthological Oddities* is his first anthology as a solo editor. He lives in Toronto.

Violet LeVoit is a film critic, novelist, and artist whose work has appeared in many publications in the US and UK, including RogerEbert.com, TurnerClassicMovies.com, Allmovie.com, PressPlay.com, Bright Lights Film Journal, the Baltimore City Paper, Film Threat, and others. She is the author of the short story collections *I am Genghis Cum* and *I'll Fuck Anything That Moves and Stephen Hawking* (Fungasm Press), and the critically acclaimed novels *I Miss the World* and *Scarstruck* (King Shot Press). She lives in Philadelphia.

Elizabeth Massie is a two-time Bram Stoker Award-winning and Scribe Award-winning author of novels, short fiction, media-tie ins, and nonfiction. Her horror novels and story collections for adults include *Sineater, Hell Gate, Desper Hollow, Wire Mesh Mothers, Welcome Back to the Night, Twisted Branch* (under the pseudonym Chris Blaine), *Homeplace, Naked On the Edge, Afraid, The Fear Report, Dark Shadows: Dreams of the Dark* (co-authored with Mark Rainey), *Buffy the Vampire Slayer: Power of Persuasion, It – Watching,* and more. She is also the creator of the popular *Ameri-Scares* series of spooky novels for middle grade readers. She is currently at work on a new historical horror novel, *The House at Wyndham Strand*, a new Ameri-Scares novel, and several short stories. Massie is a ninth generation Virginian who lives in the Shenandoah Valley with her husband, talented illustrator and theremin-player Cortney Skinner. Until her new, updated website launches, she can be reached through Facebook, Twitter, Crossroad Press, or through e-mail: emvirginia@yahoo.com

Keith Minnion sold his first short story to *Asimov's SF Adventure Magazine* in 1979. He has sold over two dozen stories, two novelettes, an art book of his best published illustrations, two story collections, and one novel since. Keith was a book designer and illustrator from the early 1990s to the 2010s, and also did extensive graphic design work for the Department of Defense. He is a former schoolteacher, DOD project manager, and officer in the U.S. Navy. He currently lives in the Shenandoah Valley of Virginia, pursuing oil and watercolor painting, and sometimes even fiction writing.

David Nickle is a Toronto author and journalist. His stories have appeared in numerous anthologies and venues including Tor.com, The Best Horror of the Year, The Year's Best Fantasy and Horror and Cemetery Dance Magazine, and been collected in two volumes: Monstrous Affections and Knife Fight and Other Struggles. His novels include *Eutopia: A Novel of Terrible Optimism*, and its sequel *Volk: A Novel of Radiant Abomination*.

Priya Sharma's fiction has appeared in the likes of Interzone, Black Static, Nightmare, The Dark, and Tor. She's been anthologised in many Best ofs, including by Ellen Datlow and Paula Guran. "Fabulous Beasts" was a Shirley Jackson Award finalist and won a British Fantasy Award for Short Fiction. "All the Fabulous Beasts" is a collection of some of her work and is available from Undertow Publications. More info can be found at www.priyasharmafiction.wordpress.com

Lucy A. Snyder is the Shirley Jackson Award-nominated and five-time Bram Stoker Award-winning author of over 100 published short stories and 13 books. Her most recent titles are the collection *Garden of Eldritch Delights* and the forthcoming novel *The Girl With the Star-Stained Soul*. Her writing has appeared in publications such as *Asimov's Science Fiction, Apex Magazine, Nightmare Magazine, Pseudopod, Strange Horizons*, and *Best Horror of the Year*. She lives in Columbus, Ohio. You can learn more about her at www.lucysnyder.com and you can follow her on Twitter at @LucyASnyder.

Meryl Stenhouse is an author of short-to-medium-sized fiction, and a huge fan of the short form. She grew up on a diet of fantasy novels and B-grade science fiction movies. She's passionate about all things speculative fiction and is a game nerd and proud of it, a pastime she shares with her family.

Jeffrey Thomas is an American author of weird fiction, creator of the setting Punktown. Books in his Hades universe include the novels *Letters From Hades, Beautiful Hell*, and *The Fall of Hades*, and the short story collection *Voices From Hades*. Thomas's forthcoming books are *The Unnamed Country* from Word Horde, and *The Punktown Omnibus* from Centipede Press. His stories have been selected for inclusion in *The Year's Best Horror Stories* (Editor, Karl Edward Wagner), *The Year's Best Fantasy and Horror* (Editors, Ellen Datlow and Terri Windling), and *Year's Best Weird Fiction* (Editor, Laird Barron). Thomas makes his home in Massachusetts.

Artist Deena Warner loves Halloween and puzzles. She's spent the last 20 years creating book covers, websites, and illustrations for publishers and authors. She lives in Staunton, Virginia, with her husband, Matthew Warner, and sons, Owen and Thomas.

Curious about other Crossroad Press books?
Stop by our site:
http://store.crossroadpress.com
We offer quality writing
in digital, audio, and print formats.